A COURT OF BLOOD AND SACRIFICE

Book one of Blood and Vengeance

Kay Marrie

Copyright

ISBN: 979-8-9910836-9-0

Prologue

12 Years Old

The nearby forest howled as a rush of wind blew from an oncoming storm. Relenting, dark clouds rolled through, shrouding the land with its eerie darkness. Lilah knew that it wasn't smart to be out in the dark, even if the sun was just hiding behind the curtain of the storm, but still, something seemed to fascinate her about the forbidden Dark Lands.

Father wouldn't be pleased to hear that she had ventured so far off from home, especially so close to dusk, and now with this storm looming above, she knew he would come searching for her soon if she didn't show up for supper. Fear was not something that came to the surface; curiosity took over any fear that should have coursed through her veins. She was just a girl after all. Curious. Adventurous. Always yearning for answers.

But she should be afraid, because living among the Dark Lands was like living among the creatures of your worst nightmares, or so the stories said. Lilah never believed Father when he would tell her the stories of the wicked and soul cursed, about the magic that coursed through their lands or the monsters who lived among the Dark Lands; that they would drink your blood and steal little girls who didn't listen. But nonetheless, she enjoyed his stories and imagined what it would be like to venture past the threshold of their land. To see one of the cursed in the flesh.

If they did exist, Lilah imagined them to have horns and fangs that protruded from an overly large snout. Her imagination ran wild with the idea of what kind of creatures Father was so scared of out there.

Just as she suspected, darkness had enveloped the land before her return to the kitchen, and so, Father howled from afar, his voice carrying through the vicious winds. He didn't sound pleased. *Better not upset him anymore*, she thought.

Lilah skipped her way up the path that led through the flat plains of her land and eventually made it back to Father in one piece.

"Lilah! Where have you been? Have you not seen the darkness coming?" Father had a butcher knife in his hand and waved it around in his fury. She could still see trickles of chicken blood dripping down the hilt and onto his fingers. She pushed past him, not a flicker of worry going through her.

"Father, I am fine. No monsters came out to grab me from the forest." She plopped herself at one of the wooden stools in front of the table and placed a woven basket filled with a bundle of herbs down. She began to sift through the herbs and pluck the leaves from the stems as she continued. "I managed to gather some fine herbs for supper tonight. Thyme. Rosemary. It should make this soup taste exquisitely."

"Do you not have any worry at all, child? Do you know what day it is?" The look in his eyes begged for her to show that she was listening to his nonsense, and usually, Lilah would just nod, smile, and walk away, but this look held more desperation than the others.

"I didn't leave our lands. I stayed away from the forest, like you insist."

He didn't seem pleased. Father kept his glare on Lilah, ignoring the fact that his cauldron of soup was bubbling over the fire. "My darling, it is a full moon tonight…a blood moon. The veils of our protection charms are weakest now. They could break through them if they wanted to. We must stay inside after dark."

"How do you know the Queen's protection barrier even works? Maybe it is just made up." She raised her brow and leaned forward, resting her chin on the back of her hand.

Lilah was too lost in the sea of desperation and fury that raged within her Father's eyes to notice that he had cupped his hands around her face. She had never seen him so distraught. It pained her to know that she caused this in him, and so she smiled and hugged him, speaking calmly into his chest. "I promise I won't go out in the dark. I won't go too far from our home either."

His tightened muscles softened around her, and she felt him push out a large exhale. "Thank you, my child. Now let's finish this soup, shall we?"

After Lilah finished helping her father cook their supper, she sat down at the table with him to enjoy the hearty goodness of her creation. Freshly scented aromas of herbs and spices danced around the cottage, enticing her to take a bite. She closed her eyes and inhaled. Supper with her father was such a simple thing, and yet she looked forward to it every night. He was all that she had now, ever since her mother had lost her battle to the mysterious flu that had wiped out half the town. That was a far too painful memory to resurface, and so she drowned out that thought with conversation.

"So, Father, I see that our garden is doing very well. Have you had a chance to taste any of our vegetables of this season?"

He nodded, mouth full of soup, and replied, "Yes. The beets that you planted are finally coming in nicely. Very rich in flavor. Can you tell that I added them to the soup?" A smile tugged at his mouth, and then Lilah took a bite of one of those beets. Rich and velvety flavor burst in her mouth, blending perfectly with herbs that she had thrown in there.

For a moment, there was silence, peace, which enveloped the air around them, and when Lilah glanced up, she noticed her father staring gently at her. "What is it, Father?" He leaned forward and stroked his fingers gently along her cheek. "You look just like your mother. So beautiful, my darling." Lilah felt the curve of her mouth twitch and leaned into his warming touch. "You even have the same birthmark as your mother, here."

He touched the side of her face, just right behind her left ear, and smiled. Her mother had the same one, shaped like a tiny heart on her porcelain skin. "I miss her, Father." When Lilah let herself think of her mother, she could feel the sadness creep into her soul like a predator lurking in the dark. Many people have been losing their loved ones over the years to a mysterious flu that has been ravishing the lands. Having her father here was the only thing that could keep her from going mad, from drowning in her sorrows.

Her father was about to speak when suddenly a screeching sound pierced through the air, breaking the silence. Lilah jumped back, almost falling out of her chair. The hammering of her heart lodged in her throat as she frantically glanced around the cottage, but her father was already up from his seat and was now standing in front of the window, clutching the dirty butcher knife.

"What was tha—"

Before she could finish, he ran for her, tore her from the chair, and carried her over to the fireplace. "You must hide, my child. There is no time." He was already opening a secret door hidden within the walls. Her eyes shot wide open when she saw a small, dark crawlspace appear on the other side.

"But what's going on? What was that noise?"

Fear was not a feeling that Lilah was used to, but in this moment, it seemed as though it was crushing her. She grabbed her father's hand and tried to pull him into the room with her, but he shook his head, gave her a kiss on the cheek, and whispered softly into her ear.

"Whatever you hear, don't make a sound, and don't come out until daylight. I love you, my child."

Before she could reach for him, she was already being shoved backward, the door slamming shut moments later, and now she was trapped in the darkness.

Faint light shone through the cracks in the wood paneling of the wall, and she could see a slight silhouette of her father standing in the living room, still holding onto the butcher knife. There was a noise that seemed to loom over the land, howling like the wind, but this was no wind, that was for certain.

Was this the sound of the cursed? Did they truly exist in this world? Lilah never truly believed the stories growing up, but now she wasn't so sure what she believed. A thundering bang clanged on the door, followed by hissing. She heard her father gasp and shift his feet.

Suddenly, the door burst from its hinges and toppled to the ground. It was difficult to make it out, but it looked as if a group of men strode through the doorway.

"Leave this place at once, demons!"

There was a heinous, and unamused chuckle that one of the men let out, intently mocking her father's demand. "You dare to speak to me that way, and I'll have your throat ripped from your body," he hissed.

There was silence. Maybe he was too scared to answer. Lilah had to clasp her hands over her mouth just to keep her ragged breaths from being heard, but she kept her eyes peering through the cracks, watching from the shadows.

"What do you want? I'll give it to you, and then I will ask you to leave."

They were now circling him, like how a pack of wolves would surround its prey before going in for the kill. These men were tall, wearing well-tailored trousers and shirts, and had a presence about them that almost drew her in. Certainly not what she had expected the *creatures* of the Dark Lands to look like.

What were they?

"We seek the girl," one of the men said flatly.

Lilah heard her father's breath hitch at the mention of her. She couldn't see his face, but she knew that his eyes betrayed him. "There is no girl here. Just me." He still held onto that knife.

"Your lies will only end in your demise. Give us the girl, and we will leave your house in peace." This time, his voice was colder, more demanding. She knew that these men were dangerous, and for some reason, they wanted *her.*

"No," Father's voice quivered. There was a resounding fear that seemed to fill the room, and these men were basking in her father's weakness. One of the men tilted his head slightly, tendrils of dark hair brushed over his eyes, and then like a viper striking its prey, he ripped out her father's throat and held the pulsating organ in his hand. Crimson red blood trickled down his wrist, twisting around a snake tattoo along his forearm. Lilah's eyes darted from the tattoo to her now dead father lying on the ground.

His body dropped to its knees, and she seemed to do the same, crippled by the shock of seeing her father's limp body, and blood pooling on the floor. She couldn't breathe. Couldn't think. What did she just witness? A stream of tears poured down her face, but she didn't dare let a cry escape her throat. She held that in, knowing that any sound would ultimately lead her to the same fate.

But what happened next, she would have never imagined. As her eyes peered through just once more, horror ripped through her nerves at what she was seeing. They were *drinking* him. Drinking from the pool of blood that gathered below their feet as if it were some kind of buffet. Pressure built up in her chest. Her body seized into a ball of despair as she curled into herself and silently sobbed. Lilah had to turn away from the view of these men drinking her father's blood, but their moans of pleasure still violated her ears.

"She must be here somewhere. Go find her!" one of them yelled. Like scattering rats, they all scurried to different parts of her father's cottage, ultimately searching for her. Lilah didn't dare move at this moment. Even the faintest of creeks could lead them straight to her, and so she lay there, tearful, dirty, and heartbroken, and just waited until their search came up empty-handed.

It wasn't long. Their bodies seemed to move at a speed unknown to any human, and once they had finished searching her home, they began to walk back out into the night. "Do you think he sent her off? Was he expecting this?"

"She couldn't have been sent far. With what riches does this man have to offer for such travels? We will search this town until we find her, and then we will be able to break the curse."

And just like that, as swift as a drifting shadow cast from the rising sun, they were gone, leaving Lilah alone with her dead father's corpse. Something from that night ignited something deep within her, a rage that burned away the little girl that once was. Now she wanted vengeance. She wanted blood, and she made a promise to herself that she would stop at nothing until she found the man who took her father's life, only to repay him with the same bloody fate.

My body curled up like a stray cat in the night as the biting cold from the Winter's wind cut through my torn, tattered cloth that hung loosely around my body. My fingers were numb and stiff, which made it difficult for me to hold myself for warmth.

It had been four days now of me being on the streets of Eldoria. Since I was found hiding in someone's garret and kicked out. I dug through old scraps of slop that had been thrown onto the cobblestone streets by the townspeople, desperate to calm the hunger that clawed my stomach.

My breath puffed out like a smog filled sky as I exhaled a sigh. Every year, during Winter, I told myself that I might succumb to the brutal death of the frost, and yet, here I was, suffering another coldly season. This year had been especially concerning. The mysterious flu was back, my fellow townspeople dropping like flies caught in a fire's smoke. Doors have been sealed in fear of spreading the disease, and so that has left me out here in the brisk of night, chattering my teeth as I hunt for some warmth.

My mind pondered on this sickness that was ravishing through our town. It was the same devastating fate my mother had met when I was little, just before my father was murdered. It pained me to think of such horrors, to know that my life had been scorched to ashes so quickly. And now, look at what I have become. A Drifter. A beggar. No one wanted to help such a piece of scum like me.

The alleyway I was curled up in shielded me from the wind that was blasting through town, but I knew that I would be able to find some food if I searched far enough. I grabbed the muslin sack that I used as clothing and hugged my body tight as I stood on shaky legs, emerging from the darkness and toward the bustling streets.

At this time of night, there was only one type of person who would dare to be up. The drunks. Royal Oak was the town's infamous pub, serving the finest beer and liquor around. I paid no attention to the addictive liquid that seemed to have these people by their throats. My eyes were set on something far more precious.

"Out with ye!" a drunken man yelled into the nightly sky, throwing his old food onto the street. My mouth watered as my eyes laid upon the slop that was now mine to claim. Any chance that I got to eat; I took it. My legs sprung forward in a frantic dart toward the food, and I dropped to my knees as I kneeled before it.

Gods, it was still warm. My finger dug into the warm mush that splattered on the ground as I began to shovel every last bit into my watering mouth. At this moment, I didn't care that the wind was whipping my bare skin like icicles. A slight moan escaped my mouth as I swallowed my last bite.

"You girl!" a drunken man yelled. The same man that had thrown this delicacy onto the streets. I craned my head up to stare into his hazy gaze. Deep creases and lines etched his face like an old map, wrinkling with the slightest of twitches of his muscles. His scruffy beard, dark as the night, was speckled with gray, indicating that he must be years wiser than me. The man placed his hand on the wall to hold himself from wobbling over.

"Pay no attention to me, I will be on my way," I said.

His words came out as a sluggish mess as he spoke. "What...er...girl, what are you doing?"

I stood and shivered as I felt the full effect of the Winter air wrap around my frail body. The man raked his drunken gaze over me and snickered. "A Drifter?" he inquired. I rolled my eyes at such a forward statement.

"Go back to your pub and leave me be." I went to turn, but he snatched my wrist with a strong grip.

"I may be drunk…erm…but I can spot a lady in need." His grip loosened, his eyes now soft and pleading. My cracked lips parted; my head tilted. Was I that obvious? But I already knew the answer to that question.

I turned to face him and arched my brow. "So bold to make such a statement," I said, crossing my arms.

"Am I wrong?" he asked.

Silence fell upon us for a moment. I didn't want to admit to this man that I had no place to go, but my silence betrayed me. "By the looks of…" he half choked on a gag and continued, "you, I would say that I am right." The man straightened, trying to mask how fuddled he was. "I have a farm just over the hills over there. I need workers. You can stay in my garret on the agreement that you shall help me with my duties."

My eyes shot wide, unbelieving what I just heard. Did this drunk man just offer me a place to stay? Work?

I had been alone since I was twelve, with no one to rely on for comfort or support, so I would be lying to myself if I said that this didn't feel foreign to me.

"Are you certain your judgment isn't being clouded by your indulgence?" The man mumbled something under his breath and snickered. His eyes burned into me with intensity as he waited for me to answer. My fingers desperately fiddled with the hoarse fibers on this cloth, practically rubbing my finger raw as I pondered.

"Are you certain?" I asked. The man simply nodded and put his sluggish arm around my shoulder.

His hot breath rushed over my ear as he replied, "I need a laborer. You need a place to stay. How more certain should I be?" I shuddered from his breath, but the idea of no longer having to suffer and starve warmed me to my core. It was Winter now, and there was no way I was going to survive this season with the disease spreading through town. Surely, the idea of this man forcing himself on me crossed my mind, but I could handle myself. There were plenty of times I had to fight men away as they tried to grope me. But something deep within me told me that I would be okay, and the only thing that I knew for a fact was that if I didn't go with him, my body would die out here in the cold.

It was do or die. I nodded my head and smiled. "Okay. Thank you." The man yelped out in a cheery laugh and started to pull me forward.

"This way my lady. I shall show you your new home."

What the fuck did I just get myself into? I thought.

I followed the man down the streets and didn't look back.

Two years later…

"You've gotta put your back into it!" Eldrich teased as I hocked a sack of potatoes over my shoulder. Ever since I followed this drunk man into the shadows, I knew my life would be different. This man spread no lies when he told me what he expected. I was to work, and in return, he would provide a steady place to stay.

At first, my scrawny arms and legs could barely lift a half-filled sack of potatoes, but now, after my two years of working on his potato farm, my muscles finally had formed. I smiled back at him, watching him take two sacks as if he were lifting a baby up in the sky. For a drunk old man, he sure was strong.

"You know, one day, I will be able to out-lift you." Eldrich loaded up his barrel and turned towards me as he strode forward. "Now don't be saying that, Lilah. You know damn well you don't want to be a potato farmer."

How could I deny him? Potato farmer? I fucking hated it, but Eldrich had become like a home to me now. I knew my face betrayed me as I tried to deny his accusations. He brushed off his dirty hands on his trousers and slapped me on my shoulder. "I see the way you have been training with my swords. You are meant to be a Hunter. Not a farmer."

"I've heard around town that more people have been going missing and even more have been dying from the flu. Do you think the cursed ones are preparing a war?" I blew out a sigh as my mind drifted to Mother, before she caught the sickness. Then, I thought of Father and how he gave his life to protect me. My eyes stung with tears, my heart burning with hatred for those *creatures* of the Dark Lands.

Eldrich sighed. He knew about my past. About my parents' deaths, and he knew I wanted nothing more than to be able to get my revenge on those who hurt them. "The ones who have gone missing, I heard, were foolish enough to go outside our barriers. As for the flu, we must hope that the gods will protect us from that."

Eldrich scratched his beard and quirked up a smile. "I see the doubt in your eyes, child, but when your heart truly desires something, the gods will find a way to make it happen. You will be a Hunter, Lilah. Now, why don't you take one of my swords and practice some more?"

The past two years, my life changed so much. I learned so much. Besides being the town's potato farmer—mostly used to make vodka for the pubs and drunks—he had another specialty that only a select few knew about. I plodded toward the shack that he used to keep his swords hidden, and pulled one free, twirling it in my loose grip.

"I've seen the way you are with that sword, and I've seen the way you watch the guard train. If you were covered in full armor, I wouldn't suspect the person behind that sword to be a woman."

"I can't just join the guard. Women are not permitted." It was true. The royal Sunfire Court guard harbored only the toughest, fiercest men to be named Hunters—the protectors of Eldoria. I wanted nothing more than to join them in their battles, but my intentions were purely selfish. I didn't want to protect Eldoria; nor did I care about our mysterious queen. What my heart truly desired was to find the men responsible for killing my father, and being in the guard would give me better access to information that I needed.

Eldrich's land was nestled right up against the lands where the Hunters trained, and so after tireless days of harvesting potatoes, I watched, mimicking their moves until I became a reflection of them. My mind drifted for a moment as I pondered the idea of being a Hunter. "Word around the street is that the Queen is going to open up the tryouts for women. Kanen has devised a very special program to do so."

My heart skipped a beat. "What? Is this true?" If what Eldrich said is true, then maybe my dream of being a Hunter in the Sunfire Court will happen. Eldrich offered me a sly smile and nodded his head.

"The people at the pub may be drunks, but they sure as hell aren't liars. I know what I heard. So, until then, I say you train like hell, that way you will be able to knock them in their asses."

I laughed. "Maybe one day, Eldrich." I set the sword back down, suddenly needing some fresh air. The windy breeze was beautiful this time of year, the fallen leaves of the towering trees catching the gentle glide of the wind. I inhaled, smelling the sweet scent of pine and…*flowers*.

My legs trailed along a delicate path that snaked the edge of our lands, my mind easing into a state of bliss. There was that smell again. *Flowers*. I didn't remember any flower fields being along this part of our lands, but sometimes the gentle wind would gift me these wildflowers, and anytime I would stumble upon them, I remembered to take a moment to appreciate them. Where was that coming from?

I let my nose follow the scent, passing by a large pine tree and coming up along a running stream. Across the other side, I noticed a beautiful red flower placed at the water's edge. I smiled, taking in the simplistic beauty. For the past two years now, I have been finding flowers delicately placed along the outskirts of our lands, as if they were beckoning me to find them. We weren't supposed to cross the barrier of our lands. To do so would risk falling into the evil that haunts the Dark Lands.

And so, my little flower would just have to stay where it was. Which was fine. I could breathe in its beauty whenever I was having a tough day. That was until the wind took it, but I knew that another would appear somewhere along the grassy field, waiting for me to find it once again. Taking a moment to soak in the beauty of the woods, of the sunset streaked sky, I closed my eyes and inhaled. It had been a long time since I have been able to just sit and enjoy the call of the wild. Feel the breeze run through my hair. Feel the wind carry nearby chirps and trills from distant flocks of birds.

I dragged my gaze along the barrier that snaked around the land. Eldrich had set up markers along to help keep me inside, so that I would not wander too far. Small stones were placed every few yards. I would be lying if I said that I didn't want to venture out there, to the Dark Lands. Something deep inside me yearned to be with the wild, a force I could not explain, pulling me to the edge.

My heart's desire was to enact my revenge on the men who killed Father. I didn't know it back then, but now, it was clear who they were. *What* they were. I drew in a deep breath, pushing out those negative thoughts that ran through my mind. *Not today,* I told myself. I won't let those memories ruin the beauty of this.

The sun was close to setting, painting the sky with warm hues of orange and pink, a wonderful sight to end this peaceful day.

I better hurry back inside before night comes.

Even to this day, Father's warnings of the night haunted my mind. I made sure to bring myself into the safety of my home before I fell prisoner to another unfortunate event. Eldrich didn't mind the night, and while he went off to his pub, I stayed nestled up in my bed, giving in to the deep pull of sleep.

"You really fight like a bitch, Lilah. Is that really the best you've got for me?"

That bastard did get a good blow on me. I spat my blood on the ground and reached for the sharpened dagger at my hip, thinking of all the ways I could spill his blood. "Are you sure you want to test me, Kanen?" I flashed him a bloody smile, but he didn't budge.

He had a reputation for being the toughest Hunter in the Sunfire Court, so I wasn't surprised that my snarky comment didn't even get the faintest of smirks. His gaze slipped to my hand that clutched the sharpened silver, and said, "If you want into the guard, you're going to have to make me bleed." And *then* he smiled.

The crowd that surrounded me roared, but the only thing that held my attention was the copper and tangy scent in the air. Dozens of Hunters had fought in this arena; crimson blood still soaked the pores of the withered concrete pillars, telling the story of their triumph into the best vampire hunter group known to man.

It was rare for a female to make it this far into the training, but they have never met a female like me. I tightened my grip on my dagger, readied my stance, and lunged at him first, jabbing Kanen with the tip, but he was too fast, swiping my hand away, slicing my cheek when he brought his sword down with a swift motion.

Fuck. That hurt.

I could feel the warm trickle of blood running down my face. Kanen smiled. "Just admit it, Lilah. This is where it ends. You won't beat me; I'm the best Hunter the Sunfire Court has ever seen."

I dared to slip a glance at the screaming sea of people behind me, all cheering for my blood to be spilled. The wind was sharp and brutal now, blowing my hair around like tiny whips in the air. If I wanted to be named Lilah—Huntress of the Sunfire Court, then I'd better make a good move on him, and fast.

No one was perfect, and Kanen wouldn't expect me to purposely take a hit to boost his ego and squander his guard. In fact, I did just that, and now I knew that he has a slight limp on his left leg, probably from all the battles that have incurred—I think I just found his weakness.

The heavy beating of my heart caught in my throat, but I swallowed it back down and narrowed my eyebrows. "Be careful what you ask for Kanen…you might just regret it." And just like that, I was a shadow lurking, seemingly turned to dust as I whipped my body so fast, Kanen barely had time to register that I had already sidestepped him and knocked him on his ass. The crowd booed and roared at their surprise that a female had just knocked the infamous Kanen Sullivan—High Hunter of the Sunfire Court—onto the blood-infused dirt ground, and now, the tip of my dagger was at his throat.

He didn't even wince—that bastard, but there was a flash in his eyes, an anger festering behind his golden irises that only I could see. He kicked me in my side, and I hissed at the pain that now shot up my hip, staggering back, just missing his sword in the process.

Oh, he wanted to play dirty. I could play dirty.

Kanen still favored his good side, trying to keep the weight off that bad leg of his, and so, I used that to my advantage. Ignoring the searing pain that now radiated through my side, I took my dagger and chucked it through the air, watching it carefully until I witnessed the tip of my blade pierce into his thigh. Kanen hissed and dropped to his knees in protest, and when he met my gaze, I was the one smiling now.

I kicked his sword out of his grip, took the silver blade within my own grip, and held it to his throat. "Kanen Sulliven, High Hunter of the Sunfire Court, I believe that I, a woman, just beat you in battle." I held the tip of the blade to his throat longer than I thought I would, offering him a playful smirk, but the only thing that I got in return was a furious glare.

No one beat Kanen. Especially a woman. But like I said, I was no ordinary woman, no. My entire life since the age of twelve, since my father's murder, all I had wanted to do was kill and get my revenge. And training on Eldrich's farm gave me the skills to do so . It was my life's mission to find those who murdered my father, and being in the Sunfire Court guard was the best place to start.

My hand let go of the hilt of his blade, and I watched it fall before him, hitting the ground until the ringing from the metal scraping the concrete rang in my ear. Around me, the crowd was now roaring in a unanimous cheer. What once was a crowd of catcalling, woman-hating men, now seemed to shift to a crowd of excited patrons.

I was the first woman ever to make it this far into the guard training, and to actually pass my final test. Kanen wasn't happy about letting women try out for the guard, but the days were changing, and so he created this test. The last test, to see if they would be worthy enough to be a Hunter in the Sunfire Court, but what he probably didn't expect was for a woman to actually beat him.

His head hung in defeat for a moment before he rose to his feet, only wincing slightly from the dagger that stuck out of his thigh. "You seemed to have proven yourself worthy, Lilah," he hissed.

It was an especially sweltering day this time of year, even if the sun was getting close to setting, my hair coating my neck like a second skin. That wind did nothing to cool me down. I pulled my hair from my face and strode forward. "Don't worry Kanen, next time we fight, I won't go easy on you."

"Just because you passed your final test doesn't mean you get to go straight into battle. You will be posted at the guard's camp until you have learned our ways and have proven yourself ready for true battle." The way he emphasized "true battle" as if something that I would never be able to achieve made my blood boil. I bit my tongue and scoffed.

Kanen leaned forward, grabbed his sword that lay on the ground, and slowly stepped away. With his back toward me, he raised his arm and yelled, "Ryker, take Lilah to her new living quarters," and disappeared into the castle. I was left standing in the arena alone, surrounded by hundreds of sweaty men. Probably not the best place for a lady to be, but before my anxiety became too crushing, Ryker—Kanen's second in command—came to my side and touched my arm.

My brows arched. "*You* are going to show me to my tent?"

Ryker just looked at me with hooded eyes, the slightest of smiles tugging at his lip, and said, "I'm assigned to all new Hunters when they first make it into the guard. I will be overseeing your transition with us to make sure you are trained properly."

I had seen Ryker here and there during my training with the guards. Ryker was only a few years older than me, and at the time, he was still in his training to be a Hunter. I remembered the way he would prance around the battlefield as if he already earned the title of Hunter. He was the best back then. That's why I would watch his fights from the shadows, studying his moves until my own body could mimic the fluid strike of a sword. Eldoria needed to keep its army strong. Ready.

Queen Margarethe kept our lands safe behind her magical border, but her infatuation with finding the hidden realm of Velorim—the Vampire King's kingdom, pushed her need for a larger army. What she really wanted was to find people brave enough—dumb enough—to go off into the Dark Lands and do her bidding. It couldn't have been a better fit for me. After all these years of taking test after test, and snaking my way up the guard's social ladder, I could finally call myself a Huntress. Fury burned deep within me at the thought of where all this began—my father's murder, and now, my time to hunt these fuckers down, had just begun.

"I can escort you to your home so that you can gather your things," Ryker said, snatching my attention from my thoughts.

My eyes fell to the ground. "I need to do this alone. Can I meet you back here in an hour?" I was expecting Ryker to protest, saying something about needing to keep me close since I was a Huntress now, but instead, he just smiled at me, and nodded.

"Sure. One hour."

"Eldrich!" I called out as I ran toward my old friend, arms outstretched.

"Lilah." His voice sounded more cheery than usual. "So? Did you make it?" I knew he was going to ask me this. This poor man—for the past month—had to endure my constant worrying about my test today.

The excitement was hardly containable, and as I drew in a large breath, I said, "Yes! I am Huntress now."

Eldrich's smile spread even wider as he pulled me into him, his arms wrapping around me the way Father used to. My head nuzzled into his chest. "I will miss you. I will miss this farm."

He pulled away and looked down at me. "Don't go talking like you won't see me again. You know where to find me and my farm. You are welcome back anytime, Lilah."

"Thank you," I said. "Actually, I can't stay long. Ryker is waiting for me. I just came to say goodbye." Right now, in this moment, I felt true happiness spread through me, through my soul, and as I met the gaze of my old friend, I could tell that he felt it too.

My legs pattered against the cobblestone pathway that led back to where I had left Ryker. I wondered if he actually was going to wait for me, but as I made the turn around the bend and saw him standing there leaning against the wall, I stopped.

"You waited for me," I said more as a statement than a question.

His head shifted toward me, his eyes brightening the moment they met mine. "Of course I waited. Did you get everything you need?"

"Mhm."

He took a quick glance at my empty hands and arched his brow. "You sure?"

"Yes. It's time to start my new life, right? Out with the old and in with the new. Besides, I didn't have much of my own things to begin with."

"The guard will provide you with everything that you will need anyway."

"Come on, I'll show you where you will be staying." He nodded his head and gently pulled my arm so that I would follow him. I couldn't help but feel the excitement in my chest grow as the realization started to settle in. I—Lilah Bennoni—was going to be a Huntress in the Sunfire Court. It's all I've dreamed of since that night, since I was forced to gaze upon the feasting of my father's blood. No child should bear such horror.

Those faces. The blood. I couldn't get that night out of my head. Just a continuous cycle of nightmares played in my mind, thinking of all the ways that I could have stopped those men from hurting my father. Still, to this day, I questioned why they were searching for me. Why me? What was so special about a little twelve-year-old girl who lived on a farm? I swore I would get answers, find the men who ripped my world apart, and kill every last one of them until they were drowning in their own pool of blood.

I didn't realize it, but I balled my fists so tight that the tips of my nails broke the surface layer of my palms. Refocusing my attention back to Ryker, I turned my head and tried to pay attention as he explained the rules of the camp.

"Training starts at sunrise. You'll want to get up before then to eat. Your new clothes will be provided to you and in your room when you arrive. You will have the day to adjust but expect to start first thing tomorrow morning with your training. And trust me, you won't be smiling then."

"Is it true that the Sunfire Court knows where to find Dravian?"

Ryker scoffed and craned his head back in amusement. "The Vampire King? You do know that in the last hundred years, no one has been able to find him, or his kingdom, right? Must be that curse of theirs." His voice was like venom when he spoke of the vampire king. I didn't blame him. I hated the vampires with every ounce of my soul. They were the ones responsible for my father's death, slithering into our house at night, when we were unexpecting.

I practically growled at the word vampire, it being like a poison to my ears. Over the past ten years, since being a naive little girl, I had learned many things that my father had protected me from. Many horrors that no one should have to know exist. But they do. Our land—Eldoria—a land of prosperous wealth and royalty, stretched far along the border of the Dark Lands, but growing up, I never knew that we had lived so close to such evil. I've learned over the years that the Dark Lands harbored creatures that even your worst nightmares wouldn't think of, one of the worst being the cursed ones. Vampires. As the people of my land went missing, whispers among the streets began, claiming the vampires have been secretly invading our towns. Maybe it was vengeance they wanted.

Legend says that their kind was cursed many years ago by a rageful queen of Eldoria, and ever since then, the vampires have been searching for a way to break their curse so that they may finally be free from its prison. I thought magic was a myth, even today, I am not so convinced that it even exists. The only thing I do know is that there are evil men that live out there in those woods, in Velorim—the Dark Lands—and one day, I will find the men responsible for tearing my family apart and get my revenge.

"Lilah?"

I blinked. I must have drifted from our conversation, because when I looked at Ryker, he was looking at me like I had three heads. His tousled brown hair was dancing freely with the breeze that was blowing through, and I couldn't help but notice the soft expression in his eyes. "Yes?" I asked.

"I said, we are getting close to the camp. No one goes out after dark, save for the few Hunters on patrol duty. Being so close to the forest, it's best to be safe than sorry."

I hurried my pace and was now walking next to him, peering at him with curious eyes. "What kind of creatures live out there exactly? I have only heard rumors. Is it true that the forest is alive?"

Ryker didn't look at me, but I could see something flash within his eyes. He kept his head straight and held out his arm, gesturing ahead. Once we reached the camp, he paused and looked at me, but his eyes hardened. "The biggest rule of them all is don't go into the woods unless you are ordered to do so. Best to just not go searching for answers, Lilah. You may not like what you find."

Ryker ducked through a doorway and disappeared into the shadows. "Wait!" I couldn't just leave it at that. My whole life I had been looking for answers about the vampires, about the Dark Lands, panhandling, and sleeping from home to home. No one ever had any idea of what truly lurked beyond the veil of the forest, only knowing what the whispered rumors have said, seemingly ignorant to the land that snaked around our kingdom. Every time I got a vague answer, it made my blood boil even more, because it seemed as if I were slipping deeper, further away from the answers that I desperately sought. "Have you been out there? What did you see?" I pressed.

Ryker sighed and nodded his head. "Come in here. Sit." He pointed to a small cot in the corner of the tent—mine I presumed—and sat next to me. "I led an expedition once, out in the Dark Lands. We were searching for something, but these woods, Lilah, are evil. There were creatures that lived there far worse than the vampires."

Ryker began to draw in ragged breaths as he spoke of being in the Dark Lands, his throbbing jugular vein pulsating fast. He was genuinely frightened of that place, which only piqued my interest more about the mysteries that haunted those lands. "What happened out there? What did you find?" I asked, drawing eyebrows together.

"There is a dark magic that lives out in the forest. Something that is ancient and angry. Many of my men that day were either lost or perished during our expedition. That was how I got this." Ryker held up his arm to reveal a long scar that started from his elbow and traveled its way to his wrist. I reached out my fingers to touch it, but he pulled away.

"What happened?"

"One of my men was taken when we were out there. I tried to follow his tracks, tried to catch up to whatever took him, but then something came from the dark and attacked me, slicing right into my arm with its teeth. I can't get his screaming out of my head." Ryker shook his head as if trying to rid himself of the memory. "I haven't been back into those woods since that night."

Tilting my head to the side, I asked, "Do you think they turned your friend into one of them? Can they even do that?" Ryker paused for a moment, as if letting my question sink in, then his eyes narrowed.

"I never thought of that. I have heard that to turn someone, it isn't as easy as just biting them. They are just rumors, but…it has to do with the magic out there. I wouldn't wish for my friend to be condemned to walk among those lands, cursed. It would be better to think of him earning a true Hunter's death so that his soul may rest in peace."

I drew in a shuddering breath and shivered. It seemed as though no one truly knew what lurked beyond the forest, save for a handful of people who were now silenced by their fear. Growing up, I made it my mission to find out who those men were and why they came after my me, but I had only learned about vampires a few years ago. Even though my eyes watched as those men slurped my father's blood off the floor, I didn't think that was what they were. I just thought they were crazy. But as I grew older, listening to the whispering gossip among the streets, that was when I started to question *what* those men were. It seemed everyone I asked shielded away from me the moment I opened my mouth about the Dark Lands.

What was everyone so afraid of? But when I pulled my gaze back to Ryker, I knew that that was real fear etched into his eyes. He saw something that was so terrifying that it pained him to retell the story. Maybe my ignorance of the creatures of the dark would be my demise, maybe I should put this to rest and forget about my vengeance. I sat there in silence for a moment, pondering about letting my anger go, putting out the fire, so to speak, but why? Why should we cower? If I were queen, I would make it my mission to find Dravian and his kingdom and destroy every last one of those bloodsuckers.

"Lilah?"

I blinked and refocused. "Yes?"

Ryker had a peculiar smirk spread across his face. "Get some sleep, okay? You're going to need it. Trust me." He stood, flashing his teeth at me, and then left in the dead of the night, leaving me to my thoughts. I lay back on the bed and interlaced my fingers across my chest, watching the rise and fall of my breathing. It was almost unfathomable to believe that after all these years of striving to be a Huntress in the Sunfire Court, that I had finally made it. Me. A girl—homeless at the age of twelve, orphaned by the hands of the vampires, and seemingly a nuisance to the castle grounds due to my panhandling—was finally a Huntress. Everyone told me that I was crazy for dreaming of such absurd things, but I knew my worth. I trained every day to learn how to be a killing machine, and now I was the first Huntress to exist in the Guard.

A smile spread across my face as I glanced up, peering through the small cracks in the canopy. The moonlight spilling through looked like tiny stars on the ceiling, waving gently with the breeze that was rolling through. I listened, the howling wind whistling through the tree branches just outside my tent. Ryker was right. We were right on the edge of these woods.

I should have been scared, but instead, I was calm. Peaceful. The Queen of Eldoria had put a magical barrier around our land, keeping away the creatures of the night. I always wondered if that were true. She claimed to have magic, that she tapped into a source that only a queen could access, but my skepticism always clouded my judgment. Was magic truly real?

If vampires were real, then why did I question magic to be real as well? I turned over, now staring at the clothes that Ryker said would be put out for me. I trailed my fingers along the hem of my mud-infused shirt and then found myself picking at the holes that decorated my pants. I didn't grab any of my clothes from the farm. Most of them were dirty and meant for hard labor. So, I only had the clothes on my back, and now, lying next to a fresh pair of clothing, that was all my own, made me almost cry. Tears began to line my eyes, but I quickly blinked them away. It was finally time to embrace the new me.

There was a clean bucket of water, and a large cloth neatly draped over a small, wooden table. Before anything else, I needed to get this dirt off me. Picking up the cloth and dipping it in the water, I began to scrub away the caked-on blood and dirt that seemed to cling to me like a second skin, and once my skin felt clean, I reached for the piles of new clothes that was left out for me.

I slipped out of my old, dirty clothes, and pulled on the fresh, clean shirt over my head, inhaling the sweet scent of linen, and then slipped my legs into my new pants. The soft texture hugged my skin in its warm embrace, and now, I finally felt as if I didn't have to worry anymore. I finally did it.

After all the years of training, all the years of being homeless, I was now a Huntress. I let the mattress of my cot hug my body as I lay back down and closed my eyes. My mind tumbled into darkness as sleep consumed me, for this was the first time that I had truly slept in peace since I was twelve.

"Lilah!"

I gasped and shot up from my bed. "What?" I barely had time to blink before Ryker was pulling on my arm, trying to get me out of bed. "Wait. What are you doin—"

"You're late," he growled.

"What?" I rubbed my eyes and peered around the room, noticing the warm orange sky emerging from the horizon. "You really meant first thing in the morning, didn't you?" Ryker was dressed in battle gear; all black leather hugged his muscles, and then iron plates hung just over his chest. He had a silver sword sheathed along his back, and his face was hardened into an almost frown.

"If you aren't ready by the time Kanen gets here, it won't be pretty. You better get up, quickly." Ryker tugged on my arm again, and I hissed.

"Fine. I'm getting up. Can I at least eat something first?"

"Breakfast was before sunrise. It's dawn now. Should have woken up on time." Ryker turned around and started for the doorway but paused as his foot reached the threshold. "You coming?"

I slipped on the boots that were lying next to the bed and stood, groaning as I adjusted to waking up so quickly. "I'm coming."

Ryker led the way out of my tent, and when we emerged, I sucked in my breath. "Holy…" I let the rest fizzle on my tongue. Hundreds of men marched among the camp, dressed in their battle gear, looking as if they were going to war. "Why does everyone look so serious?" I asked as I caught up with Ryker.

He glanced over his shoulder and smirked. "We must always be ready for battle. Would you prefer that we were just lollygagging around when the enemy attacks?"

"Well…no…but I thought our land was protected." Ryker chuckled and took a sharp right. I followed and asked, "What's so funny?"

"The Queen likes to tell her people many things to keep them feeling safe, but the truth is, her magic has been slowly dying out, and with it, our barrier that keeps us safe."

I could feel the ground thumping from the boots of the many soldiers that surrounded us, all headed in the same direction. "So, magic is real then?"

Ryker halted and held out his arm, meeting my gaze. "What makes you think it isn't?"

I tilted my head and shrugged my shoulders. "I don't know. I just always had a hard time believing in things until I saw them for myself. Like where does her magic even come from?"

"This land is ancient. Magic comes from deep within, and not everyone can access the magic. It must choose you, and even then, you must sacrifice something in return to gain access." I wanted to hear more, but a blaring alarm ripped my focus from the conversation. Ryker took my wrist into his grip and said, "Come on. We need to hurry," and pulled me into the sea of warriors.

Alarm horns were blaring in a continuous loop, and when I glanced around me, observing the warriors in the camp; they all seemed on edge. I would be lying if I said that my heart didn't skip a beat, but I was a Huntress now. I had to be tough. I frowned and continued forward, making sure I didn't lose Ryker during our trek.

"Ryker! What's going on?" I could barely hear myself speak over all the commotion, but if I had to guess, I would say that this must have something to do with the looming storm rolling through. Something shifted within the atmosphere, the sky now casting dark shadows over the land. I knew that the vampires couldn't come out during the day. The curse that haunted them made sure of that, but with most of the sunrays swallowed up by these thick, dark clouds coming in, it was almost as if it were the dead of night.

Ryker had led me across half the camp, my legs hissing in protest with every step now. Usually, I don't get tired this quickly, but after my test yesterday, and waking up early today without being able to eat a proper meal, I was *exhausted*. He reached for his sword, pulled it from its sheath, and glanced back. "When this horn goes off, that means there is a perimeter breach, which means something got through."

I gulped, my throat constricting with fear. The last time I saw a vampire in the flesh was when I was twelve, when I saw their sharpened teeth tore into my dad's throat and drank his blood from the floor. I would never be able to shake the horror that ravished me when those memories resurfaced. I had a true hatred for vampires, but hidden deep within that hate was fear. No one would ever get me to admit the fear that I kept hidden, but right now, in this moment, I felt it pushing its way to the surface.

"Did a vampire break through our barrier?"

He didn't answer. Ryker just nodded his head and quickened his steps as we were coming up on the commotion. Before he ran off into the sea of people, he told me, "Stay here." Ryker disappeared, blending in with the dozens of other warriors that crowded around. The Dark Lands seemed so close to where our camp was, and as I peered to my right, that was when I truly gazed upon the vastness of the woods. Darkness, shadows, seeped their way through the space between the trees, and even seemed to spill onto the land like spilled ink. If something was lurking within those woods, I sure as hell couldn't see them.

The wind was now blowing furiously, whipping my hair around like tiny electric bolts. I took one more moment to gaze out in the darkness of the land and then turned my attention to the commotion.

Ryker said not to move, but I couldn't just stand here and do nothing. If a vampire truly had breached our lands, and was here, this just might be my chance to get some answers about the ones sent to kill my father. I sprinted forward, shoving my way through, until I approached the alleged breach.

There stood Ryker, his warm, brown hair twirling furiously with the wind, and his face hardened into a firm line. Next to him stood Kanen, and even with the dark clouds shrouding us, his white hair still seemed as if it were glowing. He was saying something to Ryker, standing over something.

My eyes shifted to what was now lying on the ground, between them. A body. I approached cautiously, knowing very well that I was going to get an earful from Ryker once this was all over. When I made it about a few feet away, Kanen drifted his attention to me, piercing through me with his deathly glare.

"What is she doing here?" he demanded.

Ryker snapped his head in my direction and sighed. "I told her to stay by the tents."

"She shouldn't be over here." Kanen stepped over the body, blocking most of the details with his legs, and crossed his arms. "Lilah, this isn't a place for a lady to be at the moment."

The way he said lady, lit a fire within me, making my blood boil. Whatever animosity he was holding on to, he needed to let it go. Just because I was a woman didn't mean that I couldn't handle situations like this. Did he forget that I made it into the Sunfire Court guard by beating *him* in battle?

I scoffed.

Ignoring his demands, I asked, "What is that?"

Ryker glanced down but quickly met my gaze again. In his eyes, there was a hint of worry lingering beneath. "Lilah—"

"Ryker, stop. I don't need to be shielded. I'm one of you now. What is that?"

Ryker slipped a glance at Kanen who seemed furious at my disobedience, but then he relaxed his shoulders and stepped away from the body. A gasp forced its way into my throat the moment my eyes gazed upon this creature of the night.

"Is that a—"

"Vampire?" Ryker finished. He nodded his head. The body was a female; she had bright orange hair and a soft expression. Her clothes were almost normal, save for the all-black attire. In this state, she seemed…peaceful.

"Is she dead?" I asked.

"Well…" Ryker shrugged his shoulders. "All vampires are dead, but if you mean after the fact, then no, I don't believe so."

I glanced at Kanen and narrowed my brows. "Why isn't she burning?"

Kanen only looked up at the black cloud that hovered above us and pointed. "Without the sun being able to penetrate the storm, it must be offering them some kind of shield. We need to take her into holding before she wakes up."

"Wait." I stepped forward. "How did she get through our barrier? Are we vulnerable to more of *them* coming in here?"

Kanen slipped a quick glance toward the Dark Lands and leaned over the body of the female vampire, reaching for her arm. "Don't worry about that. We will set up extra patrol and Ryker will lead a group to patrol the perimeter and secure it." He nodded his head and said, "Help me grab her."

Ryker didn't break his gaze with me as he leaned forward to help lift her body from the ground, his eyes soft and almost comforting. I could feel my heart fluttering around my body from all the emotions that were swirling inside me. I had spent my life dedicated to learning the art of battle so that one day, I would be able to kill those bloodsuckers, but as I stared at this vampire, lying lifeless on the ground, my hate seemed to be replaced with something else…

Regardless of the fact that I wanted to jab my dagger through her chest, my desire for answers broke to the surface. Maybe she knew the men who killed my father. As I drew my gaze back up toward Kanen and Ryker, they had already turned and started walking off. Before I could say anything, Ryker craned his head back and yelled, "Lilah, go to training. I'll meet you there in a little!" and then disappeared.

The air around me stilled as if the sky was whispering of its impending storm coming, and just as quickly as this eerie silence enveloped the land, a flash of lightning struck, cracking through it just as fast. Pellets of rain shot from the sky now and began to pour down onto the camp. I wanted to go back to my tent and wait it out, but as I peered around me, the guard soldiers only seemed to be walking off to their posts.

"Hey!" a guard yelled, breaking me from my focus.

I snapped my head in his direction and said, "Yeah?"

He ran toward me, soaking wet and in full battle gear. Looking up at him, I had to tilt my head almost to the sky to see into his eyes. I covered my forehead with my hand to stop the rain from getting into my eyes and asked again. "Yeah?"

"Ryker sent me to get you. I'm going to show you where training is. Come on, it's this way." He turned and ducked off to the right, and so, I scurried behind him, trying to keep up.

"I'm Lilah."

"I know who you are. Everyone knows who *you* are." He turned his head slightly until I could see a faint curve of his lip. "I'm Damon."

"Oh?" I inquired. I wouldn't assume even the lowest of ranking guards would know who I was.

"You're the first female to make it into the guard. Why wouldn't we all know who you are?" Damon shrugged his shoulder and slowed his pace. "Besides, you stick out like a sore thumb here." He eyed me up and down, slowly taking in my body, analyzing it as if trying to see if I was worthy of my title.

I crossed my arms across my chest and rolled my eyes. "I'm sure I will fit right in. So, where are the training grounds?" The guard camp that sat on the outskirts of the castle grounds was *huge* and I couldn't believe that we had already walked through to the other side in the amount of time that we did. My legs screamed with every step that I took, but I bit down and pushed through the burn. I think I might have twisted something during my battle with Kanen. With barely any sleep and the ache that now consumed my muscles, I knew that this was going to be a long day.

Ahead, the sound of battle drifted through the air, men all shapes and sizes hurtling themselves at each other with weapons in their hands. The sharp clanging sound of the metal smashing into each other chimed with intensity. I inhaled and relaxed my shoulders. Excitement began to buzz through my nerves because finally, I was going to train like a real Hunter. No more watching from the shadows and sparing alone. No more trying to make it through test after test. My fingers danced along the hem of my pants as Damon and I stood along the perimeter, taking it in.

Damon went to take a step forward, but I snapped my hand on his arm to stop him. "Wait. Do you know where they are taking that vampire?"

Damon smirked. "Why do you want to know where they are taking her?"

Because I need answers, I wanted to say, but instead, I said, "I'm a Huntress now, shouldn't I know where we keep our enemy?"

Damon chuckled and nodded his head. "They took her to the commander's tent. It's over there." He tilted his chin toward my right and refocused. "Only Kanen and his second are permitted to enter. Don't get any stupid ideas."

Damon must have seen the look in my eyes. There was no way that I was going to admit what I was planning to do, but when everyone goes to sleep tonight, I was going to pay our little friend a visit. Maybe she knows the men who killed my father. This was finally my chance to get some answers. Before I knew it, Damon had walked off toward the battlefield, and as I gazed upon the sea of Hunters, dancing in battle, I couldn't help but gulp. Finally, it was time to train like a real guard.

Chapter Three: Time for Battle

Lilah

The storm that had been shrouding the land had now drifted away, a mere speck among the horizon, and with the clouds no longer looming above, the sun now blazed down with its intense heat.

I swiped the beads of sweat from my face and tightened my grip on my sword that Ryker had given me, my body screaming as I tried to keep up with my battle partner. Ryker was a beast of a Hunter, knocking me on my ass more times than I could count.

"You're looking a little tired over there, Lilah. Are you ready to tap out?" He smirked.

I scoffed and readied my stance. "Not a chance," I replied.

The air crackled between us, promising an inevitable battle. Ryker's battle armor flashed under the white light of the sun, almost blinding me with its intensity. The heat during this particular time of day was unforgiving, and with the heavy weight of my own armor pressing on me, I was *dying*. I noticed a flicker of movement coming from him. A shift. And I knew that he was preparing another hit, but before he had a chance to lunge, I brought my sword up, slashing down in his path.

Ryker barely had enough time to lift his sword to catch the brunt of my hit before I knocked him on his ass. We had been sparing all afternoon, and finally, I had been able to show my skills. Ryker hit the ground hard, slamming onto his back and dropping his sword in the process. The air expelled from his chest as he gasped.

I stepped forward, Ryker groaning before my feet. I pointed the tip of my sword to his chest and smiled. "I believe I would call this one a victory."

I heard a faint chuckle escape from his mouth as he kneeled, pulling himself up from the ground. "Don't get too ahead of yourself now. That was one win. You will have to do that ten more times before you move on to the next level of training."

I rolled my eyes. As of right now, I was one of the lowest levels of the Hunters of the Sunfire Court. My goal was to be at the top. The best. "Well, I hope you are ready to be knocked down ten more times then."

A small curve of his mouth twitched as he leaned forward to grab his sword. "Don't worry. You'll have plenty of time to practice. We've been at this for hours. Let's go get something to eat."

He didn't have to tell me twice. My stomach growled the moment the word *eat* left his lips. It had been days since I had a decent meal. I clenched my stomach, feeling the emptiness taking full effect inside me. My mind drifted back to the time before Eldrich came into my life. Living as a Drifter, food was something that I had to fight for. Hunt for. There were times when I wouldn't eat for days, and when I did eat, it was mostly scraps left out for the rodents.

Ryker slid his sword back into its sheath and nodded. "Come on. I'll show you where we all relax." I did the same, slipping my sword back into where it belonged. Ryker started for the exit, passing through sweaty bodies and drifting swords. I nearly had to duck to avoid being hit by one of the Hunters sparing. Through the field, the clang of metal against metal echoed across the land, the sound of battle calling out to the Huntress deep within me. I still couldn't believe that I had made it into the Sunfire Court guard. Me. The first Huntress.

Still, there was something pressing on my mind, something that I could not seem to ignore, and Ryker would know the answers to my questions. He was Kanen's second after all. "Ryker," I called out. He halted and turned until he met my gaze, curiosity flashing under his eyes.

"Yes?" He lifted his brow.

"The vampire. Did she wake up yet? Do we know why she was here, or what happened to her?" Ryker sighed as if he knew this was coming but didn't want to answer. I pressed, not breaking my pleading gaze with him. This could finally be my chance to find answers.

I waited for him to respond.

Ryker shifted, as if he was uncomfortable with sharing any information with me about the female vampire that he had locked up, but as he looked at me, I could see in his eyes that he was going to give in to my plea. He rolled his eyes and dropped his hands. "You can't repeat this to anyone. If Kanen finds out that I mentioned anything, he will have my head."

Ryker leaned forward, the heat of his breath caressing my ear as he spoke. "We have the vampire locked up in Kanen's tent, and as of right now, I believe she is still asleep. Our guess is that when she tried to cross our barrier, the magic must have knocked her out."

"I thought you said our barrier was supposed to keep them from entering at all." I tilted my head.

"It was, but something has been going on with the Queen's magic. We think that there are weak spots now through our perimeter. Vulnerabilities, and with the magic depleted in those spots, it allowed the vampire to cross…"

"But not without hurting her," I finished. Ryker nodded and now I was left with more questions than answers. If the Queen really did have magic, how come it was all of a sudden depleting, growing weaker? Why were the vamps trying to come into our lands? My curiosity swirled around my head like an unforgiving storm as I tried to come up with reasons as to why this could be happening.

"No," Ryker hissed.

"No, what?"

"I see that look in your eyes. You are not going to see her. Kanen would never allow it."

Was I that obvious? I had better practice a better facade next time. "I don't know what you are talking about. I have no intention of going to see the vampire," I lied.

Ryker drifted his gaze along my body, inspecting me from head to toe with a frown smeared across his face. "Good. The last thing you need to do is piss Kanen off even more."

"Is this it?" We were coming up on a vast area laden with tents aligned in a half circle. At the center, a large crowd was gathered around, seemingly ignorant to the fact that we were walking up. Ryker offered a devilish grin and nodded. "We call this the Core. This is where the Hunters will come to relax. Enjoy. Over there, we can go grab some food."

It took everything in me not to squeak with joy as I gazed upon a banquet of food lying out along a large table. My mouth instantly began to water as the vibrant colors and sultry scents drifted in my direction. I inhaled, pulling the scent in, when the gentle touch of Ryker's hand on my shoulder broke my focus.

"Smells good, huh? Come on, I'll show you around." Ryker led the way, and I followed. As I approached the table, I felt my tongue dance with excitement. Food that I had never seen before lay before me, beckoning for me to give my tastebuds what they so desperately desired. Ryker handed me a wooden plate and said, "Have whatever you want," and then drifted off to his left.

I stayed where I was, completely overwhelmed by the options that I had. Growing up, most of my meals consisted of leftovers, stale bread, and if I was lucky, a nice bowl of warm soup. In my wildest dreams, I would never have expected to ever stand before a feast and be given the option to choose to eat *whatever* my heart desired.

I reached for an apple—so red that it reminded me of spilled blood. It pulled me in, my mind getting lost in the memory of my father. I held the apple in my hand for longer than I should have, staring into its hypnotizing sheen before placing it on my plate. Next, I grabbed a frost-dusted pastry with a jelly center. My stomach growled more intensely the longer I stood here. I needed to find Ryker and find somewhere to sit.

I dragged my gaze along the camp, passing by Hunters sprawled out along the ground as if they had no worries in the world. For a moment, I had forgotten the cruel world we lived in, completely drawn into their bliss.

"Like what you see?" Ryker spoke from behind me, startling me from my thoughts.

I gasped and shot my head to his direction. "Never sneak up on a Huntress. Might not end so well for you next time."

Ryker laughed. "Well, it's good that you didn't have your dagger in your hands, or else I might be on the ground."

I couldn't help but snort and roll my eyes. "So, this is where you all come to…what? Hang out after almost killing each other?"

Ryker took my plate from my hand and grinned, walking over to an empty stone table off to the side. "Here, come sit in the shade." A beautiful, tall tree towered over the table, casting just enough shade to keep us from baking under the sun. I gladly obliged and sat down, immediately feeling the release of tension from battling for half the day.

"Your body will eventually get used to our training," Ryker said.

I blinked and refocused my attention on him. "What?" I asked.

"You are sore, aren't you? Don't worry. It's to be expected. Give it a week or so and you will be doing backflips after battle practice."

"It's that obvious, huh?" I rubbed my aching shoulder and tilted my chin. Underneath, my body screamed for a release, yearning for something to take the pain away, but I couldn't allow myself to succumb to being weak. I gritted my teeth and straightened up.

With a mouth full of food, Ryker nodded and said, "Well, to me it is. Your body language is different. I can tell you're in pain. After we eat, why don't you go rest? We can just start from where we left off tomorrow."

"Are you sure?" Ryker was right. My body felt as if it had been trampled on by a horse and then fell out of a tree, and as I continued to rub my shoulders, the aching only seemed to intensify. I hissed, nodding, accepting his offer.

"Yes, I am sure. I will tell Kanen that I have you on grounds patrol. He won't question a thing."

"Where is Kanen, by the way? Is he still with that vampire?" The wind around us was blowing furiously through the lands, whipping tendrils of my hair around my face. I tried to pull the pieces back, but to no avail. Ryker too was feeling the intensity of another storm approaching.

He gazed up at the sky, and said, "We should go soon. That storm is coming in fast," ignoring my question.

Ryker stood and I followed. "Is Kanen with the vampire?" I pressed.

Ryker looked at me through his tousled hair and grinned. "Not anymore. He had business to take care of. She is locked up." He hardened his stare, held it on me longer than I wanted, and said, "Don't worry. If you are concerned about her escaping, trust me, she won't."

"How can you be so sure? They supposedly have superhuman strength." I wasn't for certain but when I had learned of their existence—delving into a dark world of secrets and myths, searching for answers since my father's murder—I had learned among my years of being a Drifter that these particular vampires could snap your neck with a single flick of their wrist if they wished it. A buzzing feeling hummed through my body whenever I thought of the vampires, of the secrets they must hold. It was like a puzzle waiting to be solved, and I couldn't wait to crack open that knowledge.

"Trust me. She won't be able to get out of her cage without this. The cage is infused with our protective magic." Ryker reached into a small, black leather pouch and pulled out an iron key. My eyes went wide. If I could get my hands on that key, if I could go talk to the vampire, maybe she would be able to tell me something about that night my father died. I could feel my pulse pick up, but I didn't dare let my excitement show on my face. Instead, I hardened my expression and tightened my lips.

"Oh. Well, that's good to hear then. I guess I'll see you later. Which tent is yours?" I asked selfishly.

Ryker didn't think anything of it. He nodded his chin to his left and pointed past the Core and to a row of larger tents among the wall of the backside of the castle, and said, "Mine is the one way on the left, right next to Kanen's. If you need anything, just come ask."

He offered a soft grin and turned away. I knew that I should feel guilty for what I was going to do, but I needed answers, and I had waited ten years to finally have a chance to fuel my desire for vengeance. I stepped away and headed back to my tent, back to where I would plot a way to speak to this mysterious vampire.

Chapter Four: Escape

Lilah

Around me, the orange-yellow sky soon melted away until I was left gazing upon a blanket of stars; darkness had seeped its way into every corner, and with the darkness came silence.

Most of the Hunters had left their training fields and gone off to their tents to rest for the night. I knew most were probably succumbing to the deep pull of slumber, and even though my body begged for me to give myself to its desirable pull, I forced myself to stay awake.

I traced idle circles along the seam of my shirt, playing with the edges of my sleeves. There wasn't much else that I could do until I knew everyone had fallen asleep. My gaze shifted outside my tent, as I stared at the moon, watching as the distant storm clouds seemed to pass right by. A brilliant white crescent dangled above the camp like a charm, gifted to us from the stars. I drank in its milky essence and rubbed my eyes, letting the hours slip by. Now, judging by its position in the sky, it had to now be the middle of the night.

I knew Ryker was now probably asleep, so the only people that I had to worry about seeing me were the guards posted on night watch. Being on the edge of the camp, I could hear the moments that their feet would stir up the fallen leaves. They came in intervals, in twos, so I knew that the guards were paired up. If I timed this right, I could slip away and lurk among the shadows unnoticed.

It had been about ten minutes since I heard the last pair scurry by, and so I waited, counting the seconds, knowing that my chance was coming soon. Just as I suspected, the faint sound of boots rumbling among the grass echoed from the distance. I quietly slipped on my boots and prepared to leave just as they had passed.

Chattering soon was right at the back of my tent, but I didn't pay any attention to their conversation. The moment their voices drifted away, I took my chance, darted from my tent, and headed for the darkest part of the grounds. The midnight air was crisp, causing a trail of goosebumps to appear along my arms. That's how the weather was here in Eldoria, brutal heat during the day and bone shattering cold in the middle of the night. It was a foreboding of what was to come—Winter. The most brutal of seasons here.

Every step I took, I took with caution and stealth, carefully moving silently among my fellow Hunters. If I were to get caught, I was not sure what would happen, but finding out even the slightest hint of who murdered my father was worth the risk. Kanen's tent was on the farthest end of the grounds, past the Core, and along the castle wall—I remembered that much.

There was not a soul in sight. Silence enveloped the air around me and closed in. I sucked in my breath, afraid to make the faintest of sounds. First, I had to get the key from Ryker and then find my way into Kanen's tent.

Gods, please let them be asleep.

I was getting close. The Core was now behind me, and as I slowed my pace, I was now just approaching the outside of Ryker's tent. Crouched behind a bush, I peered around to make sure no one was around. I blew out a sigh and relaxed my shoulders when I realized that it was only me. This was going to be a piece of cake.

As I stood and started for the opening of his tent, I heard a noise, and I practically jumped in the air from the startlement. Before I could run and hide, I tripped over my foot and fell backward right on my ass.

"Lilah?"

Shame washed over me. Disappointment. I couldn't believe I fucked this up. I glanced up through my tangled hair and sighed. "Hey, Ryker. Sorry...Uh..."

"What are you doing out here?" he asked. Ryker kneeled down and lent out his hand, pulling me to my feet once I slipped my fingers through his. "Are you okay?" He seemed more worried about me falling on my ass rather than the fact that I was out here lurking in the middle of the night. I brushed the dirt from my clothes and laughed.

"Yeah, I am fine. Sorry about that. I uh...tripped."

"Right," he said, his eyes narrowing, now analyzing my body. "What are you doing out here so late?"

I had no time to think of what to say. I panicked. "I came to see you," I lied. Ryker's expression changed from worry to something else. Excitement? I wasn't sure but I did see a slight smirk for about half a second. It was his eyes that seemed to shift, gleaming with intensity.

"You did?" He leaned against one of the trees outside his tent. "Well, it's the middle of the night. What did you need?" Ryker crossed his arms lazily across his chest and softened his expression. Then my eyes watched as his fingers played with the small leather bag that hung on his belt, completely oblivious to the fact that I had my gaze locked on it.

Shit. I needed that key to convince the vampire to give me what I needed. And the only thing that I could think of in this moment was using my charm to get what I wanted. I flicked my hair off my shoulder and smiled. "I just wanted to see you. I wanted to…thank you, for uh…such a great training session earlier."

It took everything in me not to laugh at the horrible acting I was putting on, but when I met his gaze, I knew he had bought it. His throat constricted in a swallow as he offered a devilish grin. "Ready for more training then?"

"Actually," I said, stepping closer. "I was thinking of something else." I closed the space between us in a slow stride toward him. Ryker straightened his posture, the curve of his lip twitching slightly. Loose strands of his hair caught the wind. As my body reached his, I hovered my mouth slightly over his, whispering, "I was thinking of this." I laced my fingers into his hair, pulling him in until I slipped my tongue into his mouth, his lips parting for me desperately. His soft groans told me his desperation for my touch was something that was there. His wanting pleasure. And I gave him just that.

He deepened the kiss, more fervent with every breath, and I caught his escaping moans with my mouth as I let my body take control. Even though I was doing this as a distraction, I was surprised to feel how much my body liked being touched by him, but just as quickly as our kiss had started, it had ended.

My body slowly pulled away and I felt the lingering swollenness of his lips pressed against mine. I smiled, a genuine smile, and said, "Thank you," and started to walk away.

Ryker caught my arm. "Wait!"

When I turned around, I could see that I had him under my spell, his eyes pleading for more. "Where are you going?" he asked.

I glanced at the stars that hung above us and smiled. "It's late, remember? I need to get some rest. So do you. I'm not going easy on you tomorrow."

There was that devilish grin of his. I could tell I had succeeded in my plan. Ryker only nodded, kissing my hand, and said, "Well then, goodnight my lady. I will see you on the battlefield," and then turned back into his tent.

A wave of relief washed over me as I realized that I hadn't gotten caught, his small leather pouch now dangling between my fingers. My grip on the pouch tightened as I crept my way toward Kanen's tent. My heart was now slamming against my ribcage as I approached. I knew that I would have to somehow sneak past him—without waking him, and if I succeeded, I still needed to convince this vampire to give me answers. She could easily kill me after I let her out, but this was a risk I was willing to take. For Father.

Before I entered the tent, I slipped one last glance over my shoulder, just to make sure that Ryker hadn't come back out. To my relief, he hadn't. There was a dim glow coming from inside, the warm orange hues dancing among the shadows. My fingers delicately pushed through the flap of fabric that hung over the entrance as I peered inside.

It was quiet. Peaceful.

Kanen's tent was *huge*, stretching about the size of four of my tents, and when I turned my gaze to my left, that was when I noticed him, sound asleep. Even in his sleep he looked furious; his hand clutched a medium-sized sword firmly on his side. I guess Hunters truly were ready for battle at any given time.

Suddenly there was a shuffle. A noise coming from the darkened corners where the lamp's light didn't touch. I sucked in my breath and almost staggered back from fear. A moment passed before my body loosened, and then I heard it again.

Hissing.

Was that the—

Before I could finish that thought, two brilliantly bright yellow eyes were looking right at me. I blinked, picking at the seam of my pants in a nervous tick. I knew who those eyes belonged to, but I didn't want to admit it. All my life I had sworn that I would enact vengeance on their kind, on the bloodsuckers who murdered my father, but as I stood in the presence of one, I only felt myself shrinking with uncertainty.

"I won't bite," she hissed. Her voice was merely a whisper among the wind, but it felt as if she had pressed her lips right up to my ear to speak. I tightened my grip on the little leather bag in my hand and slowly plodded toward her.

Her fingers laced around the metal bars that held her in as she pressed her body closer to me. A faint curve of her lip twitched when I stepped closer. Sweat beaded on my brow and dripped into my eye; weird since it was so cold this time of night, but I wiped it away and gulped. I wondered how the magic holding her in worked. The metal bars weren't burning her, but maybe she just couldn't pass the threshold without opening the lock.

She was so…beautiful; her vibrant orange hair reminded me of the leaves that had fallen from the trees in the nearby gardens. I traced my eyes over her features, taking in the beauty, the delicacy, of her expression, but once my eyes fell upon her eyes, that was when I saw her for the true predator that she was.

"Came to torture me some more, human?" she flashed me her sharpened canines and tilted her head. Her fingers danced along the metal bars, one by one, tapping her nails in a rhythm.

My body shifted away, and I froze. "I uh…"

"Or have you come here to quench my thirst? I am feeling quite parched." There was a wicked gleam in her eyes, one that promised all the things she could probably do to me if she weren't behind these bars. The longer I stood there before her, the more I questioned if I were about to make a terrible mistake.

"Is that what they did to you?" I asked, going back to what she first had mentioned. I hated these creatures, but still, it didn't feel right to torture someone.

She inclined her head and smiled. "They did lots of things to me." Her fingers slipped up her sleeves and exposed fresh wounds along her forearms. I reached forward—on instinct—and she hissed as she stepped back.

"Shh, please," I begged. "I came here for something. To make a deal with you." I pulled the key from the leather bag in my hand and dangled it from my fingertips. She immediately focused on the key and then shot a deathly stare in my direction.

"Speak," she demanded.

I gulped. No one ordered me around like that. My fingers closed around the key, and I put it back into the bag, back into my pocket. "First," I said. "Don't demand anything from me. Second, I need something from you first."

Her jaw was set in a hard line as she nodded her head. "Fine. What is it that you want?"

"My father was murdered by your kind ten years ago. I want to know who killed him. Do you know anything of a man named Geraldi Benonni?"

The vampire smiled when my father's name slipped through my lips, as if she knew exactly what I was talking about. "I may know something about that name. What do I get in return?"

This time, I laced my words with demand, my voice coming out as an almost growl. "Give me any information you can, and I will let you go. On the condition that you don't harm anyone on our lands. You simply must go back to where you are from."

I was playing a dangerous game, making deals with a creature of the night, but I may never get another chance like this. Silence settled over us, casting a wicked eeriness to the atmosphere, but I didn't let myself succumb to her games. My eyes narrowed in on her as I waited for her to take me up on my offer. The corner of her lip twitched up in a half smile, knowing damn well that she was feeding off the amusement of making me wait.

"Now or never. Your choice."

I almost started to walk away when I heard a quiver in her voice. "Wait. I know of something. A rumor of that night." I raised my brow at her. "Where I am from, my king has strict rules of speaking of things that you did not witness, but I remember hearing something about a way to break our curse."

Was she talking about the curse that the ancient queen had put on the vampires? The one that would cause their flesh to burn in daylight? Was that why they were at my home because Father knew how to break it? I vaguely remembered them mentioning the curse and the girl, who I assumed must have been me, but what was my connection to all of this?

No. That wouldn't make sense. If Father knew, then they wouldn't have killed him. The mentioning of my father made my heart flutter in ways that I couldn't describe, but my body did want to sit from the building tension that I was now feeling.

"Was that what those men were doing? Looking for a way to break the curse?"

The vampire smiled and nodded her head slowly. "I heard that there is something among your lands that is legend to be able to rid my kind of this curse, but I don't know *what* it is. They must have been searching for answers that night."

"Who were they? The men that killed him," I pressed. The vampire's mouth twitched as her eyes went blank for a moment. I could tell she was trying to remember anything else of what she heard of that night, but when she met my gaze again, I knew that that was as much as I was going to get out of her.

"I don't think I ever learned that much of the curse, or of that night. I tend to keep to myself." Her eyes drifted to my hands. She was searching for the key, pleading for me to release her silently, but I had more questions before I was going to commit such a crime.

"Why were you crossing our borders?" I held my stare on her, dangling the key only a few feet away from her face.

She scoffed and rolled her eyes. "You humans. Always wanting more. I gave you what you asked for. You should release me."

Before I could speak, the sounds of a body shifting behind me stole my attention. Her eyes flicked past my shoulder, narrowing into a predator's stare. I turned my head, but to my relief, it was just Kanen turning over. For a brief moment, my eyes flicked to the empty bottle of—what I assumed to be—liquor half spilled onto the ground. Lucky me that he chose tonight to get utterly fuddled. I knew he had Hunters patrolling the area, so I needed to get this over with before he woke up or someone found me. I needed to get this over with before he woke up. "Why were you crossing our borders?" I asked again. I wasn't going to let this go.

The vampire wrapped her fingers around the cage poles and flashed me her canines; they were as white as bone, glimmering under the flicker of the lantern's light. "I was forced to cross over to your land. The magic that protects your precious land is dying. My king sent me to find out for myself how vulnerable your barriers truly are."

Did she say forced? I wanted to ask more questions, but she hissed with impatience. I flinched and nodded. "Fine. I will let you out. You promised you will go straight home to your land. Go far away from here and don't come back."

I lifted the key, placed it in the lock, and twisted. There was a click and then before I knew it, the vampire had her body pressed against mine, pinning me against the wall of the cage. Her lips hovered above my ear, breathing heavy, deep breaths. "You smell so good," she hissed. "I should suck you dry right here." My fingers carefully searched for something that I could use to stab her; maybe it would give me time to run, but just as I was about to panic, she pulled away and grunted. "But I won't. A deal is a deal."

I let loose a large breath and relaxed my body. "Wait," I whispered. "What is your name?"

She glanced back at me and smiled softly, and said, "I'm Sadi," and then whisked away into the night.

Kanen was stirring more frequently now, and I knew that if I didn't get out of here soon, that I would be caught and labeled a traitor. Now that I had some information about the night of my father's murder, I could start to work on finding the missing pieces.

Before Kanen had any more chances to hear me scurrying through his tent, I bolted outside.

Thankfully, it was still dark, and if I had to guess probably only about one in the morning or so. Before I poked my head completely outside, I took a final glance around to check for the patrolling Hunters. They came in intervals, and I knew it was about time for them to pass by here again soon. They still must be far away enough. Leaving the tent, I stepped stealthily as I approached Ryker's tent. I still would have time to sleep a few hours if I hurried back to my tent, but one thing had to be done first though. I retraced my steps back the way I came, and as I passed by Ryker's I dropped his small leather pouch by the front entrance of his tent and took off. When he wakes, he will just assume that he dropped it, and I could go back to being the Huntress that I was.

Again, more alarm horns were blaring; chaos was ensuing outside just before the ass crack of dawn; the sunlight barely peaked through the horizon. I knew what all the commotion was about—Sadi had escaped and now the Hunters were going ballistic because they had lost their prisoner. If anyone found out that I was the one who let her out, I don't know what would happen. There were hundreds of footsteps stomping by my tent, as if running through the fields in a frantic search.

There was no use. She was gone, but I was a little closer now to getting what my heart so desperately desired. I rubbed my eyes and sat up, knowing damn well that my sleep was over, and slipped myself into a clean pair of pants and shirt. There was a small dagger with an attachment that hooked onto my belt lying on my dresser. I snatched it up and hooked it through the belt loop before stepping outside. I would have preferred a sword, but I didn't have time to get fully dressed in my gear.

There were Hunters everywhere, dressed in full battle gear and scurrying around like they were in the middle of a war. If I hadn't known what was going on, fear would have definitely have ahold of my emotions, but instead, I just gazed upon the chaos and froze.

"Lilah!" I heard a familiar voice call out. It was Ryker. He was running toward me, his tousled hair bouncing with every step. I had almost forgotten that I kissed him until my eyes met his and then fell to his lips. Did I start something that I wasn't sure I wanted?

"Are you okay?" he asked. He reached out his hand and touched my arm gently.

"Yeah, I am fine. What is going on?" I asked.

"The vampire escaped somehow."

I pretended to be surprised and even widened my eyes when he told me this. "What? How could she escape?"

Ryker's head darted all around while he scoped the land and then returned his attention back to me. "Kanen had her locked away, but when he woke up to check on her this morning, the cage was opened. The lock was gone. We think she must have broken it somehow and taken it with her."

That clever vampire. She knew that if she left the lock, then Kanen would know immediately that it must have been opened with the key. Taking it gave them the false idea that she broke it and took it with her. I could feel my lip starting to curve into a smile, but I forced it back to a hardened line. "Well, aren't they super strong?"

"Some are, some aren't. Their kind have rankings and different levels of power. It's possible that she could have been strong enough to break out of that cage, but we assumed since the magic in our barrier had knocked her out like that, that she was one of the weakest of her kind."

"Never underestimate your enemy," I said.

Ryker smiled partially and pulled me off to the side. "It won't be crazy like this for much longer. Kanen already has sent out half the men to search our grounds for her. The others will be posted on watch."

"Well, what are you going to do?" I asked, crossing my arms.

"Kanen needs me for something, but don't worry. I am going to have Damon stick with you today. You still need to train."

I sighed and rolled my eyes. "Really? You are going to make me train today? I want to go out and patrol with the rest of the Hunters." Ryker ran his fingers through his hair and said, "You will. In time. But now, I need you here where I know you will be safe."

His fingers found their way down my arm and now were tracing idle circles along the tops of my hands. "About last night," he started, but Damon came from behind him and clapped him on the shoulder.

"I'm ready for practice whenever you are." Damon lifted his gaze toward me and offered a devilish grin.

"You aren't worried about the vampire escaping?" I asked.

Damon scoffed and unsheathed his sword. "No, I'll be ready if she comes. Right now, my only job is to make sure I knock you on your ass at least ten times." He offered me a wink, and that was the moment I told myself that I was going to kick his ass. Respectfully.

Lilah

 It had been hours since Ryker left me and Damon to train while most of the Hunters went off to search for their lost prisoner. I knew Sadi was long gone, and glad at that. The longer I stayed in the presence of such evil, the more I could feel my hatred burning a hole in my chest. I needed an escape, and training gave me just that.

"You're holding back," Damon said, his voice calm, but I could tell he was challenging me, his eyes demanding as he stared me down. I twirled my spear effortlessly between my fingers—thanks to the many years of practice with Eldrich's secret armory.

"Afraid you'll hurt me?" He flashed me a devilish grin.

I smirked and tightened my grip on my spear. "Not a chance. I just don't want to hurt your ego. You Hunters do get embarrassed pretty easily."

Damon didn't go easy on me. He gave me everything he had, swinging his sword with brutal precision. I danced around him, spinning my spear in a blur of movement as I dogged his strikes. For every powerful strike Damon threw at me, I countered, my movements just as unpredictable and sharp as his. I fought with precision and speed, while Damon relied on power and endurance.

We had been going at this for hours now, and due to my lack of sleep, I knew that my fighting would be off. Every muscle in my body screamed as I tried to keep up with my battle partner. I knew I had to cause a distraction to beat him, and so I lifted my spear upward, bringing his attention to the sky and as I had his guard drawn to my spear, I swiped out his legs from under him. Damon crashed to the ground and groaned as he rolled onto his hands and knees. I could have gone easy on him, but I was a ruthless Huntress, and I needed to win. Charging forward with renewed fury, I slammed into him with my body and knocked him over once more, blood now dripping from his busted lip.

He smiled and wiped the stream of red dripping from his mouth. "Seems I underestimated you," he said. I gave him a chance to get back on his feet because a true Hunter won their battles fairly. He picked up his sword and twirled it in his hands. "Ready?" he asked. "Ready."

Our weapons clashed, crackling through the air like lightning striking the ground. Sweat now dripped from my face; I licked the salty liquid from the corner of my mouth and kept my gaze locked on Damon, circling him as if he were my prey. I was looking for a weakness, something that I could use to win this fight, but there was nothing that I could see in this moment.

My breathing became ragged as I drew in another large breath. I needed to end this fight soon before I collapsed from exhaustion. Damon began to circle me, smiling a wicked smile as he met my eyes, and I flashed him the same expression right back.

"You know, Lilah, I didn't think you would fight this tough." Damon readied his stance as if he were ready to pounce.

My lips curled into a smirk. "You won't make that same mistake again," I said. Before he could strike, I lunged my spear forward so fast that I almost couldn't believe it was me and jabbed right into his hand.

Damon dropped his sword and hissed. He acted quickly, trying to pick up his sword before I had a chance to take him out, but like I said, I was fast.

My body came hurtling forward and crashed into him, knocking him off his feet. Damon staggered back and almost toppled on his ass. Clearly winded from the hours we have spent battling under the brutal sun. I brought my spear upward and charged for him with no mercy, but just as the tip was about to meet his flesh, he held up his hands. "Okay. You win."

Immediately, I dropped my spear and smiled. "I what?" I mocked.

Damon flashed me a wicked grin and rolled his eyes. "I said you win. You beat me in battle." He was breathing heavily and hunched over as he tried to catch his breath, his hand now dripping a small stream of blood onto the ground.

A new wave of pride swept through my body as I realized that this meant I was moving up the ranks. I stepped forward and held out my hand. "You fought hard, like a true Huntress," he said as he shook it.

I nodded and smiled. "Thank you. You were a tough partner to beat."

Damon chuckled and swiped his hands through his tousled hair. "Let's take a break. We need to eat and wash." I watched as my battle partner picked up his sword and strode away from the battlefield. I knew where he was going. He was headed to where all the Hunters went to wind down—the Core.

Chapter Six: The Core

Lilah

After I had found a small creek near my tent to wash the dirt from my body, I slipped on some clean clothes that Ryker had left in a chest for me and made my way to the Core. My stomach growled, and this was the first time I truly took a moment to appreciate that I didn't have to steal food. Even though I had spent the past two years with Eldrich, all those years living as a Drifter had done something to me. There was always the feeling that it wouldn't last with him. That one day I would be kicked out and forced back to the streets. But now, I didn't have to worry or lurk among the shadows and eat what had been left out for the rodents. I no longer had to go hungry, wondering if this would be the last time that I would eat.

My fingers clutched my stomach as I smiled, coming up on the group of Hunters lounging around. It was a lot emptier than I remembered it, but I had to remind myself that more than half our army was sent on patrol.

My eyes scanned the area until I found the banquet table laden with food, passing the Hunters that were lost in their conversations. Instantly, my mouth watered as I eyed bowls of fruit that looked as if it had just been picked, soft, warm bread, and clean vases of water.

I needed this.

I grabbed myself a plate and piled on as much as it could hold and made my way over to the same stone table that Ryker had shown me. I liked it over there. It was calm, peaceful, and completely off in its own vicinity.

The tree above me cast the most wonderful shadow which kept me from literally cooking under the blazing sun rays. If it were not for the clouds rolling through and my new tree friend, I probably wouldn't be able to stand this heat. This time of year, was odd—when Summer began to transition to Fall. I knew Fall was here, and Winter would soon be approaching, bringing about a wicked cold that seeped into your bones. Every year, I barely managed to survive the freezing temperatures, but now that I was a Huntress, I had no doubt that they would give me what I needed to stay alive.

As the hues of warm steam lifted from the freshly baked bread hit my nose, I melted. It smelled so good. My fingers ripped a piece away and shoved it into my mouth. I was lost in the moment of my desires, completely focused on the ecstasy this food was causing me when I felt someone place their hand on my shoulder.

I flinched and shot my attention behind me, but as soon as I saw Ryker standing there, looking rather defeated, I loosened my shoulders. "Ryker? What are you doing back so soon?" In his eyes, there was an emptiness that I hadn't seen before; a hollow look of despair that lingered from his gaze.

He blinked and looked away as if he knew I was analyzing his gaze. "We called off our search for now. Our Hunters searched every corner of the castle grounds, and we didn't find anything."

When he returned his gaze to me, a small smile tugged at his lip. "I heard you beat Damon in battle today. That is hard to do. Damon is one of my best Hunters." Ryker took a seat next to me and placed his hands on the table.

"Well, he sure didn't go easy on me," I joked.

Ryker looked at me and I knew by his expression that he was here for a purpose, not to just hang around. "I think you are ready for the next level of training. I have a new mission for you."

"Oh?" I inquired.

"We can go over the details in a little bit. Finish your food and meet me at my tent when you are done." Ryker stood and smiled at me before walking off. His silhouette disappeared into the horizon and now I was left alone wondering what my new mission would be.

It didn't take long for me to finish the rest of my food; my belly was now nice and full, a feeling I thought I'd never get to experience in my life of being a Drifter— before Eldrich found me. Sure, the old man kept food on is table, but it was *nothing* compared to this. Ryker's tent wasn't far from the Core. Maybe only about another ten-minute walk or so. Besides, the fresh air was nice to walk through.

In the distance, I could see Ryker leaning against a tree; the same tree I had kissed him under. I brought my fingers to my lips, almost feeling the reminiscence of his soft touch. Guilt crept its way through my nerves as I thought about how I used Ryker like that. It's not that I couldn't see myself pursuing something with him, but I had bigger things on my mind right now.

He lifted his head and smiled when he noticed me approaching, his hands fell to his sides, and he straightened his posture. "You ready to hear about your new mission?" he said. Ryker started walking toward his tent when I noticed something small on the ground by the entrance—the leather pouch. He hadn't noticed it was missing yet. My eyes darted away before he could see me looking at it, but I think I was too late, because he chuckled and said, "Oh, my bag. I must have dropped this on my way back from our search." Ryker leaned forward and picked up his leather bag and refastened it to his belt. An exhale of relief expelled from my chest knowing that I had escaped any suspicion of what I had done. To Kanen, to the Hunters, Sadi escaped on her own, and that was exactly how I wanted that narrative to stay.

"I hope whatever it is, there is shade involved." I laughed and stepped closer. Now that I was only a few feet away, my eyes noticed the finer details of his face; the hard lines between his eyebrows, the speckles of dirt that had been splattered across his skin, and the look in his eyes, a desperation for something. I couldn't pinpoint what exactly that could be.

This man that stood before me wore his façade like armor, masking the true emotions that lingered beneath, but the more time I spent with him, the more those layers were peeling back. "Oh, trust me, there will be plenty of that. And if I am honest, I would be lying if I said I wasn't worried for you to come along on this mission, but Kanen insisted."

"Kanen? He is the one who approved this?"

Ryker nodded his head. Now I was really curious as to what I was supposed to do. I followed Ryker into his tent and the first thing that I noticed was how he had decorated the inside to resemble the forest. There were small pots with new tree saplings growing in the corner and soft grass where his boots didn't trudge up mud. He even had flowers placed along one of his tables, which made me smile softly.

"I like your tent," I admitted.

He laughed nervously and ran his fingers through his hair. "Thanks. I like to bring nature into my place as much as I can. It reminds me of how peaceful things can be out there sometimes. Which brings me to why I brought you here."

He turned to face me and placed his hands on my shoulders, meeting my gaze.

"Well, what is it then?" I asked.

Ryker drew in a large breath, and said, "Kanen wants you to come with one of my groups. We will be going into the Dark Lands."

I bit the corner of my lip, wide-eyed. I had never been in the Dark Lands and from our previous conversation, Ryker hadn't been back to them since that incident. The closest I ever came to them was the night my father was murdered, and even then, I could feel the oppressive weight of its eeriness holding me down. That place was filled with creatures that your worst nightmares wouldn't dream of, so I would be lying if I said I wasn't even the slightest bit scared.

"Why are we going into the Dark Lands?" I asked, tilting my head.

Ryker paused for a second, as if thinking of what he said next very carefully, and replied, "We will be testing our barriers, expanding our lands, and looking for clues as to why that vampire had trespassed into our lands."

"And you think I am ready for this?" Ryker didn't answer. I pressed. "You don't?"

His eyes met mine, desperate, yearning, and said, "That's not it. The Dark Lands are dangerous and I..." his voice trailed off. He shook his head. "It doesn't matter. I think you have proven to be a fantastic fighter, which is why Kanen suggested you come along for this mission."

I didn't want to pry any more. I simply nodded my head and sighed. "So then, when do we leave for this *dangerous* mission?" That got a smile out of him.

Ryker grabbed a small bag from his table and tossed it into my arms and then grabbed one for himself. "We leave right now."

What? Right now? I didn't even have time to prepare myself for what I was about to get in to, but if I was being totally honest with myself, I was scared shitless.

Chapter Seven: Into the Woods

Lilah

'You must never go into the Dark Lands.' **Father's voice** still haunted me with this warning, even today.

All light was seemingly absorbed by the shadows that loomed within the Dark Lands, a wall of contorted, twisted trees sunk deep within, giving off a warning to those who dared to enter. I fingered the strap of my bag that crossed over my chest as I stood before such horror.

The smell of rotting leaves littered the mossy ground, its sweet and pungent stench gliding through the wind, but that wasn't all that was rotten. I knew rotten flesh when I smelt it, and these woods reeked of death. Ryker must have noticed the look in my eyes and leaned closer to whisper in my ear. "Don't worry. The creatures of these woods tend to stay in the center. You'll be fine. We are expanding our perimeter charm and searching for clues on the missing vampire. You see anything, you tell me right away. Understood?"

I nodded.

Truthfully, I wanted to run away; all of those warnings Father gave me as a little girl came rushing to the surface. These were the very woods that harbored the monsters who ripped my father apart, and now I was about to willingly step right into them. I was a Huntress now, which meant that I could not show fear. I'd be damned if I let it show on my face. My nose tipped up, chin tilted, and I drew in a breath and took a step forward, stepping over the threshold of our protective barrier.

The air stilled the moment my body fully left the safety of Eldoria, as if it were wrapping its invisible fingers around me and pulling me in. My breath quickened and my heart rose to an abnormal speed but suddenly my attention was caught.

"Alright," Ryker announced. "We do this quick. With precision. And get out before dark comes."

I looked up at the sky and squinted. I would assume we had another couple hours or so before darkness came. Normally, for a mission this dangerous, we would have left earlier, but Ryker said Kanen insisted to start now, that if we waited until tomorrow, Sadi's tracks might not be there anymore.

The group of Hunters started forward and Ryker followed. I was the last to fully walk into the woods but when Ryker glanced over his shoulder, I hurried my pace and made sure I kept up.

The sounds of swords unsheathing rang throughout the darkness, and as we ventured deeper, the light slowly diminished with it. One of the Hunters lit a fire in their lantern and held it up so that we could see better. Warm orange hues cast among the trees. It was weird how even though it wasn't night, the darkness in this forest seemed to shroud the light around us. Only occasionally would I see the beams of light peering through the canopy.

"How are you going to expand our perimeter?" I asked curiously. Ryker glanced at me and pulled something from his pocket—a small dagger, encrusted with deep red rubies. I widened my eyes and watched as he stabbed the tip into the dirt, whispering something under his breath.

"What is that supposed to do?"

Ryker glanced up at me while kneeling and said, "This dagger belongs to the Queen. The magic she has can be transferred to objects. The Queen wants more land; she wants to eventually take over the Dark Lands. When I place this dagger into the dirt, it infuses our magic into the ground. What I was whispering was a protective spell."

I scoffed. "That's it? It's that easy?" Surely, it should take more than a little spell to expand our protective barrier.

Ryker arched his brow. "What is so funny?"

"Oh, it's nothing. I just never truly believed in the whole magic thing. I thought it was made up to make us feel safe. Even as a little girl, my father would talk about the barriers, but I didn't *really* think there was a magic wall keeping those *things* out. But if it's that easy, why haven't you done this sooner?" He chuckled and stood, removing the dagger and placing it back into its holster.

"You mean extend our barrier?"

I arched my brow. "Mhm."

"Well, it's real, and so are all the myths you probably heard growing up. But our magic has to be replenished. The Queen lets her commanders know when there is enough for the spell, and then we are sent out to extend the barrier. The farther out we go, the more magic we need. And truthfully, I never thought to question her about the spell. It does seem simple, but this is how it has been done for many years."

The men from our group had split up and dispersed among the forest to search for clues about the missing vampire—Sadi, leaving Ryker and I alone, in the dark.

"Step one…complete. Now we just need to search a little longer before we go back to camp." He offered a soft smile and brought his lantern higher so that we could see better among the shadows. All light seemed to be swallowed but the towering trees and interwoven canopy that shielded us from the white blast of the sun. Each step through the rustled leaves upturned a waft of a sweet and pungent odor from the mossy ground and rotting leaves. I crinkled my nose to get rid of the smell and kept my gaze outward. Ryker veered left and so, I veered right, keeping my pace slow and delicate. My eyes stayed glued to the ground, careful not to trip over the twisting roots that seemed to break from the surface.

There it was again. That familiar smell in the air. The wind had blown just enough in my direction to carry the sweet scent of flowers to my nose. My favorite smell. I inhaled and let out a breath, calmness washing over me. I followed the wind, scanning the forest for my special gift, and that was when I saw it.

A small red flower nestled up between two rocks, its vibrant sun-kissed color standing out like a flame among the shadows. My feet glided over to it as I bent down to pick it up. The petals fluttered in the wind as I twirled the velvety texture between my fingers, lifting it to my nose and taking in the warming scent. For years now I have been finding these treasures from nature. And every time I came across one, it brought back a sense of peace within my body.

I craned my head back to see how far Ryker had walked off too—not far. His silhouette still shifted among the trees. I decided to make my way over in his direction to see if he had found anything interesting. Over here, there was nothing out of the ordinary that I could think of to report, save for my little flower, but Ryker wouldn't care about the wind blowing this into the woods. I placed my flower back down on the moss under my feet and left it behind.

"Anything?" I shouted.

Ryker snapped his attention to me and shrugged his shoulders. "Not yet. It seems pretty quiet today. I haven't made my way over there yet. Come join me. Four eyes are better than two." Ryker nodded his head to the area ahead of him. My feet scurried to catch up with him as we both walked off, searching for clues of where Sadi could have gone.

Ryker and I spent at least another hour or so searching the woods for clues of what direction Sadi had gone in, while the other Hunters veered to our left to search more area. I played along with my ignorance, although, I was curious which way she escaped to. Velorim—Dravian's kingdom—hadn't been found in over one hundred years, which had gotten my curiosity piqued. How could that be? But then again, being out here while the sun was setting truly set in the reality of the dangers that lurked within these lands. I could feel the world shift its energy, slowly changing to something more sinister as the sun began to set. I knew we were out of time with our search as I peered up through the canopy, watching the blue-sky fade.

"What exactly are we looking for?" I asked.

"Traces of her…anything that could tell us which way she went, really." I nodded my head and started to scan the area. I followed a small trail that led deeper into the woods, the crackle of branches snapping under my feet *clicked* and *cracked* with every step. Ryker was right behind me but stayed silent.

There was nothing that I could see that indicated any kind of reminiscence of her, but I kept looking; I had to make it believable that I didn't know where she was. "Where *does* the Queen's magic come from," I asked, breaking the silence. "I mean, I know the magic comes from the land, but how does she get it?"

Ryker grunted. "I don't know. Only a handful of people do, but they are her closest guards. She is very secretive when it comes to her magic. I'm not sure why. The only thing that I know is that her ancestors had an artifact that granted the magic, but in order to dip into its power, they had to give it something in return."

"So, she inherited the magic then?"

"Yes. Born into power. Lucky her." I heard Ryker scoff as we continued forward, which made me chuckle. Before I could respond, I heard a twig snap to my left. I snapped my head in that direction, but the darkness swallowed the landscape, making it impossible to see that far.

"Did you hear that?" I asked.

"Yes. Shhh," he whispered.

"Was that one of our Hunters?"

Ryker didn't answer, but by the way the energy shifted around us, I already knew his answer was going to be *no*. My heart started to thrum; my fingers now gripped my small dagger tightly as I listened. Reaching over my shoulder, I unsheathed my sword and held it firmly with my other hand. Two blades were better than one in my opinion. Ryker followed the noise, but I stayed right where I was as I watched his silhouette slowly disappear into the shadows.

"Ryker?" I whispered.

I pulled my hair up into a high bun to keep it from sticking to my face and glanced around—

A scream ripped through the air, a terrifying and bloodcurdling call for help. I gasped and almost dropped my dagger in the process. That was when I heard chaos ensuing all around me. Horrifying wails of desperation rang through the woods, and I knew that those were the cries of the other Hunters. I began to run toward the direction that Ryker had gone, fueled by my adrenaline that now coursed through my body.

"Ryker!"

There was no answer, but I could hear echoes of hissing and screaming all around me. I wanted to curl into myself; flashes of my father's death came rushing to the surface, but before I let myself get pulled in too deep, I felt a hand tug on my shoulder.

"Lilah." It was Ryker, looking sweaty and beaten. He was breathing heavily as if he had been fighting something big. My eyes looked him up and down. "What is going on?" I cried.

He leaned down and put his finger on my lips. "Shh. They will hear you. It's an ambush. The vampire must have sent more to our borders. I didn't think she would have after what happened to her trying to cross our barrier."

"Did you see them?"

"No, but I am assuming it's them. We need to get you out of here." Ryker grabbed my arm and pulled me up and we began running through the dark. The screaming was all around us, and as we made our way to the exit, an eerie silence started to fade into the air. I stopped running. "Why did the screaming stop? Are they—"

"Dead?" he finished. "I need to go make sure they made it out. There is some magic in our weapons, which offers us some protection from the vampires. My men are well trained. Let's just get you out of here and then we will go make sure the rest of the group made it back over our barrier."

Before I could take a step, something swiped me out from under my feet, my back slamming onto the ground, ejecting the air from my lungs. My bag was tossed across the ground and just out of my reach, and as I blinked away the stars, I realized that my sword had flown out of my grip. I gasped and clenched my chest. Coughing, I called for Ryker. His name came out as a pathetic whimper, but I heard something hit him from behind too.

"Lilah…" his voice called out. He sounded weak. As I lay on the ground, trying to catch my breath, that's when I heard something large plodding toward me.

The ground shook with every step it took. I scrambled onto my hands and knees, but when I glanced through my tangled hair, it was no vampire that I was staring at. What stood before me looked nothing short of monstrous.

I heard Ryker suck in his breath behind me, but my breath had been stolen from my chest. Its snout snarled back in a growl revealing a set of razor-sharp teeth. Saliva dripped from the tips as if its hunger for me took control. Its eyes were pitch black, glossed over with a translucent sheen; I could see my reflection in its eyes.

"Lilah, run," Ryker struggled to say. I heard him fumble for his sword, but he sounded weak. There was more hissing surrounding us now and I knew that there were more of these creatures stalking us. "How do I kill this thing?" I whispered.

"You have to sever their spines or puncture their brains." The hissing grew closer and this beast in front of me was shifting its weight. It was going to pounce. Within a heartbeat, the creature snapped its jaws toward my face, but I rolled, missing its teeth just barely. I gasped and hurried myself to my feet as quickly as I could.

I took off running as this thing came barreling toward me, towering over my petite body like a fucking bear. Ryker's screams echoed in the distance, and I wondered if he would be able to fight his way out of here but quickly snapped my focus back to myself. I was headed deeper into the woods, way past our barrier now, and I had no fucking clue where I was going.

In my hand, I held my dagger firmly, just waiting for any of those fuckers to come and try to eat me. I will be ready. I dared to glance over my shoulder and immediately regretted it because I kicked a branch and began tumbling down a hill. Branches smacked me in the face. My body slammed into a row of small boulders on the way down, and I was pretty sure I had cracked a rib.

As I lay here at the bottom of the hill, I held my breath as I heard the creature come to the edge. It was searching for me, but if I stayed quiet, maybe it wouldn't see me. It was too dark for me to see exactly where it was, but I could hear the rustling of the leaves and snapping of twigs above me. Silence lingered, and that was when I knew that it must have given up. I exhaled.

Tears were now streaming down my face as I lay here, broken and bleeding. Every inhalation felt as if a hot knife was stabbing me in my chest. My head throbbed, and I was pretty sure I gashed it open on one of those boulders on the way down. My vision began to grow cloudy and eventually darkness started to creep its way into my head.

"No," I whimpered. *I can't pass out. I can't die out here.* My fingers dug into the dirt beneath me as I tried to support my weight and roll over, but a searing pain in my side stopped me from doing so. I hissed as I plopped back down on my back, lying like dying helpless prey. Was this how I would die? Would I finally meet my father and mother in the afterlife?

The canopy above me was so thick that the light spilling through looked like a sky full of stars, offering just enough light to see shadows and not pitch black. My eyes were adjusting and the longer I lay here, the more I could see. This forest seemed to have a presence about it, an eerie essence to its trees. I could hear them moving, feel the ground shifting. Was this why no one has ever been able to find Dravian's kingdom? Was it protected by the everchanging Dark Lands? As I tilted my head to the side, I saw something glimmering just a few feet away—my dagger. It must have fallen from my grip during my fall. My fingers reached for the dagger, but it was too far and with my injuries, there was no way that I would be able to reach it.

I sighed.

A tingling rush flushed through my body, and I felt my lips go numb. *Oh no,* I thought. This was not good.

As that numbness spread into other parts of my body, a darkness now started to spread into my mind. I knew my body was about to pass out, maybe even die; I didn't know at this point, but nonetheless, I knew I would be dead either way.

I tried to cry out for help, but my voice came out a pathetic whimper. My eyes blinked away the tears that now started to gather as I felt myself get pulled deep into darkness. The last thing that I heard before being consumed by the blank void was the crunching of leaves behind me as something approached.

Chapter Eight: Taken

Lilah

I felt warm, tight muscles wrapped around my body as the wind blew through my hair. My head was throbbing as if my head had smashed into a rock…then I remembered that was exactly what had happened. Everything came rushing back to me in flashes.

The woods. The creatures. Falling. I fell down a steep hill and injured myself badly, and the last thing I remembered was lying on the ground and something was coming—

I sucked in my breath as I realized something was holding me. *Someone.* I screamed and darted my gaze up as a pair of glowing blue eyes glared right back down at me.

"Welcome back," he hissed.

My body took control, writhing and wiggling, trying to break free from his grip, but his fingers only dug in deeper, causing my skin to ache.

"Please," I begged. "Let me go." I could barely speak, let alone fight my way out of his arms. Weakness had a firm grip on my body and all I could do was pray that whatever this was, I wasn't going to be eaten alive.

"Shhh," he said.

I sucked in my breath and stayed quiet.

It was still so dark. I couldn't make out the features of whoever was holding me, but his eyes had the same glow as Sadi's did, which only told me one thing. Whoever this man was carrying me through the woods; he was a vampire.

My father always warned me of the creatures of the Dark Lands, but he never told me *what* lived out here. Only that they all would eat my flesh or drink my blood any chance they'd get. I had only learned about the true nature of the vampires when I was older and living with Eldrich. His warnings still lingered in my head. *'They will rip your throat right from your body.'*

Was that what he was going to do to me? Bring me back his lair and drink my blood? The memory of my father's throat being ripped out came to the surface. A painful knot formed in my throat as I held down a sob at the thought, followed by a fuming anger in my core. I hated the vampires for what they did. For what they were. They should all burn in the Dark Realm as far as I was concerned.

It took all my strength to not let my anger seep from my mouth. I didn't want to piss this thing off just yet. When the thrumming of my heartbeat finally simmered down, that was when I could hear the sounds of the dark. The growls and hisses that seemed to lurk just beyond the shadows, and as I listened closer, I could tell that we were being followed.

Suddenly, we were falling, my breath hitching in my chest at the shock of the drop, and just as quickly as we fell, we hit the ground just as fast.

The vampire landed without even an ounce of wobbling off balance, and immediately pulled me into the shadows, down a long, stretched cavern deep underground. Was this where they slept? Underground like the pests of the planet? As if he could hear what I was thinking, he said, "You are to stay here until they pass." His voice came out deep, almost a growl. Demanding something from me as if I was his slave.

I was in too much pain to fight back, so the only thing I did was nod my head. His eyes burned right through me with their intensity as I looked up at him. Down here, there were torchlights hung along the wall every few feet or so. Dim light cast along the shadows, allowing me to finally see this monster for who he was.

But when I traced my gaze along his face, monster was not the first thing that came to mind. His jaw was sharp, defined, hardened into an almost frown as if he too were holding back his anger, and his eyes were the brightest blue I had ever seen in my life. They looked like they were plucked right from the stars themselves and placed on his face, but the predator in him lingered within his gaze as he stared at me. I could see it clearly now how he looked at me. How I must be something his kind desperately craved to feed on.

I brought my hand to my neck and held it there in response to the deathly stare. He set me down in the corner of the cave and walked away, turning his back toward me and sat on a wooden chair on the opposite side. Watching me.

I felt barely alive, half conscious, and completely bone shattered, and this bastard was just going to set me down and watch me suffer? *Screw him!* All I could do was let the hatred pour from my eyes as our eyes met in fury. He hated me and I hated him. That was for certain.

I opened my mouth. "Don't speak," he interrupted. Demanded.

Being the stubborn woman that I was, I didn't listen. I needed answers and I wanted them now. "Who are you?" I managed to ask through the pain.

The vampire crossed the room so fast, it was as if he had turned into dust crossing the cave, and then his body was right up against mine. His teeth snapped out and mouth snarled back as he yanked my head by the roots of my hair, pulling my head to the side. A whimper escaped my throat as I felt the sting of his grip on my head tighten.

I felt his hands pull my hair back—he was probably getting ready to finally drink that sweet liquid of mine—and he pressed his mouth against my skin. The heat of his breath caressed my skin in a sickly feeling, his sharpened canines just barely nicking my neck. I sucked in my breath and froze. What was he waiting for?

He inhaled and growled at the same time. I could tell he was angry but why wasn't he drinking my blood yet? If I was going to die, I'd rather just get it over with instead of being tortured for days. I felt his grip on my hair loosen and him step away, his fuming anger lingering like the smell of death.

"You're lucky," he growled. I wanted to speak, but another wave of darkness was creeping over me. My lips began to feel numb and then slowly, the rest of my body followed. I was passing out again, and there was nothing that I could do about it.

Lilah

I awoke to an empty cave and silence. The vampire was nowhere around and to my surprise, my body felt as if it were finally starting to heal. *How long have I been asleep for?* There was still a throbbing ache in my head and when I lifted my hand to feel where I had hit that boulder, the gash still felt sore and swollen, but not nearly as bad as before. My fingers were coated in dried blood and dirt; I didn't even realize it until now.

Okay, gather yourself.

How bad was my situation? We were ambushed in the Dark Lands, I was chased by some monster that was trying to eat me, I fell down a hill and practically broke my body and almost died, and now I was trapped in a cave underground, taken prisoner by some very angry vampire.

Shit.

This was bad, but I wouldn't escape by giving up. I was a Huntress, and I needed to remind myself of that. I should be the feared one, not the other way around. When I went to stand, my legs wobbled a little but didn't give out. Another indication that my body was healing. Again, I wondered how long I had been down here. The thrumming of my heartbeat picked up as I became more alert.

I went to stand and take a step forward, but a shackle clamped down on my ankle. I sighed. "Fuck!" I threw my hands into the air.

"That wasn't part of my plan, but if you insist, I can make that happen."

I shot my gaze to my right and immediately fell back against the wall. The vampire must have come in while I was distracted, and now he was staring at me from across the room with his arms crossed over his chest. I was surprised at how fine he dressed in his silken black shirt and trousers.

My mouth went dry when I tried to swallow. "Excuse me?" I seethed.

He pushed off the wall and stepped closer, closing the space between us, a smirk tugging at his mouth. "I think I heard the word fuck. I said, if you insist—"

"Don't you dare fucking touch me!" I pulled back, bringing my body as close to the wall as I could.

He leaned forward and reached his hand out, gliding his knuckles along my cheek. "I can do whatever I want," he growled.

"What is this? Did you bring me here just so you could, what…kill me?"

Raising an eyebrow, he said, "If I wanted you dead, I would have left you in the woods to the true monsters that roam them," his voice cold. "I could have just killed you, but I didn't." A hint of desire gleamed within his eyes as he spoke to me. "I'm curious if you will accept a compromise."

"I want nothing to do with your kind," I spat.

The vampire scoffed and stepped away. "It's better than the alternative. I could easily throw you right back up there. The umbragores would pick up your scent from a mile away." He sniffed and then smiled. "I could smell you from even farther away." So, that was what that creature was.

I felt so violated the way he could smell me like that. I pulled my arms into my chest and hugged myself tight, trying to cover as much of myself as I could. "You said compromise. What kind of compromise?"

His piercing gaze locked onto mine, and he smiled, flashing his wicked teeth, reminding me of the true predator that he was. "There is something that I need from you. Once my needs have been fulfilled, I will see to it that you go back to your home." His voice came out like ice, cold and sharp.

Rage began to burn within me, igniting a fury I didn't know existed until now. Being so close to one of these bloodsuckers truly had put my hate for them to a whole new level. I kept my eyes darting around the room, searching for anything that I could use to kill him. "What is it that you want from me?" I managed to ask through my gritted teeth.

The vampire smiled at me, ignoring my question. "Let's just say that you are far more special than you know, Lilah."

My breath hitched. My eyes went wide. "How do you know my name?"

The vampire strode toward me, and I immediately regretted asking that question. He leaned down, bringing his face close to mine. His black, tousled hair just barely covered his eyes as he let them burn into me. "I know lots of things, and how I acquired these things are none of your business." He tossed something in my lap and snarled. "Now eat. I need you healthy."

He went to leave the room, but my curiosity took control. "Wait," I called out.

The vampire turned with narrowed brows. "Yes?"

"What is your name?" He looked at me as if I had just asked him something very personal. "You know my name. I think it's only fair that I know yours too." I crossed my arms and waited for him to drop the scowling expression and at least give me this. After what seemed like an eternity staring him down, I saw his shoulders slack and him roll his eyes.

"Nyx," he stated, and then he stormed out of the room.

Chapter Nine: Darkness

Nyx

I could feel my darkness deep inside me, clawing at my core, just begging to be released. The more I tried to ignore it, the more I felt the shadows of my soul consuming me. Father would strip me of my power nonetheless if he knew I had somehow figured out how to let my darkness break free again.

Something I wish would happen, considering I was doing this monster's bidding. Even though I haven't stepped foot in his precious castle in years, he still had a fucking grip on me. Oh, how I wish I could break the hand that commanded me and feed it to creatures of this godsforsaken forest.

I had to leave Lilah behind. Her blood was too strong. Too…tempting. Something about seeing her so angry did something to me, made me feel uneasy. I wasn't one to open up, but I wasn't a monster either. It was just easier this way, keeping her at a distance. Safer. Leaving her alone would do her some good anyway.

She needed to rest and heal before we got moving. First, there was something that I needed to do.

I glanced over my shoulder as I walked through the forest, carefully stepping in places I knew wouldn't upset the trees here, because this place was *alive*. I haven't fully figured it out yet, but I knew there was something beyond my comprehension when it came to this forest. Over the years, I had learned what it liked and what it didn't like.

One of those things being stepping on its roots.

There was a flicker of movement up in my right peripheral, but the moment I glanced up to see what that was, I heard a *crack*.

Fuck.

Removing my foot very carefully from the broken roots that I just snapped, I quietly spoke to the forest like some fucking lunatic. "Don't worry. I meant no harm to you. If you let me pass, I will make sure to plant a new tree soon." Sometimes I talked to the trees. Sometimes I believed they actually listened to me. Other times, it seemed as though this forest was just as bloodthirsty as I was.

A shift in the energy around me crackled in the air, the trees now contorting in a way that I knew they were preparing to attack. Before I could see it coming, a large branch rolled through the air and smacked me right in my fucking face. Pain exploded through my nose and down my jaw. I could feel the warm trickle of blood oozing from the gash along my skin. Another root began to snake its way around my ankle and pull tight, knocking me to the ground.

I grasped at the roots as they slithered their way like snakes to my body, ripping and twisting them away just as more came rushing for me. I got to my feet and began to run, ducking and weaving as the trees of the forest shifted to meet my face with their branches. Shaking my head, I knew I should have just stayed back in the cave, but if I had stayed, I don't know if I could have controlled myself.

Just a few more feet until I came over the bend and where I would find my small patch of herbs. Only around a certain location of the Dark Lands have I been able to find these herbs. And when steeped into some water, they could help soothe the body. Even as a vampire—a cursed soul—I still needed help with healing at times. Especially living out here. Sometimes blood was scarce, and even though I technically could eat food to get my energy, blood worked a lot faster.

Right now, it was Lilah who I was worried about. She needed help with healing. Her wounds have been difficult to take care of. Giving her some of my blood could be an option, but that always came with a risk. When someone was injured, and then drank cursed blood, they always risked the possibility of being turned or it not working at all.

I glanced behind me and noticed that the trees had stopped their advances on me, slowly retreating as if they lost interest in me. Leaning over, I scooped a small handful of petals from this patch and shoved them in my pocket. The moon was still out, gifting me just enough milky light to see the forest without having to use my predator's vision. My chest huffed out a breath. Now, it was time to make it back through in one piece. Watching as carefully as I could, I kept an eye on my feet as I walked back to where I had just come from.

If only she knew the struggle I just went through for her.

Chapter Ten: Wicked Games

Lilah

Being down in this hole, in the dark, removed all sense of time, but if I had to guess, Nyx had been gone for at least a few hours now. I cracked open my eyes—I'm pretty sure I dozed off—and glared around this stuffy cave.

Stagnant air swirled around and every time I inhaled, it felt like I was inhaling remanences of dust particles. A cough expelled from my lungs and once that was over with, I slugged my body back into the wall and slid down. How did I let this happen to me? How could I be so careless? As my mind racked around insults to myself, I took my finger and started to draw a flower in the dirt. I never thought I would miss such a simple thing, and yet, here I was—a Huntress— missing a little red flower.

Maybe it was the lack of fresh air down here, or the fact that I might never get to see the beauty of nature again, but my heart was truly missing the simplicity of them. I let my finger swirl around in large swoops until my eyes fell upon the only thing that I had to admire from inside this cave.

Thoughts of Eldrich crossed my mind. That sweet old man who took me under his wing. Was he going to miss me? Then, Ryker took over my thoughts. I couldn't get him out of my head either. Couldn't stop thinking about the way his lip curled ever so slightly when he spoke to me, or the way his soft lips felt on mine. Was he dead? This was the painful truth of letting your heart open up. In the end, it always gets shattered.

Suddenly, my attention snapped up when I heard rustling from down the hall. Bright blue eyes emerged from the shadows, and immediately I scoffed and rolled my eyes. "How long have you been watching me?" I asked flatly.

Nyx stepped forward with his hands in his pockets and leaned up against the wall across from me, a slight smile tugging at the corner of his mouth. "Long enough, little flower."

"You can stop watching me like some smug statue," I hissed. I curled my hands back into my lap and locked my gaze onto him, trying to ignore the throbbing ache in my head.

Nyx cocked his head to the side. His eyebrow raised, amused. "But why? You are so amusing to watch."

"What is your purpose for even keeping me down here? Just so you can watch me like some pet?" Fury started to gather in my chest. Every second spent looking at him made my blood heat. When the time was right, I was going to kill him before he killed me. I saw him look away for a moment, as if biting his tongue.

"I don't want a pet, little flower."

"Then what?" I yelled. What could he possibly need from me? Why couldn't I just leave? If I wasn't a pet, and wasn't a prisoner, then what was I to him? He was silently staring at me with those piercing blue eyes of his, analyzing. Watching. I continued. "And if you are waiting for me to beg for you to release me, well, you'll just have to kill me now because I won't do that."

"That would be a waste of your breath anyway, and I would much rather you save your breath." Nyx stepped forward and stopped just a few feet away. "I didn't take you to hurt you, Lilah."

My eyes became glossed with tears, burning my vision as I glanced up into his eyes. "Then why? Why did you take me? Why are you keeping me locked down here like some slave?" Tightness wrapped around my lungs and throat. My chest heaved with uneven breaths as I let myself lose control into a sob. I waited for Nyx to answer, daring to look at him with pleading eyes.

Gone was his smug smirk, his mouth now a firm line, and eyes softer, more concerning. "I'm keeping you down here because I am trying to keep you alive."

I scoffed. "Alive? Really?"

"You don't believe me?"

"How should I believe you when you have me chained to this wall!" I yanked on the chain and dropped it just as fast, letting the echo of the metal hitting the ground ring around me.

"I can't let you go. Not yet." I wanted to speak but I winced from a sharp pain that shot through my head. I gasped and hurled my body forward as the pain grew intensely. My hand cupped where I had smashed my head on that boulder, as if that would be any help.

Nyx was over to me in less than a heartbeat. "What is it? What is wrong?" he asked, his gentle hands analyzing my wound.

"My head," I managed to breathe.

Nyx stood and headed toward a small table along the far end of the wall and pulled something out of his pocket and placed it in a small wooden bowl. There was a small cauldron hanging over a small fire nestled into the wall. Weird how this cave seemed so much like a home to him. It even had a bed. Then he grabbed the cauldron and poured some of the water into the bowl. "Here, you need to drink this," he said while picking up the bowl and handing it over to me.

"What is this?" I asked.

"It will make you feel better. I promise." At this point, the pain was so unbearable that I didn't have it in me to fight him on this. My shaky hands took the bowl from him and lifted it to my mouth so I could sip. I sloshed the liquid back with a guzzle and placed the bowl on the floor. "What was that? What did I just drink?"

Nyx grazed his knuckles along my cheek and spoke, "That will make you better. I promise."

A warm, tingling sensation buzzed through my face, causing my mouth to go numb, and then suddenly my vision was starting to go black. "What was that, Nyx?" I asked again, my voice now wavering, but the only response I got from Nyx was, "It will make you sleep."

The last thing that I managed to do before the black void consumed me was whisper his name as it faded on my lips.

Lilah

I woke to the smell of smoke and the comfort of a warm fire. Nyx was in the corner of the room, adding wood to keep the flames going. His back was to me, so he couldn't see that I had woken up. My brain was still a little foggy but then it all came rushing back to me. *He drugged me.*

I groaned as I sat up against the wall which caused Nyx to immediately snap his attention to me. "You drugged me," I seethed.

"You needed to heal."

I scoffed. He just thought that he could do whatever he wanted with my body. "You should have told me what that was."

"Would you have drunk it if I had?" His brow arched, curious.

I rolled my eyes. "No, I would not have."

"Which is exactly why I didn't tell you what it was."

"What if it killed me?"

Nyx laughed and strode toward me with his hands in his pockets. "It was healing herbs. A practice used among *your* kind. There was no danger in taking your pain away and offering your body some time to heal."

As angry as I was, the pain had subsided, and I was grateful that my head no longer felt as if it were being smashed between two boulders. I lifted my hand to where my scalp had split and gasped as my fingers grazed over an almost healed wound. "It's almost healed." My eyes went wide.

"Like I said. You needed to heal and sleeping just helps your body even more." Maybe he didn't want me dead after all...

"Why didn't you leave me back there in the woods?" I asked, breaking the silence.

Nyx smiled, but it soon faded. "I don't need to explain myself."

Rage fumed in me, filled me up to my throat. "Oh, so now you are too good to answer my question?" His arrogance seeped off of him like the stench of cheap booze. If anyone deserved answers, it was me for fuck's sake. "Would you rather me have left you out there, to save yourself?"

"I could have managed. I didn't ask to be saved."

"That's usually how that works, isn't it?" His lip curled up into a devilish grin. I wanted to throw another insult his way, or throw a dagger into his chest but a deep growl ripped its way through my stomach as hunger consumed me, breaking my focus. My fingers clasped at my shirt in an attempt to ease the pain, but I knew that the only thing that would calm this feeling was food.

As if reading my mind, Nyx said, "I need to get you more food. I'll be back." And just like that Nyx disappeared into the shadows, leaving me alone once again in this forsaken cave.

Lilah

I spent the next—what I assumed to be—week lying in this cave, chained to the wall.

Nyx kept me fed and hydrated just enough, but it was far from what my body needed. He didn't talk much. His anger drowned out any opportunity to try to get to know him, which shattered my plan at making him see me as something to protect. Keep alive. Maybe even let go. But no, I was still chained to this wall.

It was like clockwork, waiting for the sun to rise— and I knew it had risen because that was when he would come back into the caverns. The curse that the Queen had put on his people forbid them from going into the sun, scorching their skin if they tried to disobey. I knew this much because that was what my father spoke of, of a curse that would burn the creatures of the Dark Lands. I just had no idea he was talking about vampires until that day I found out they were real.

"Are you going to tell me what you are keeping me for? My people will come looking for me." I pulled my knees into my chest and linked my arms underneath. Nyx stood along the far end of the cave, just staring at the wall.

"Nyx," I yelled.

He flashed a deathly stare in my direction but didn't answer. "You can't just keep me down here forever. Whatever you need me for, shouldn't we just get it over with?" I saw something deep within his gaze that seemed to shift. Had I gotten through to him?

"It's almost time. Don't worry," he said, giving me a wicked grin.

I hated how beautiful the vampires were. Maybe it was how they attracted their prey, lured them in until they got close enough to bite. I straightened at his comment and pried. "You didn't tell me what you needed me for. Are you going to tell me now?"

"The more you know, the harder it will be to let you go," he admitted.

"So, I am your prisoner then?"

Nyx ran his fingers through his hair and sighed. "Lilah, if I wanted to hurt you, I would have already. I'm not your enemy despite what you may think. These chains are for your protection."

"Then what are you?"

"Something you wouldn't understand yet."

There was a gleam in his eyes, a plea for my acceptance. But I had heard of the vampires and how they slowly hunted their prey. His presence was charming, his body...immaculate, and his face? Fucking gorgeous! The perfect snare to trap me into his charm. He had his hair slicked back in a clean swoop, looking rather perfect. If I didn't know he was a vampire, I would fall right into his charming trap. I rolled my eyes, unamused at his comment and scoffed. "Whatever..."

Nyx hissed at my comment and crossed the room in less than a heartbeat. He had his palms pressed against the wall as his face stood only a few inches from mine. I drew in a shallow breath, but not once did I break my gaze with him. I was over his shit by now and ready to get the fuck out of here. His looming presence over me washed over my body like a shadow stretching beneath the dying sun—dark, inescapable, and suffocating in the most intoxicating way.

The air was suffocating, thick, causing my skin to break out in gooseflesh. My eyes flicked down to where his throat hovered above my head, how every swallow caused his throat to bob slowly, as if he were savoring the scent in the air. If only I had my dagger, I could slice his throat open right here and escape. When I broke my gaze and looked away, Nyx shoved away from the wall. "You want out so bad…fine. Let's go," he growled.

Nyx pulled a key from his pocket and undid the metal cuff on my ankle. The area around my ankle was sore and bruised from being chained to this wall for who knew how long. I rubbed my aching skin and stood. "Thank you," I said. Nyx didn't even look in my direction as he swooped his hands underneath my body and lifted me to his chest.

I could feel the heavy rising and falling of his chest as his breath washed over me, his hands tightening around the curves of my waist, fingers digging deep into my skin. He carried me until we were standing in the spot underneath the hidden opening. There was a moment where he paused, as if he were feeling a shift in the air, but it faded just as quickly as that look flashed into his eyes. Before I knew it, we had lifted from the ground—as if he had some kind of crazy jumping ability—and we were now back standing among the forest.

He placed me down and started walking. I could tell that the sun was still out by the way that small beams of light spilled through the thick canopy above, but most of the forest was dark enough that Nyx could avoid going into them.

"Wait," I called. "Can't you just use your vampire speed to take us wherever we are going?"

Without even glancing back, Nyx grunted, and said, "You wouldn't want me to use it. Using our abilities like that can overexert our bodies, causing us to get…hungry. Besides, I wouldn't be able to navigate as easily if I were using my *vampire speed*."

"Where are we going?"

Nyx didn't look back, his back to me, as he kept moving forward. I hurried my pace because I knew those umbragore creatures were probably still looking for me. I'd take my chances with the vampire with an attitude.

"You can't just ignore me the whole time," I said to him as I matched his pace. Nyx side-eyed me and smiled.

"Tell me, little flower, what is it that you want to talk about?"

I rolled my eyes at the fact that he couldn't even call me by my name. "My name is Lilah, not little flower."

When he didn't respond I took the opportunity to keep talking. "First, I want to know what we are doing. Why can't I just go home?" I heard him sigh as his shoulders tensed.

"If you must know, like I said, I need you for something."

"Okay. But what *is* that something?"

"You are valuable here. The King has set a bounty on your head," he said.

I sucked in my breath. How would Dravian know who I was? Why in the hell was there a bounty on my head? So many questions now swirled around in my mind as to what I just heard Nyx say.

My heart began to thrum with anger; my face turned hot. "Why the hell would your king be interested in putting a bounty on me?" I swiped my loose strands of hair from my face and tucked them behind my ear. I could see Nyx watching me from the corner of his eye.

"You ask a lot of questions," he growled.

I scoffed and rolled my eyes. This motherfucker. "I can ask as many damn questions as I please. Now tell me, why would there be a bounty on me?"

"He thinks you are a descendant of the Veyl bloodline. If that is the case, then you are more valuable than you think."

"So, you are collecting your prize for my bounty?" I scoffed, undeniably furious at the fact that I was being marched to my inevitable death. Nyx slightly craned his head back so that I got a glimpse of the side of his face, but didn't fully meet my vicious stare.

"It's more than that, Lilah. I don't want to harm you."

I lifted my eyebrows and rolled my eyes. "Really, because it sure as hell seems like you couldn't give a fuck about me."

Nyx halted and sighed. When he turned his body to face me—for the first time—I saw something other than rage burning deep within his eyes. "Lilah…"

"What? Why don't you care? Why do you act like nothing matters to you?" I hissed.

Nyx paused and sighed. "I have lived longer than you may think and over time, feelings become a distant memory. Where I am from, it is different…"

I swallowed. "That sounds lonely…"

"It's better than the alternative."

"Which is?" My eyes burned into him.

"Letting your heart open up. If you let your feelings get in the way, that is when you can get hurt." Nyx's words faded into a whisper as he gazed off into the forest. For once, his words resonated with me, leaving me thinking that we may not be so different. I understood the reasons to guard your heart. I had experienced so much heartache that I didn't think my body would be able to handle another loss. Better not to care than to care and get your heart ripped from your chest.

"So, that is why you act like this? To guard yourself?" I didn't believe him for one second that my life mattered to him.

"If I wanted you dead, I would have already killed you. Your blood…it's almost impossible to resist. I have to stay guarded or else…"

He didn't have to finish for me to know what he was going to say. Mr. angry, sexy vampire didn't trust himself to get to close to me. I gulped and took a few steps back, not wanting him to catch my scent drifting in the wind.

"What is my blood supposed to do anyway? Why does your king think I have…whatever it is that you were talking about?"

"Veyl," he corrected. "If it's true then you will be the most hunted person in the last hundred years. There is no way to tell until we test it."

"Then why the hell are you taking me to a place where I will be the most hunted person? I am a damn good fighter but there is no fucking way that I will be able to defend myself from an entire kingdom of vampires. You are delusional if you think that I am going to do anything that you tell me to."

When the time was right, I needed to find a way to kill him before he dragged me to my certain death. I shook my head, consumed with utter rage and disappointment at this point.

"Lilah," Nyx pleaded, his voice deep and smooth. That voice could pull me out of my rageful fit with just the smoothness alone.

"What?" I asked.

"You wouldn't understand. Dravian has a certain control over me…over all of the vampires. I cannot just ignore his demands, but I have a plan, and it requires you to be alive. To stay alive."

What the hell was he talking about? Before I could ask, Nyx slammed his arm into my chest and pushed me against a tree, pressing his body into mine. I could feel his breath as he stared down at me with a hunger in his eyes, his teeth gleaming from the saliva that coated his mouth. I drew in a shuddering breath.

"What are you—"

"Shh," he pressed his mouth to my ear, speaking softly and demandingly. "It will hear you." His voice came out as a low growl, and even though this predator had me pinned against the tree, I wasn't scared. Not of him. This past week, spending my time alone with this "monster" had unsurfaced a new perspective of these creatures.

Sure, he was grumpy and guarded, but the more time I spent with him, the less I...feared him. His eyes were locked on something, something in the distance. I couldn't see but maybe that was because of my human eyesight. His fingers held my arms firmly against the bark as we stood there in silence; the only sound was the low growl that reverberated from his chest. Then I saw it. The same creature that had chased me in the woods—the umbragore.

Its body resembled that of a bear mixed with a rat, its long-pointed mouth decorated with sharp, jagged teeth. Its skin was like the skin of a rat's tail—hairless, and its eyes were black as death itself. They must still be hunting me. I thought we would have lost them when Nyx threw me into the hole. I felt his eyes burning into me and so I looked up and met his gaze. His eyes spoke of something deeper than what he was putting off. I always had this way of reading people when looking into their eyes, as if I were looking into their souls, and Nyx, well, he didn't seem to be as dangerous as he was trying to put off. Was this one of their tricks? Could he sense my distrust? Did he have the power to change how I felt about him?

The grip of his fingers on my arms loosened and he pushed himself away. I stood there still up against the tree for a moment, scared that the umbragore was going to hear me move. "It's gone," he said flatly.

I let loose a breath and stepped forward. "Is that the same one that was chasing me?" I asked. Nyx glanced back and tilted his head to the side.

"Most likely. The umbragores are notorious for being stubborn with their hunts. They can track their prey for weeks sometimes. It probably smelled your scent once we left the cave."

He wasn't lying. He had said that those creatures would smell me. So maybe he was trying to keep me safe. Nyx shifted his attention up through the canopy and hissed at the sunlight that was peering through. I could see parts of his skin that looked as if they had gotten burned. I reached for his arm to see more clearly, but he pulled his arm away.

"Don't mistake me protecting you as kindness. I need you for something. It is as simple as that."

Immediately my concern for his burns were tossed away, replaced with my fury once more. "Fine. Burn for all I care." I crossed my arms over my chest and seethed at his arrogance.

Nyx shoved out a sigh. "You shouldn't touch me, little flower."

"You shouldn't tell me what to do." I pressed my face closer to his, not once breaking my glare.

He stepped closer now, meeting my gaze. "You are reckless. Stubborn." His breath washed over me like a warm blanket in the Winter air.

"You are bossy," I said.

Suddenly, the wall between us shattered. His eyes were heavy and daring, but his mouth soft, not truly matching the look in his eyes. Our mouths were close, so close that I could feel each exhale from his nose. "Tell me, why am I so important? What is it that you want?" Nyx's voice shifted, his voice soft and tender.

"My little flower—" he brushed his knuckle along my cheek and tucked my loose hair behind my ear. "You don't want to know what I want—"

The breeze blew viciously through the forest which caused Nyx to sidestep a large branch that snapped from the tree above us. His arm flung out with precision as he knocked the branch off its path and caused it to land off in the distance. This was a stark reminder that I wasn't safe out here. That at any time, something could snatch me away from this world. As the silence once again hung over us, my mind shifted to a lingering question in my head.

"What is Veyl?" I asked, breaking the tension between us. His lip twitched into a snarl and then it turned into a wicked smile.

"Your Queen doesn't tell your people much, does she?"

What did he mean by that?

"If you are who my people think you are, then you're a descendant from an old bloodline."

Disbelief and shock were the two and only things I was feeling right now. My parents were just ordinary farmers. We didn't even live on the castle grounds. I'm sure that Mother would have mentioned this to me if it were true.

"What? You don't believe me? Ever wonder why my kind came searching for you when you were young? My king has been searching for you for years."

Tendrils of his hair caught the wind, dancing furiously around his face, but my attention was stuck on what he had just said.

"When I was young? Do you mean when my father was murdered by your disgusting kind?" I seethed.

Nyx hissed and snarled back his lips. His pointed canines promised what kind of animal he could be. "Be careful," he warned. I didn't want to be careful. What I wanted was to slap that snarl right off his face and leave him. I pressed my eyes into his until I heard him groan.

"You humans are so stubborn," he hissed under his breath. "I wasn't there. I've only heard rumors of that night, but apparently Dravian sent some of his men to retrieve you. He has been searching for you ever since."

"Why in the hell would Dravian think that I am a Veyl?" My father's farm was no way large enough to be noticed by any neighboring kingdoms. Hell, our own kingdom barely acknowledged our existence, but then that got me thinking. Was Father trying to keep me hidden by having us live so far away from people? He would never let me go into the woods and when we did go into town, I was always to cover up.

"He believes that your bloodline is the only known thing to break the Queen's curse on my people."

I blinked, not fully registering what he had said to me. "So, the stories are true then," I said more as a statement than a question. Nyx narrowed his brows as if he didn't know what I was talking about. Of course he wouldn't know the gossip of Eldoria. "I grew up hearing about a curse put on the creatures of the Dark Lands by one of our queens. That they wouldn't be able to emerge during the day, forever a slave to the night."

Nyx just stared at me with those intense eyes as I spoke of the legends that I heard. "Your queen is far more evil than us *creatures* of the night."

That piqued my curiosity, and I wanted to know more about what he meant by that, but suddenly something hard smacked me in the side and knocked me to the ground. Searing pain shot up my hip and into my ribs as I tried to take a breath in, my wounds from my attack still healing, and now, getting hit all over again felt as if my bones cracked once more. I groaned, kneeling in the dirt.

"What was that?" Before I could look up, Nyx had lunged forward, hissing and growling at something in the distance. My body hurt and I could barely move again. I lay there on the ground trying to see what he was fighting off, but when I felt someone throw a bag over my head and cinch it tight, I knew that we had just been ambushed.

"Nyx!" I screamed.

My legs kicked and thrashed against the body of what I assumed to be another vampire, but this time, he wasn't so friendly. "I've been searching for you," his breath hissed in my ear. The only thing that I could see was the black fabric that clung to my face, my breath suffocating and heavy. Someone had my arms yanked behind my back and I felt them tugging on me to move backward. "Get off me!" I managed to scream. This only enticed them more as their heinous chuckle to my cries echoed around the air.

"She's a fighter," I heard one of them say.

Another voice called out, "She smells like sugar. I bet her blood tastes sweet." That comment made my heart drop to my stomach. This was definitely an attack from vampires, and they definitely wanted to cause me harm.

"Nyx!" I called again.

I felt the vamp press his mouth to my ear again. This time a low growl reverberated from his chest as he spoke. "Your little buddy is probably dead by now, and if you don't stop screaming, I will rip out your tongue."

I sucked in my breath and let the tears roll down my cheek. How did my life come to this? How did I get myself here? His hands pulled tighter, and I groaned from the pain it caused me.

"Please let me go."

"Why would I do that? You've got a bounty on your head, girl. You are worth a fortune where I am from." My lips parted and I was about to speak when something cracked right into my skull, and then everything went black.

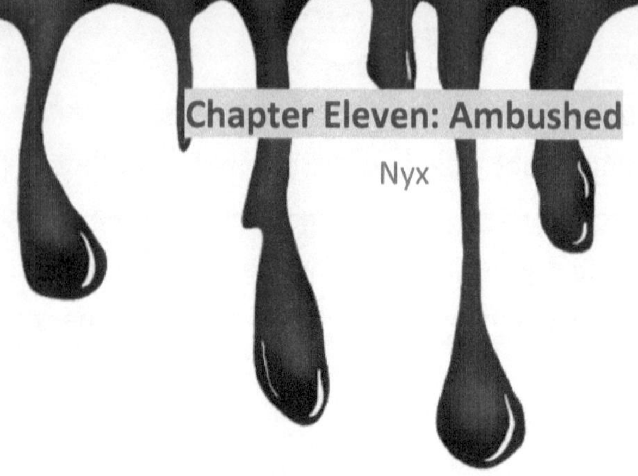

Chapter Eleven: Ambushed

Nyx

Strong hands gripped me around my face, covering my mouth and eyes with a bag as someone—maybe even two people—dragged me away. If only I hadn't been so careless to let my senses down.

I was distracted…

A low growl ripped from my chest as I tried to sling these two off of me, but with my darkness caged inside me like a wild beast, I didn't have my…usual strength.

"He is a feisty one. Make sure you tie those tighter so that he can't escape us," I heard one of them say through a chuckle. The fact that this bastard was laughing made my blood boil beneath my skin.

"Looks like everyone has heard of the bounty on your little friend. She's pretty too. Maybe I'll fuck her before I kill her," the other voice slithered in my ear. That made a terrifying scream rip from my chest as I bucked my body against theirs.

"You lay one fucking finger on her and I swe—"

"Or what? You won't do anything. Not after we are done with you. There won't be anything of you left."

His grip on me tightened on me as he continued to drag me farther away from Lilah. I could hear her screams fading away. Drifting with the wind of this godsforsaken forest.

"Go help Alerice. I've got this one."

Suddenly, I was slammed against something hard and before I knew it, things were wrapping around my body until I couldn't move. Breathing grew tighter the more pressure that was put around my chest, and then the sack that was thrown over my head was pulled away, revealing my captor.

His crooked smile gleamed at me with the promise of suffering. His eyes glared at me as if I were his next prey. His next thing to catch. "Well, well, well. I don't believe it. The Dark Prince in the flesh." He began to slow clap, letting the echoes of the slapping of his hands reverberate around us before he brought his attention back to me.

I didn't take my glare off him.

"Word on the street is that you were cast out by Daddy. Too bad Alerice wants you dead. You'd be worth a fortune among our kind." He stepped away and his eyes slowly traced around me, watching the roots of the trees snake around my body. "It helps having the forest on your side. Don't you think?"

"You can't kill me. The treaty forbids it," I growled.

"Oh, but I can make you wish you were dead. Besides, the creatures of this place will smell your blood from a mile away and finish the job for me."

The vampire bellowed out a wild howl into the air before slamming his fists right into my face. My jaw cracked on impact, blood splattering on the nearby trees. Again, and again. He attacked me with brutal force, slamming his fists into my face, my torso, my groin, everywhere until my body felt like it was going to crumble. And with these fucking trees holding me down, there was *nothing* that I could do.

My vison was blurry, but I could see that he had stepped away for a moment to gaze upon my body like some twisted art exhibit, as if he were admiring his own fucked up creation. I spat out the blood that was pooling in my mouth and managed to slip out two words. "Fuck. You."

"Not today, Dark Prince. But I will have your little friend screaming for you as I shove my cock inside of her. But you won't be there to save her. She will be passed around, tormented all the way until we deliver her to Daddy."

The darkness inside of me wanted to break out. It wanted to rip this fucker limb from limb, but it was too deep. Too locked away to access. The only thing that I could do was listen, my eyes barely able to stay open to watch his next move. And as if he could sense me trying to do so, he cocked his head to the side and smiled, saying, "Good night," and then slammed a rock into my skull.

Chapter Twelve: Hostage

Lilah

I was fading in and out, whispers and threats danced around me as my mind started to come back.

"We should just kill her now," one of them said.

"Not yet. We could use her."

"Well at least let me have a little fun," a third voice spoke.

My arms were shaking, and my chest began to rise and fall as my heart rate picked up. My hands were tied behind my back, and I still had something over my head, but I could see light peering into wherever we were.

"Shh, I think she is waking up." I heard steps stomping over to me and I sucked in my breath, holding as still as I could. *Shit.* They saw me moving. Someone snatched that bag off my head and when I glanced up through hazed eyes, that was when I stared into the face of evil.

She couldn't have been older than twenty-two, however, I had no idea how long she had been stuck at that age. I traced my gaze over her body, slowly taking in the monster that stood before me, and when I got to her eyes, I froze. Like a predator lurking in the night, her eyes burned into me with a hunger, flashing a brilliant glowing orange. There was nothing I could do except sit here.

"Hello," she purred. Even the curve of her mouth twitched up slightly as she spoke, trying to trick me into thinking she was anything but a predator. I gulped and fiddled with the rope that had my hands tied behind my back. If only I had my dagger…

"Who are you," I asked through a ragged breath. There was that smile. I knew it was coming. Vampires loved to toy with their food before devouring on the flesh, or so the stories told. Her canines poked out from behind her lips as she curled them back even more.

"Alerice. Yours?" She tilted her head as if she were studying a captured animal on display.

I inhaled and replied, "Lilah." My eyes darted to one of the males in the back who had now just crossed the room. He was holding something in his hands, but it wasn't until he got closer that I knew what it was—a knife, its tip gleaming from the refracting beams of light that sporadically spilled into wherever we were. He pulled off a thick cloak and hood and set it down on a table and stepped over to me.

"What are you doing?" I shook my head.

He only smiled at me with a wicked smile as he closed the space between us. Alerice glanced over her shoulder and said, "Should we do that?"

"It's not like she will be able to outrun us," he replied. She shrugged her shoulders and stepped away as the man approached. His features were a lot rougher than hers. A long scar trailed down the side of his cheek and his eyes were the color of blood. The heat of his body pressed into mine as he lingered over me. Was he going to kill me? Stab me? Rape me? The way this vampire dragged his eyes over my body sent my stomach twisting in knots. Before my mind went too far with theories, he yanked my arms out and took the knife and sliced through the rope.

I rubbed my aching wrists and glanced back up at him. His face was set in a hard line as he snarled. "You try to escape; I will catch you and make you wish you were dead." I nodded my head in silence while sitting on my knees. They ached from being on the hard ground, but I didn't dare move, not now.

"What is it that you want from me?"

He had started to turn away but when I asked this question, his body paused and turned back slowly. "Maybe we should test the theory now," he said, shooting a deathly glare at the other two vampires. There was a shift in the air, and I felt the tiny hairs on the back of my neck spike as the energy shifted.

The third vampire pulled back his cloak and hissed as his teeth shot out from his mouth. "Finally, I've been waiting all day for this."

Gone were the somewhat human faces and now I was only staring at the true monsters that they were. The three of them came hurtling toward me and before I could scream and run away, Alerice slammed me against the wall, pinning me with her body. Tears burned as they gathered in my eyes. Her hand was pressed against my throat and her mouth hovered just above my collarbone. Her breath washed over me as she inhaled my scent.

"I wonder if it's true," she purred. "If you truly are a Veyl..." her voice trailed off.

The other male shoved her out of the way. "Move! It's my turn to play." He was a blur of darkness, moving with terrifying speed, and before I knew it, his fangs were out, and now *his* body was pinning me against the wall. His lips curled back, and his breath caressed my skin. I felt a sharp sting as his teeth sunk into my flesh, and I let out a yelp as I tried to fight him off. A searing pain shot from my neck and down to my legs, causing me to collapse into his arms. He was an animal, ravaging me like I was his prey, his teeth sinking deeper the more I tried to fight. Warm liquid pooled around my collar bone; I knew that that was my blood streaming down my body. Everything started to go fuzzy; my vision went blurry, and my body started to sag into him.

He was going to kill me. Blackness started to creep its way into my vision, my mind slowly going in and out, and just as my body succumbed to the darkness, a familiar face came crashing into where we were. My eyes closed shut, a dull tingle now trailing over my body, but I could still hear the voices around me.

"I think you stole something from me, Viktor," a male voice hissed. I recognized that voice. The arrogant tone, the rasp; it belonged to my other vampire captor—Nyx. Something crashed around me, as if someone threw a glass jar across the room and shattered it along the wall. Then, chaos ensued.

"Why the hell is he still alive?" Alerice yelled. Before anyone answered, my body hit the ground in a slump as the vampire dropped me. I felt my body slam against the stone wall before it rolled to the side, causing a splitting headache to rage through my head.

"I swear I left him bleeding to death for the creatures out there. There was no way he could have escaped—"

"Well, he did escape you idiot!"

"Looks like he fucked you up pretty bad though," one of the males mocked.

"I'm here for what is mine, and then we will go. Don't make me hurt you," Nyx growled.

"Everyone has seen the bounty on her, Nyx. I could smell her blood the moment she stepped foot in Velorim. You don't think I was just going to let that go, did you?"

All around me, bodies were thumping and crashing, hisses and snarls danced around with their threats, but my vision stayed black, my eyes too heavy to open and see the horror for myself.

"You're wrong about her. She isn't who you think—"

"Shut it!" the female—Alerice—shouted, interrupting Nyx. "I could feel her magic the moment she walked into our lands. All it needed was its source to come over the threshold and that would activate the magic that has been dying. There is no denying it, Nyx."

I heard Nyx growl in fury. What did she mean by she could feel my magic? I didn't have magic in me. The only person I knew who claimed to have magic was my queen, and even then, I was skeptical.

There was a groan. "What's the matter, Nyx? Did our little umbragore friends tear you up too bad?"

Someone grabbed me by my hair, a whimper escaping my chest, as I felt my body get thrown over someone's shoulder. I was too weak to fight, going in and out of consciousness. "Put on your cloaks," she hissed. "The forest thins out where we are headed."

"Give me back what is *mine*," Nyx demanded.

A heinous chuckle echoed around the room as one of the males spoke. "What does the Dark Prince want with her anyway? It's three against one. You won't be able to get her from us. Just leave, Nyx."

"I can't do that," he growled.

Did he say Dark Prince? Ugh my head hurt so bad; I couldn't think straight. Maybe I was hallucinating all of this. My breathing was slowly becoming harder to do, each inhale more difficult than the last. Whoever was holding me shifted their body to the left, as if dodging something, and that was when I felt us slam into the wall. I groaned from the hit.

"Alerice!" Nyx snapped.

"Take the prince out," Viktor hissed.

"With pleasure, Viktor," she purred. It sounded as if two feral beasts were caught in a battle, their growls and snarls screaming through the air. It was brutal and all I could do was listen helplessly, dangling over Viktor's shoulder. Bodies were shuffling and thumping against the wall. The ground vibrated from their brawl and Viktor seemed to be joining in on the fun, because I could feel our bodies thrashing around amidst the chaos. I whimpered, letting out a small plea as my body ached from the brutal hits it endured. I wanted this to end. My body begged for peace. For relief.

Finally, the screaming stopped and now silence fell upon us. My heart sank. Did he win? Was she dead? But by the chuckling my captor was doing, I would assume it was the other way around. "Poor little Nyx. Not so high and mighty now, huh?" I heard the other male vampire growl. "Your precious king isn't here to save you this time. What are you doing out this far from home anyway?"

"I heard your father banished you from Velorim, you pathetic excuse for a prince," Alerice mocked. They said prince again. *Father. King.* Did that mean that Dravian was Nyx's father? Which meant that the Dark Prince was the one who kidnapped me.

"Shall I finish him off?" Alerice asked.

Viktor scoffed and said, "We can't. Not without consequences. Leave him for the umbragores to find him. He is practically dead anyway. Let's go."

Darkness was creeping over me. My mind was now going in and out and I felt our bodies move as if we were rising up from underground, which meant that I was being taken by another vampire, but this time, I think that he planned on causing me harm. "Hold on tight," he growled and then blackness engulfed my mind as we took off into the woods.

Lilah

"I think our little friend is waking up," a female voice purred.

My eyes were heavy, but I tried to open them as best as I could. It felt as if something had exploded in my head and my body was aching from the attack. The moment I was able to crack open my eyes, that was when I realized that that voice was Alerice. I frowned at the sight of her. Who was she talking to?

My eyes shifted to the corner of the room and that was when I made eye contact with one of the males in the back, his short tousled brown hair curling around his features. Along his neck was the start of a very elaborate tattoo that twisted around his shoulder; I wondered what it meant. He was the other vampire, the third one, and I don't think I got his name. His eyes were burning into me with a vicious stare. I gulped, too afraid to move.

Alerice strode over to me and kneeled before me, smiling with her wicked expression. "Welcome back, Veyl." Her voice was clipped with anger, and even though she was smiling, her face held a promise of death. I was certain she was the leader of the group by the way her presence loomed throughout the room. I groaned, cupping my head.

"What are you planning on doing with me?" I dared to ask.

My eyes darted around the room, first meeting the gaze of Alerice, then to the vampire in the back. This room was empty, and there was nothing from what I could see that I could use as a weapon. Slowly, my gaze kept scanning the room. Viktor must be around here somewhere. As I peered around the room, I slowly realized we were somewhere above ground. I could tell by the beams of light that spilled through the boarded-up windows. Alerice noticed me gazing toward the window and smiled.

"Must be nice to feel the warmth on your skin," she growled. "I wouldn't know though." I could hear the arrogance pouring from her words.

"I had nothing to do with your curse," I snapped.

The third vampire stood and threw his chair to the floor, his chest heaving with big, heavy breaths, and his eyes not once breaking their gaze on me. Alerice held out her hand and shouted, "Enough, Zev!" He cocked his head to the side; the corner of his lip twitched slightly. He was toying with me.

"Come on, Alerice. I want to see for myself what she tastes like. Let me test her out. Viktor said it was the best damned blood he had ever tasted."

Zev came forward with his hands in his pockets and a dark green cotton shirt hanging loosely over his taut muscles. He reached for me, and I winced, pulling away from his touch. "Don't worry," he breathed. I could feel the heat of his breath lick my neck as he spoke. "I can make you like it if you want." His fangs dropped and his neck craned back as if he were about to feast on my blood. A wail ripped from my chest as I felt his fingers clench into my shirt and pull me into him, but the moment the tip of his fangs nicked my skin, a crashing sound exploded from the other side.

Zev dropped me to the ground and hissed. Alerice staggered back and screamed as a beam of sunlight now shone through a gaping hole in the ceiling. It was the only thing that kept me safe at the moment. "What the fuck was that!" Alerice screamed.

Zev was darting his head all around, as if searching for whatever destroyed their place, but then a familiar voice purred, coming from around the corner. "What's wrong Alerice, didn't get your snack?" His brilliant blue eyes met mine behind a dark cloak. His face hid beneath the shadows, but the glowing in his eyes gave him away.

"I thought he was good as dead." She shot a deathly glare at Zev who was standing just at the edge of the sunlight.

"He was practically dead. I made sure to tear him apart, leaving just enough for the umbragores to get him."

"You fucking idiot!" she hissed. She snapped her head back toward Nyx, and said, "Don't you fucking touch her. She is mine now." My eyes darted from one side of the room to the other and back again, completely unsure of which vampire to trust. Both of them kidnapped me, and both wanted to use me for my magic—which I didn't know that I had. Nyx pulled back his hood, blood dripping down his face, his dark hair a hot mess and forced a smile.

"I don't think so. I had her first."

"I am no one's to claim!" I screamed. I finally have had enough of this bullshit. There was a beam of light protecting me now and I knew that they would get burned if they tried to cross over, so I took this as my opportunity to run. My body ducked around the corner and ran down a narrow hallway until I came up to a door.

Without even thinking, I slammed my shoulder into it, barreling all my weight to break through the wood, and smashed through to the other side. Immediately, I slipped onto the ground and coughed from the hit. My lungs begged for air as I gasped, trying to gain back control. The only thing that I could hear was screaming. I knew it was a very pissed off Alerice and an equally pissed off Nyx. No chance I was going to stay here and find out who wins this fight. It was daytime; this was good. I had plenty of time to figure out how to get far enough away from them and find my way back home. No time was wasted as I sprinted for the woods, not glancing back as I left the chaos behind me.

These woods had a mind of their own. The ground shifts after I walk over it, branches are always somehow slapping me in the face or poking me in the side, and I swear they were doing it on purpose.

I continued to walk forward with my arms crossed over my chest, delicately squeezing my elbows. Hours must have passed now, and as the sun started to set, the crisp Fall air was now creeping through. My arms were covered in small scrapes or cuts. These trees would just randomly snap or fall down right as I was passing them, or I would somehow find myself tangled in a web of twisted branches.

I knew that this forest was taunting me. Alerice even said that I awoke something when I stepped over the threshold into the Dark Lands. Maybe she wasn't lying. Maybe everything she had said was true. The creaking got louder; I glanced over my shoulder nervously, but still, I didn't see anyone following me;

there was this lingering presence in the air that seemed to be stalking me though.

My hair caught the gusts of wind that managed to blow through the forest, whipping around furiously. Darkness was descending, the golden rays of the sun slowly being swallowed by the night sky. Curiosity and fear burned into me as I wondered what other creatures lived out here. Hunted out here.

I needed to find somewhere safe to stay for the night, but where? It was nothing but a vast, eerie forest in every direction. My heartrate picked up and my breathing followed. I took another step forward when my breathing hitched in my chest. I screamed. Something sharp sliced right into my ankle and I hissed as I staggered back.

"What the hell was that?" I asked myself.

I was bleeding.

While I examined my now bleeding ankle, I felt another sharp pain strike me in my side. I cried out as I fell to the ground. My hand shook, cupping my ribs and when I pulled my hand forward, that was when I saw more blood. An aching pain now radiated down my side, and I now had a limp from my ankle being cut. I needed to get out of here. I think it was the trees attacking me.

My pace picked up once I got back on my feet and I quietly told myself that I would find somewhere safe soon. Then I saw it. A massive, twisted tree craned its branches back and came swinging at me full force.

I ducked my head, just barely missing the hit, but what I didn't expect was for it to come back around. A loud crack exploded in my head as I was knocked to the ground from the tree branch hitting the back of my head. I yelped in pain. Crawling, I pulled myself forward through the dense forest ground. My hands clawed at the twigs and dirt, but something wrapped itself around my right wrist and yanked me down. Then my left wrist was caught by another tangle of vines snaking its way from the woods and clamping down.

I shook my head. This couldn't be happening right now. The trees were literally attacking me. Now, I was on my stomach and my arms were pulled tight, forcing my face into the dirt. I tried to kick my way out of this but then my ankles were too restrained by the evil vines. I cried out, knowing that no one was listening.

The tug started to grow more intense, pulling my limbs until it became painful. Through gritted teeth, I screamed out, "Help!" I couldn't help it. My body was going to be ripped apart if someone didn't come and find me. Before the pain became unbearable, I heard something coming up from behind me. Their footsteps echoed through the dark woods; I silenced my cries. What if the umbragores had finally found me. Or Alerice.

Now I regretted calling out in agony, but before my fears consumed me, a familiar voice rung through the air. "You really shouldn't be out here alone, Lilah."

I sucked in a gasp. Nyx. "Shut up and just get me out of this," I growled. Nyx stepped in front of me and wiped a handful of blood from his face and dribbled it into the dirt before grabbing a fistful of the vines that were tangled around me. He pulled hard until the majority of them began to snap and rip away. I gasped in relief as my left arm had been freed. "That's no way to treat your rescuer," he mocked, ripping the rest of my body free from the grips of the vines.

I clenched my teeth and flinched from his touch as he pulled me to my feet. "Don't fucking touch me!"

"A simple thank you would have been nice." His voice was clipped with anger. I rolled my eyes and stepped away from him and away from the tree that had me pinned. My eyes raked over his body, his torn clothes, his...bloody face. *How did he escape them?* I thought. Being around Nyx was trouble for me and I needed to get away from him. I needed to get out of this damned forest.

"Why would I thank you, when I know you are here to take me against my will again?" My fingers dug into my pants as I tried to keep my anger under control.

Nyx arched his brow. I leaned in and said, "That is what you are doing here. Right? You are kidnapping me to use me for…" I trailed off.

"What makes you think you are a prisoner?" he asked, stepping forward.

I tilted my chin up. "You took me against my will. You said that you were going to use me for something. What else would you call that?" I crossed my arms.

Nyx scoffed and rolled his eyes. "I would call that saving your ass from being eaten. If I hadn't found you, those umbragores would have and then you would have been long dead by now. As for being my prisoner, like I said, I do need you. I wouldn't call you my prisoner, Lilah. You are my prized possession." He lifted his hand and grazed his knuckles down my tear-streaked cheek.

"I need you for something important. And as much as it pains me to do this, I have to." He was close now. Too close for my liking. The curve of his lip twitched slightly as if he were holding back a smile. My gaze traced over his features: his bloodied-porcelain skin, his sharp features, until I rested my gaze into his eyes. They were the most brilliant blue I had ever seen in my life, and for a moment, they took my breath away. There was a predator in there, staring back at me, but in this moment, I saw something else hiding behind those eyes. Something yearning for release.

"What are you doing?" I breathed.

He stepped closer, closing the space between us; his body now pressed against my chest, pinning me against a tree. Nyx took his hand and grabbed my neck firmly and leaned into me, breathing. "I can smell you," he growled. "Your blood smells sweet, like honey." He closed his eyes and inhaled my scent, practically moaning from the aroma that I must have been giving off.

My body shook as this predator had his hand gripped around my throat. Heat pooled in my center. My heart fluttered in my chest. The graze of his fingers played delicately along my skin as I inhaled a shallow breath. My eyes opened slowly, going to his parted mouth. The tips of his fangs glistened under the moonlight, through his parted lips. "Nyx…"

"Don't speak," he demanded. I thought he was going to sink his fangs into me right then by the way his breath caressed my neck. I could tell he wanted a taste. And in some twisted part of my soul, I think I wanted it too. My fingers dug into the tree my body was pinned to, preparing for that sharp sting, but then, Nyx pulled his body away and growled. He held out his hand and stepped away. The warm trickle of blood blazed down my body like tiny rivers, carving a stream of enticing, sweet liquid. I groaned as the ache from my cuts radiated throughout my body.

"How badly are you hurt?" Nyx must have noticed the pain etched into my eyes. I was a Huntress. I shouldn't feel pain, but my body betrayed me, because right now, it was consumed with it. "I'm fine," I growled.

"Lilah—"

"It's nothing," I lied. Truthfully, I felt like I was going to collapse. After everything that I have been through, I don't know how I was even still walking.

"You're bleeding. I can smell how much you have lost. Let me see."

Hesitation racked its way through my mind, but as Nyx carefully reached out his hands to inspect my wounds, I felt my body sag against the tree, giving into his touch. "Fine," I said through gritted teeth.

His hands grazed over my skin, caressing every inch as he looked for all the places that I was hurt. I would be lying if I said it didn't feel good. My entire life I was a loner, never touched by another man, but now, as I felt his fingers give me that simple pleasure, I craved more. More of him. What the fuck was going on with me? I was supposed to hate these fuckers.

"I can try to help you heal them. I just need to be careful on how much I give you," he said. Before I could ask what he meant, his fangs dropped and he had already ripped a tiny puncture wound in his wrist, letting the blood drip to the ground. "Hold out your tongue," he demanded.

"What?"

"My blood will help your body heal faster. Just do it. You will only slow us down like this." His eyes raked over my wounds as if he were inspecting a hurt child, ignoring the fact that *he* looked as if he needed medical attention too. His eyes blazed into me, and I knew that he wasn't going to take *no* for an answer, so I did what he said, reluctantly holding out my tongue. My body was trembling knowing what I was about to do. I was about to go against everything I believed in. Nyx must have seen the worry that lingered in my eyes because he froze, and said, "Don't worry, little flower, my blood will only heal you. Not turn you. I will make sure not to give you too much."

I didn't have time to ask for the details before the drops hit my tastebuds. I almost gagged knowing that his blood was in my mouth, but almost instantly I could feel my body's pain subsiding. Was this how I healed so fast down in the cave? Did he give me his blood while I was unconscious? I brought my finger to my mouth to wipe away the excess drips that missed my mouth. The pain that had snaked its way through my body slowly began to fade, fizzling away until it was just a lingering memory.

"Just come on. We need to find somewhere safe for the night. These trees are the least of your worries." I gulped and nodded. My heart was accelerating, and I wasn't sure if it was from fear or from something else.

I caught up to my captor—although Nyx would beg to differ, insisting he was my savior—and matched his pace. "What happened to Alerice and the others?" I asked.

Nyx side eyed me and smiled. "I left them tied up. Viktor…I snapped his neck and threw his head into the forest while he was on watch."

A gasp forced its way into my lungs. "You what?"

Nyx stopped walking for a second, a low growl now rumbling from his chest. "He hurt you. Bit you."

"You killed him because he bit me? Do Alerice and Zev know he is dead?"

Nyx turned his head toward me with a furious look in his eyes and said, "I killed him because he touched you *and* bit you. I assume they will be figuring it out pretty soon if they aren't already dead by now."

So many emotions were now colliding through my mind. This monster—vampire—did another thing to protect me, which got me thinking that maybe they all weren't as vicious as I assumed they were. A few seconds passed, my mind drifting away, but then I heard Nyx hiss as if he were in pain. When I looked over at him, that was the first time that I noticed that *he* was injured just as badly as I was; beside his bleeding face, his leg was covered in blood, and he was limping. "How badly did they hurt you?"

Nyx turned his gaze to me and flashed me a devilish grin. "Why? Are you concerned for me, human?"

I scoffed. "No...I mean...I don't know." That stupid bastard. Next time I won't ask if he was hurt if he was just going to mock me. I gritted my teeth as we continued forward through the woods. We must have traveled miles from Eldoria by now. I wondered if Ryker was okay, or did he suffer a horrible death by the umbragores? I could still feel the lingering touch of his lips on mine, the heat of his skin so close to me. My heart ached at the thought of Ryker lying in the woods, alone, bloody, and hurt. I dug my fingers into my arms as I tried to shake my thoughts away. And the others…were they all dead too? Or were they alive somehow, searching for me?

The trees continued to creak and shift in unusual movements, which told me that they had some kind of consciousness, but with Nyx around, they didn't seem to be attacking me. I nodded my head. "How come the trees aren't trying to kill me now?"

Nyx kept his gaze forward and continued his stride. "We have rules here in Velorim, one being that no soul must kill the Dark Prince or King, at least not without consequences. They won't kill me…"

"But they *can* hurt you? Right? There must be a loophole," I asked.

Nyx smiled and glanced down at me through his tousled hair and said, "You catch on quick." He drew in a deep breath and continued. "Sometimes, the forest leaves me alone. But when it seems to be bloodthirsty, I just have to give it an offering."

"Like a sacrifice?"

Nyx chuckled. "Something like that. It likes blood. Just like all the other creatures that live out here. Give it enough and it may just buy you some time."

My mind went back to something that he mentioned. "The Dark Prince?" I asked, but then it hit me. The conversation Alerice had with Nyx back at that cottage. She had referred to him as the Dark Prince. And then I vaguely remembered the mentioning of Dravian before, which meant that the son of the vampire king had kidnapped me. My eyes went wide; fury raged inside my core. Dravian was known for his ruthless reign, and I would be damned if I let his *son* take me anywhere.

I stopped dead in my tracks, letting Nyx continue forward, but once he noticed I was no longer following him, he stopped and sighed, turning around with furious eyes. "What are you doing?" he growled.

"I'm not going anywhere with you. Your king, your father, sent people to kill my father. Why would I trust going anywhere with you?"

He could have a secret agenda and be leading me straight to my inevitable torture for all I knew. My arms fell to my side as I picked at the hem of my pants in a rageful tick. Anytime memories of my father flushed through me, it filled me with so much hatred again. There was so much blood, the color red spilled onto the floor and into my mind, forever scaring me with the last memory of him. My breathing picked up and so did my heartrate. My eyes burned as tears began to gather, but I refused to cry in front of anyone, especially a vampire. I turned my head to blink away the tears, but it only took that moment of looking away for Nyx to bring himself close to me again, grabbing my face with his hands. He rubbed his thumb along the side of my tear-streaked cheek and forced me to look at him with glossy eyes. But when I met his gaze, he didn't look at me with pity or anger. His eyes spoke to me of something else that was deep within, as if he also didn't know what he was feeling.

"I am not going to hurt you, Lilah." The way he spoke my name sent a river of goosebumps up my arms. Up my neck. I felt him wipe away my tears and then he brought his other hand to cup my other cheek. I should be scared in the presence of such a monster. I should take my chance and find a way to kill him before he kills me, but instead, I froze. My body was frozen from fear, my mind screamed at me to run, but my heart…

"How do I know that you won't hurt me?" I asked. "How can I trust you? I don't know how to trust you," I cried. Nyx trailed his fingers along the side of my cheek and down my neck, causing a slight moan to escape my mouth. I closed my eyes and inhaled deeply. His touch was electrifying. I couldn't explain it. Maybe it was the magic in the air making me feel this way.

The trees around us began to creak and twist along with the heavy winds that blew through. My hair caught the gusts, but Nyx tucked my wild strands of hair behind my ear. His lips pursed into a smirk as he said, "Let me show you that you can trust me," as he leaned into me. My lips parted for his, my chin tilted to meet him, and then I felt his mouth on mine. The moment our lips touched, a fire exploded within me, traveling down to my core. A slight groan escaped his mouth as he pulled me in more, deepening the kiss. My body was now pressed up against a tree as his hands grabbed me by my waist in a firm hold. Twisting my fingers in his hair, I pulled him into me as he hovered his mouth just above mine.

The pleasure. Oh, the pleasure that I felt from this man was something I didn't know I was denying myself. His soft groans against my mouth undid me. Unraveled me into something I didn't know I had locked away deep inside. My leg wrapped around his waist, pulling him into me more, and gods…he was *hard*.

"Nyx," his voice faded on my lips. He felt so good; his touch, the way his body held firmly onto mine, the way his velvety voice spoke to me. But then his fingers dug into my skin deeper, pinching me and causing me to flinch. He hurled forward and hissed.

"What's wrong—"

"Stop! Stay away," he groaned. Nyx held out his hand to create space between us. When he lifted his head to look at me, it was as if I were staring into the eyes of a monster. His pupils were dilated, shrouding the brilliant blue irises, and his fangs dropped.

I stepped forward and reached out my hand. "Nyx."

"No!" he growled. He turned away from me and began to breathe heavily. "Your blood…" his voice trailed off. "It's almost impossible to resist." My hand lifted to my neck, slowly grazing the sore wound of where Viktor had sunk his fangs into me, thinking that Nyx probably almost did the same thing. The battle within me ravished my emotions, pulling me in so many different directions. I grew up not trusting the vampires, hating them for what they had done, but I was starting to realize that Nyx might be telling me the truth when he said that he wouldn't hurt me. Whatever he had planned for me, maybe it was something good. Maybe he would protect me from his father.

"I trust you," I said, stepping forward. I knew that now. All my life I wondered what creatures lived out here among the darkness, tethered to it in some sick and twisted way. This place, it pulled me in even before I knew the truth, and after my father's murder, well…I just couldn't wait for the day to begin my hunt for those responsible.

But Nyx? He wasn't the same as the other monsters that roamed this forest. There was something about him that drew me in, captivating me in a way that I never knew he could. "I don't want to hurt you," he said. I placed my hand on his shoulder and gently pulled his body up, scanning the rest him and noticing that he was still injured.

My eyes met his. "You're injured. Will my blood help?" I asked. I didn't know why I was curious about my blood. Why would I want to think about Nyx sinking his fangs into me? I hated the vampires for what they did to my father but now, my heart was telling me something different. I pulled my hair over my shoulder and tilted my head until my bare neck was exposed. Nyx hissed and flinched, looking away.

"No," he growled. "I may not be able to stop."

"You need to heal." I stepped closer. I could tell that his body was in pain. That he had been struggling to make it through this forest.

"I'm fine." His voice was clipped with anger. When I reached for his shoulder, he didn't flinch this time. Instead, his eyes slowly traced up my arms until it met the pulsing vein along my jugular. The darkness in his eyes washed over his brilliant blue, a primal beast waiting to be revealed. I saw his lips curl back, exposing the tips of his fangs, as if he had no say in what his body was about to do. I hated the vampires, but now, I think I trusted Nyx.

"Feed." I ordered. I needed my savior strong and healthy if we were going to get out of this place alive. A low, guttural groan rumbled from his chest as his body crashed into me. Nyx gripped my neck with his hands and tilted my head to the side, inhaling my scent.

I barred my teeth and waited for the sting. I knew it would hurt a little. "Are you sure?" his breath washed over me. I didn't speak, but when I nodded my head, that was all he needed to know that I wanted this. "Please," I managed to beg.

One second, Nyx had my body pinned up against a tree and the next second, his mouth came crashing into me, sinking his fangs into my neck. I hissed the moment his teeth pierced my flesh, but that sting quickly faded, being replaced by a sweeter sensation. Warm trickles of blood ran down my neck, pooling at my collarbone. My body felt as if it were floating on a cloud, a tingling sensation radiating down the center of me. I wanted more. More of him. More of his touch.

The waves of pleasure that seemed to crash through me sent my body over the edge. My lips parted for his, desperately waiting to get another taste. Nyx must have sensed my desire for him. His fangs retracted as he pulled away from my neck, blood coated the sides of his lips. He licked the sweet trickles from the corner of his mouth before bringing his lips to mine. I felt his tongue slip inside, offering me the sweet and coppery taste of my own blood as he explored my mouth with his. "Nyx…"

"I can make it cause you pain…" he groaned. He pulled away and licked the pooling blood from my neck and I moaned as his tongue glided over my skin. "I can make it cause you pleasure…" Nyx brought his mouth back to mine and captured my escaping moans with his lips.

My back arched against the tree and my leg curled around his back, pulling his body into me. The hardness in his pants pressed against my aching spot. It felt as if my body was being licked and kissed on every sensitive area all at once. I moaned and brought my hand up to my neck as I caught a stream of my blood on my finger. Nyx curled his fingers into my hair and pulled my head to the side as he cupped his lips around it and sucked the blood clean.

My breathing picked up from the intensity of the desire for him that now was flowing through me. I was fully under his spell. A prisoner to the pleasure that the Dark Prince had gifted me. I didn't want this feeling to end, but just as quickly as it started, Nyx pulled away. His eyes flashed back to his glowing ice blue color, a stark contrast to the darkness that now surrounded us. He looked as if he were listening to something.

"Nyx, what is it?"

"Shh," he said. His hand cupped over my mouth. Nyx brought his lips to my ear and whispered, "Something is watching us."

Chapter Fourteen: Stalked

Lilah

What had I done? I let a vampire drink from me. All those years training and hating the vampires now seemed like a distant memory. Being out here in the Dark Lands has done something to me. Shifted my perception.

The bark from this tree was digging into my back but Nyx's body was still pressing against mine. I could see the animal within his eyes as he scanned the area. He said something was watching us, and I wanted to know what that something was. Fear began to creep its way over my nerves as the eerie silence of the forest settled upon us. It was as if the trees could sense danger lurking and were listening for the predators of the shadows. My breathing slowed and my hearing picked up. Whatever spell Nyx had me under was still lingering through me, washing over my body like a wave of pleasure that I had never experienced before.

He said that he could cause me to feel pleasure instead of pain, and if this was it, I didn't want it to end.

I felt high. Utterly fuddled. My heavy eyes glanced up at him as he looked as if he were staring at something with anger in his eyes. But right now, he looked like a god to me. I had never seen a man look so attractive under the moonlight. My lips were swollen and numb from his kiss, desperate for another taste of him. I reached up to touch his face, but his hands pushed mine away.

I scoffed. That got his attention for a second. He shifted his gaze to me with an intense stare and brought his finger to his mouth. I knew he was telling me to be quiet, but the only thing that I could think of was how good I felt. How I didn't want this to end. Before I could get another thought in, something came barreling into us from the shadows, knocking me to the ground. My body felt limp and heavy; it was way more difficult to move right now. *Fuck.*

I groaned as I rubbed my head. Nyx was knocked off to my right. He was already up on his feet looking as if he were circling something. I could hear the growl that was rumbling from his chest, but as my eyes scanned the area, I still couldn't see anything. Maybe it was too dark for my human eyes to see, but there was moonlight spilling through the canopy.

"Nyx," I whispered, bringing myself to my feet.

He didn't break his gaze, but he answered me. "Lilah, the venom in my bite won't last much longer. You will be able to think more clearly once it fades. You need to listen to me. There are vampires looking for you. Not just Alerice and Zev, but other groups too. Dravian has put a bounty on your head. These woods —
"

Before he could finish, something crashed into him and both their bodies went flying through the air. It was all a blur. I staggered back, but my back bumped into something; I realized that it wasn't a tree. My breath caught in my throat as I realized that there was someone right behind me. Before I could turn around, I felt lips press against my ear, and whisper, "I found you, little pet. Thought you could escape me?"

"Alerice," I breathed. Her wicked laugh swirled around me, tormenting me. That meant that Zev was the one fighting Nyx right now. "But...I thought he killed you. How are you here?"

Alerice threw her head back and chuckled. "Your stupid boyfriend should have finished the job if he really wanted us dead. Nothing like a little blood couldn't fix. Oh, and by the way, speaking of him, I am sure he has told you the reason he kidnapped you. Right?"

I spun around until I was staring right into those glowing yellow eyes of hers. "What do you mean?" I growled. Alerice had her fingers dug into my arms so that I couldn't run. Her lip curved up into a wicked smile as she tilted her head to the side. Whatever venom from Nyx's bite that was in my body must have finally been flushed out by my adrenaline, because now, I was clear minded.

"You do know that he plans on delivering you right to Dravian, right?" She flicked her dark hair over her shoulder and smiled. "Only difference is that he can't help it. His Daddy gave him an order, and he must obey. But for the rest of us hunting you, we are simply doing it out of sport. If anyone is going to deliver you to Dravian, it's going to be me. I want my prize."

She dug her nails into me deeper and I whimpered from the pain. "You stupid human. You are so fragile. There was no way you were meant to survive out here. Don't worry. When I suck you dry, I will make sure that it hurts."

"Alerice!" I heard Nyx yell. I snapped my head in his direction only to see him pinned on the ground with

Zev's massive body on top. Alerice simply smiled and turned her attention back to me.

"Don't you fucking touch her! Lilah, don't listen to her!" I heard him curse under his breath as he struggled to get up from Zev's body.

"It's too late for your little prisoner. She is mine now and I plan on delivering her to Daddy just as you were planning."

My eyes began to water as the betrayal began to set in. How could I be so stupid? was starting to believe that Nyx was trying to help me, but he was just good at manipulating me to get what he wanted. He was so vague whenever I asked about where he was taking me, what his plans were. "Is it true?" I asked through gritted teeth. When I glanced over at him, he was silent, head hung in shame. I scoffed and blinked away my tears, realizing that I got played. I knew I hated the vampires. I knew I should never have trusted them.

"I was never safe," I said.

"It's not what it seems, Lilah. Don't let her get into your head." But when my silence filled the air, I heard Nyx curse again. "Fuck! Alerice, I should have ripped your head off just like I did to Viktor." Alerice flinched at the mention of Viktor, but that was about it. Her eyes went dark as she turned toward him, plodding over to his body that was pinned to the ground.

"And yet you didn't. Your mistake. Now I have what is yours and you will be left here to rot in the ground. The sun should be rising in a few hours. I'll make sure that you get a good view for your final moments." Alerice snapped her fingers at Zev, and he nodded his head. Zev whispered something under his breath and let a small vial of blood pour into the ground. I watched as the twisted tree branches and roots snaked through the ground and wrapped around Nyx like a vice. He hissed as his body became encased the same way that mine once was. Even though I was furious with him for hiding the full truth from me, I didn't want him to die.

I went to run forward but Alerice pulled me back. "You aren't going anywhere, pet."

My eyes met Nyx's, his eyes searching mine. "Lilah, I'm sorry."

"Enough. Let's go." And just like that, Alerice wrapped me into her grip even tighter and carried me away.

Lilah

The vampires were known for their supernatural abilities. It was all rumored back in Eldoria, but now I was beginning to see some of those rumors to be true. One being speed. Alerice was fast. She had carried me through the Dark Lands so fast that everything around me only looked like a blur. I remembered how Nyx mentioned that using their speed like this would make them want to feed, and I couldn't help but worry if that was what she was going to do next. We were moving too fast to make out any landmarks, or for me to really tell which direction I was going in. I couldn't tell how many miles we traveled or what time it was. Everything was a blur, but then I sensed her slowing her pace. There was a cliff up ahead that I could now see. Zev stopped first, right at the edge and glanced back, his muscles shifting under the moonlight. Man, he was jacked. "Have you told them?" he asked Alerice.

"Not yet, but they will find out soon. You kill anyone who touches what is mine."

Zev nodded his head and then looked right at me and smiled. "Welcome home," he growled.

I sucked in my breath. As Alerice brought me closer to the edge, that was when I saw it. A city under the moonlit sky, nestled in a valley between two cliffs. The city looked as if it were made of bricks and stone, just as Eldoria was, and I could see orange flames flickering along the city and lighting the paths. Was this Velorim? The lost vampire city? Had I found it?

"Is this—"

"Velorim? Yes. Trust me, you won't be looking so bright eyed once we get down there. Remember," she pressed her mouth to my ear, "everyone down there has been searching for you. And I am sure some will try to hunt you."

I gulped as fear now came crashing through me. What had I gotten myself into? How the fuck was I going to get myself out of this? I wondered if Ryker was searching for me. Maybe he didn't die during the attack. I wondered if he would even be able to find this place. Probably not.

I needed to channel my inner Huntress and figure a way out of this myself if I wanted to live. I just hoped that Alerice would give me enough time to do so. She pulled me into her chest again and said, "Let's go."

I watched Zev drop over the cliff, disappearing into the night, realizing that she was going to hurtle us over the edge. I went to step back, but her body stopped me. "Don't worry. It will only last a second," she hissed as she threw both of us over the edge.

My stomach felt as if it went into my throat as we fell free from the cliff. I screamed but the sound was drowned out by the wind shear that surrounded me. Alerice was right. It only lasted a few seconds and then we hit the ground with a heavy thud. My hair was a tangled mess, and my heart was beating fast. I sucked in my breath as she tried to pull me forward. Zev started on a path toward the city, his silhouette slowly disappearing into the shadows. No wonder no one has been able to find this place. It was hidden in between two cliffs. For a city filled with blood sucking predators, it was quite beautiful.

Just like them. Beautiful on the outside and vicious on the inside. It was a way to lure their prey in close enough to strike. And I was about to enter the predators' lair. "I can't," I said. I tried to pull away, but Alerice just rolled her eyes and dug her fingers deeper into my flesh. The pinch caused me to flinch. My arm ached from her grip, and I knew that her fingernails had pierced my flesh.

"Don't worry little pet. I am going to keep you for myself. Put this on." Alerice took her cloak off her shoulders and threw it over my shoulders, snapping it in place. Then, she reached into her pocket and began smearing a paste that smelled like pine on my skin. "It will mask your scent," she said, as if reading my thoughts. Once she finished, she pulled the hood over my head and shoved me forward.

"Keep your head down and don't speak. I can guarantee that if someone spots you, they will probably kill you, so you better stay close."

I scoffed. "Aren't *you* going to kill me? Why should I stay with you?"

I heard Alerice chuckle as she walked forward in front of me, now leading the way. Her head glanced over her shoulder as she answered. "Believe it or not, I have changed my plans for you, which now requires you to be alive." I sighed. "That doesn't mean that I won't have my fun with you though."

We were now coming up to the outer parts of the city and the closer we got, the more I felt my fear crushing me. It was night—the moon just past the highest point in the sky—which meant that it was the midafternoon for the vampires, since they couldn't go out in the daytime—all thanks to a queen's curse put on them by my kingdom. No wonder they hated us so much. I would hate us too if that meant I could never feel the warmth of the sun kiss my skin. A wave of dizziness washed over me as I kept moving forward. How long had it been since my last meal? Since I have had water? I could feel my body slipping away, and if I didn't get some soon, I might not be able to make it any farther. My fingers clenched into fists as I buried my anger deep within. It would be stupid to act out on it now, although, the Huntress in me was begging to be released. Soon. First, I needed to play along and see for myself what this city of Velorim was about and see if I could gather some intel for the Sunfire Court. I might as well make myself useful while I was here, and once I return home, I will be able to deliver the ultimate news: the location of Velorim. I will be the best Hunter, even better than Kanen.

We were coming up on the city. There were no walls like Eldoria had. I guess they didn't have monsters that came hunting them at night, so there was no need to hide behind the towering bricks. We slipped right into an alleyway and popped out through a busy street. Hundreds of vampires surrounded me, and in this moment, I had never felt so vulnerable, surrounded by predators that would probably rip me limb from limb. If only they knew who was walking past them right now.

I was surprised at how normal everything seemed. There were shops and vampires walking around, smiling, as if they were just on a casual stroll. It was different from what I expected. Honestly, I don't know what I expected. Maybe dungeons and sacrificial lairs, bodies hung up to feed on, but not this. Alerice leaned closer to me. "Beautiful. Isn't it?"

I silently nodded and kept forward. She made a right turn, and we walked past another group of vampires all laughing and sitting around a table, drinking from carved wood mugs and food on plates in front of them. *Wait.* They eat food still? One vampire took a sip from her mug, licking a small drop of red from the corner of her lip as she chatted like it was just a normal fucking day. The liquid inside was a deep red, which I presumed to be blood. Seeing the blood brought the anger back into me. They had to get it from somewhere, which meant that I was not safe from that fate, just as Alerice had said. A female vampire glanced up at us and nodded her head. Alerice smiled at her, but I looked away, afraid that she would recognize me for who I was.

Dravian put a bounty on me, and I wondered how they would know who I was. How did they ever know who I was? Memories of that night when my father was murdered came crashing back into me. They were searching for me that night. I always wondered why, but I guess now I had my answer.

"Keep up," she hissed. I must have slowed my pace while lost in my thoughts. My feet scurried faster to trail behind her closely. Wouldn't want to linger too far away and get caught. My lips pressed into a firm line as I held back speaking. So many questions now swirled in my head, but I didn't dare speak around so many bloodsuckers. Alerice took another turn, but this time it was down another dark alleyway. The moment my body shifted into the shadows; I halted. My breath caught in my chest as fear rose in me. Where was she taking me?

Alerice looked extra annoyed and rolled her eyes as she stormed over to me and yanked me forward. "I said this way. If you don't keep up, then I will just have to hurt you."

I gulped. "Where are you taking me?" I managed to ask.

There was a slight curve of her thin lips as she spoke. "You'll see."

Her fingers grabbed onto my wrists and pulled me to follow her through the dark. There was a door coming up to our right; she paused in front of it and knocked. Just as I thought it couldn't get worse, Zev opened the door and shot a deathly glare in my direction followed by a wicked grin. "Welcome home, pet."

Confusion set in. How did he get here so fast? "Where are we?" I asked again. Zev stormed out from the doorframe and grabbed my arm in a firm grip and pulled me through. I gasped, expecting to be thrown into a dungeon of some sorts, but when I walked through the threshold, my body relaxed a little when I realized that I was in someone's home.

Alerice closed the door, locked it, and walked forward. "Is this your…home?" I glanced around, my gaze darting from corner to corner as I took in this vicious monster's lair. But to my surprise, it was quite…eclectic. A small kitchen hung off in the corner, then there was a gathering room with a few plush seats and a table that were nestled up by a lit fire. The warmth from the flames offered me a little bit of comfort on this brisk night. Alerice plopped herself down on her chair and picked at her fingers, smiling.

"This is where you will be staying for now," she said flatly.

I was confused. "I thought you were bringing me to Dravian. Isn't that what you said?" I asked.

Zev stepped forward and took the other seat, not once taking his deathly glare off me. "We were going to at first, but then I started wondering what was it about you that was so special to him. It must be worth a fortune if he was willing to put a bounty on your head. We want to see for ourselves what kind of powers you possess first before we let you go."

I crossed my arms over my chest and scoffed. "I don't have any powers. I don't know what Dravian wants with me," I said, knowing that I was lying to myself. The moment I stepped over Eldoria's protective barrier, I felt something inside me shift. Something connected to the land that was hard to explain, and since then, there was this growing hunger inside me that I couldn't explain. Was that my magic? If it were true, then what *could* I do? That got me wondering the same.

I watched as Alerice's nostrils flared and a frown spread across her face as she eyed me up and down.

"You stink. Go wash up in our washroom," she said bluntly. Alerice pointed to a door on the back wall and pinned me with her eyes.

What did she expect from me after being dragged through this fucking forest for days? I wasn't going to argue though. I could use a good wash, a good pee, and maybe even way to brush my teeth. "Okay," I replied. I slowly walked to the washroom and locked the door, enjoying the peace for a moment.

After I finished washing myself, I exited the room and immediately my heart sank as Zev and Alerice just glared at me like I was something they wanted to eat.

"So, now what? Are you going to lock me in your dungeon?" I scoffed.

Zev smiled and shared a devilish glare with Alerice before standing and yanking open a wooden chest. He reached inside and pulled out a thick metal chain with a large cuff. I stepped back and held out my arms. "Please," I begged.

"I am only giving you what you asked for," Zev snarled as he rushed me.

I tried to run but couldn't get farther than a few feet before meeting the flames of the fireplace. Strong hands gripped the back of my head and threw me forward to the ground. A whimper escaped my throat as I felt Zev clamp the metal cuff around my neck and secure it into place.

Even though my anger for Nyx was fresh, I couldn't help but wish he were here to take me away from this. Maybe he was tricking me so that he could deliver me to his father, but he had not once hurt me. The last thing I saw before being snatched away was Zev sitting on his chest as the trees wrapped around his body. Once the sun came up, which was only a few hours away now, he would be burned. My heart ached for his death that I knew was inevitable and there was nothing that I could do in this moment. With these two predators watching me, the only thing I thought to do was to get some needed sleep. I knew that they needed something from me, and wouldn't kill me until they got their answers, and so, I curled into myself on the ground and let darkness wash over my mind until the only thing I felt was the warmth from the fire behind me.

Lilah

"Here," Zev hissed as he threw a piece of bread in my face, waking me from my slumber. I cracked open my eyes only to be reminded of where I was. He placed a glass of water next to me as my eyes raked over him with a deathly glare. Despair sunk into me as I realized that it wasn't just a bad dream. My stomach growled as I peered at the fluffy wheat bread that was before me. My lips parched for the glass of water. As much as I hated taking anything from them, I knew my body needed this nourishment. My shaky hands reached for the water, and I tilted my head back as I guzzled down every last drop. The bread was warm and fresh, better than anything I had eaten in a while. I tore away pieces slowly, letting the warmth melt into my mouth until there was nothing left.

Zev watched me the entire time. His face was set in a hard frown, brows narrowed onto me, and he didn't so much as blink. "Happy?" I scoffed.

He shrugged his shoulders and stepped toward me. "No," he growled.

"Oh Zev, having some fun with our pet?" she asked, striding into the gathering room. She wore dark leather pants and a fitted corset that clung to her like a second skin, but her cloak was the color of dark blood, draping over her body like a waterfall. Her hood was up, which had my curiosity piqued. Zev grabbed his cloak and slung it over his body as well.

Alerice picked up some clothes that were lying out and she kneeled down, handing them to me. "Get dressed. Your clothes are filthy."

"Are we going somewhere?" I asked, snatching the clothes from Alerice. Neither one of them answered me but by the way they were dressed, I assumed we were about to head outside in the sunlight. They both turned their backs, so I took that as my cue to put these clothes on. Not my usual style, but it would do, I guess. Zev took a key from his pocket and unlocked my chain, releasing my neck from the heavy metal. I rubbed my aching skin, as if my touch would relieve the soreness that lingered deep into my muscles—it didn't. "Like I said, I want to know just how far your magic goes.

There is someone I want us to see who might be able to tap into your magic."

"And then what? You'll let me go?" I knew she wasn't planning on it, but I still liked to piss her off with the tone of my voice. Alerice snarled and went for the door. "I am never letting you go. Keep your hood up and head down. There will still be some vampires up this time of day."

Bright, white light exploded into the room the moment she cracked open the door. Both Alerice and Zev had their entire bodies covered with their cloaks and their heads down, and yet I still heard them hiss at the sunlight. "Let's make this quick," he growled.

I followed and threw my hood over my head, trying to blend in. I stepped off the ledge and followed them down the alley; with the sunlight out, it was less eerie here. I kept my head down and eyes forward, as they said to do, and tried to take in the scenery around me as much as possible. They may be looking for their friend, but I was looking for a way out of here.

They didn't know it yet, but I could be a feisty thing and soon I was going to let my Huntress out of the dark.

"It's up here," Alerice said with anger etched into her voice. This kingdom was *huge*. We had walked for what seemed like hours now and only crossed maybe half of the structures in Velorim. My legs ached with every continued step, begging for me to give them a break, but there was no way I was going to let them know how sore my body was. That would be a weakness I refused to reveal.

Alerice was right though. There were some vampires out at this time of day—not many, but still, enough to make me bow my head in fear of being spotted. So far, no one had suspected a thing. Zev walked up to a gate off on the outer parts of the city and opened it, gesturing for us to go through. Alerice went first and then Zev's eyes met mine. He didn't have to speak to order me to follow. I could tell by the way he glared at me with those vicious eyes of his. I nodded my head and went through, trailing up behind Alerice as she followed a dirt path up to a small cottage.

"Where are we?" I asked.

"A friend's."

I scoffed. To her it was a friend, but a friend to my enemy was my enemy, so I knew I needed to be guarded. My body stiffened. Alerice and Zev went to the red painted door, and I couldn't help but wonder where they got that paint from. Maybe it was blood from a victim. *It would make the perfect medium*, I thought. Zev knocked twice and stepped back, leaving some space between him and the door. A few seconds passed but then I heard the wood creak as someone opened it from inside.

A woman poked her head out as Alerice whispered something to her. Her face was covered with a cloak, but I could tell that she nodded her head. The door swung open and Alerice reached for me and pulled me inside. Here I was again, trapped inside another "home". More like prison, but it beat being stuck in the Dark Lands. This woman removed her hood and glared at me with hooded eyes. She looked to be well in her fifties, which meant she must be very old. The corner of her mouth curved upward as she flashed her sharp teeth at me, reminding me of who I was in the presence of.

I didn't say anything, but I knew she was establishing her dominance. For now, I would play the submissive weak role. My eyes scanned the area for anything that I could use as a weapon, silently from the background.

"Did anyone see her?" the woman asked.

"No. No one suspected a thing."

"This is risky. Have you heard of the bounty on her? If Dravian finds out—"

"Marla, enough!" Zev snapped.

The old woman shot him a deathly glare at his disrespect. "Zev, this is not the place to be doing this. You brought this human into my home, and now you expect me to go against our king?" The way Marla said human made my skin crawl, as if I were an insect waiting to be squashed. How dare she.

"Marla," Alerice stepped forward. "Don't you wonder what makes her so special? Maybe we could somehow harness her abilities. Her magic. Use them on ourselves." So, this was why Alerice has kept me alive? Because she wanted to harness my abilities? whatever that meant. All I knew was that I needed to get out of here. As the three of them drifted toward the corner of the room, talking in hushed tones, I took this as an opportunity to look for anything that I could use to make my break for it. Once Alerice got what she wanted, there was no doubt that she would kill me, or turn me into Dravian. What I did know was that even though they could use their cloaks to walk around in the sunlight, they had to move slowly, or else it would blow off the fabric that kept them hidden from those brutal rays.

There was a hot kettle on Marla's stove top, its whistle blaring to let us know that the temperature was more than scalding. My eyes were glued onto it as I watched Marla step away for a moment to pour some tea. *So, they do drink tea...*I cocked my head to the side as curiosity struck me. I always thought that as vampires, they could no longer eat human food, but that had proven to be far from the truth. I had seen it passing through the city. Vampires eating meals, drinking liquids that weren't the color of red.

I was intrigued to say the least. Marla poured the steamy liquid into two mugs and steeped some herbs in them as she handed them over, continuing her conversation, paying no attention to me. One foot slid, then the next, until I was able to slowly creep my way over toward the kettle. With them lost in their conversation, they hadn't noticed me reaching for it, and within a heartbeat I was hurtling the scalding hot liquid right toward them, watching as a wave of boiling water splashed through the air.

The sound of tortured screams filled the air as the three of them hit the floor in agony. I couldn't help but smile at their suffering. I grabbed a butcher knife that was lying on the counter and swung it as hard as I could in a downward motion, taking Marla's head clean off from her body. Her head rolled to the side as blood pooled around Alerice and Zev. Alerice was too preoccupied in her screaming and clawing at her face to notice that I had just severed her precious friend's head. Too bad I wouldn't be here to hear her cries of despair once she realizes her loss.

I shoved through the front door and took off running as fast as I could down the cobblestone roads. *Now*, she was going to kill me, so I better run fast. It was a ghost town in this part of the city, thank the gods for that. I don't know what I would have done if I were to have run out in the middle of night. Just as I turned a corner, a shrilling scream pierced the air and I knew that Alerice had just found her dead friend's head, and with that scream lingered a rage that seemed to snake through the town and catch up with me. The predator was now out, and she was going to hunt me down.

My legs pattered along as fast as I could make them, ignoring the searing burn in my muscles. They would relax once we are out of Velorim. But like I mentioned, this place was massive. How the fuck was I going to find my way out of there? I made a right down an alley, then a left, then turned the corner again to my left. My breathing picked up along with my heartrate, but I didn't let that slow me down. Sweat began to drip down my neck, down my cleavage, and even down the lower parts of my back.

Vampires had a keen sense of smell, and I knew that I was creating a trail the more I let my scent linger in the air. I came up on a dead end and stopped and threw my hands up in frustration.

"Shit!"

My head darted from side to side; I was trapped down a maze of alleyways and stone walls. Alerice couldn't run in the sun, but I bet she was walking pretty damned fast.

"So, we meet again," I heard a voice smooth as velvet purr. I sucked in my breath and turned around, meeting the eyes of someone I now knew. I wouldn't have forgotten that vibrant orange hair or the porcelain skin anywhere. Or the fact that she was the first vampire I ever spoke to. "Sadi," I breathed. She took a step forward, a smile playing along her lips. Her fangs were out, and she wore a black cloak over her head, but her glowing eyes showed me that she was starting right at me.

"Lilah, was it?"

I gulped and nodded my head. "How did you find this place? Your kind has been searching for my kingdom for many years. And yet here you are, walking around our streets as if you own the place." She tilted her head to the side.

"I uh…"

"No need to explain," she purred. Sadi stepped closer now, closing the space between us, pinning me up against the brick wall behind me. "I can smell them on you. The rebels, we call them. They don't like to abide by Dravian's rules, and therefore we cast them out like bad blood. Their scent is all over you." Her lips hovered over my racing pulse, and she licked her lips. "I can smell something within you. You aren't entirely human. Did you know?"

"What do you mean?" I managed to ask.

"Have your people told you nothing? About the curse? About how your Queen even has magic?" I glanced down as her hand came over my chest, stroking my skin like she would like a pet.

"What are you talking about?" For as long as I knew, only the Queen was gifted magic from an heirloom handed down her family. I never questioned it because I never really thought it to be true. Living as a Drifter all those years would turn anyone into a skeptic.

"Your precious Queen doesn't have a magic bone in her body, and yet she protects her citizens with it. Doesn't that cause any curiosity in you?"

"I never thought—"

"Right," she cut me off. "You are so blind to follow your orders and praise your precious Queen."

"I wasn't following orders when I let you go," I snapped. "I could have let them kill you or burn you, or whatever they do to your kind." I crossed my arms across my chest, ignoring the fact that she was so close to me.

"I remember, which is why you are still alive right now. I'm no monster, despite what you may think of us." Sadi stepped back bnd smiled. "Looks like you could use some help." Before I could ask what she meant, Sadi cinched her hood around her face until only a small hole was visible and then wrapped her arms around me, pulling me into her chest. *That's handy*, I thought. She was as fast a striking bolt of lightning as she ran us out of the city and away from Alerice and Zev. There was no doubt in my mind that my scent trail was lost back there in the alley.

Sadi dropped me at the edge of a lake, just on the outer parts of the city that bordered the Dark Lands and stood over me. "You need to jump in." She pointed to the water. "What?" I barked.

"Your scent. I can smell you still. If I can, they will be able to too." She nodded her head to the city, her face still hidden beneath the darkness of her cloak, and I couldn't tell if now that she had used her speed, if she were holding back the urge to feed on me.

"Okay," I said as I peeled back the layer of my clothing until it was dropping to the ground. I leaned my head back and inhaled the fresh air as my skin soaked up the warm rays of the sun, a sensation Sadi probably never had the pleasure of knowing.

My toes plunged in first, feeling the brisk coolness of the temperature shock me to my core. During this time of year, we'd be dead in less than thirty minutes out in this water, but I did as I was told. I wanted to hide my scent just as much as Sadi seemed to too. Besides, I could use a good wash. It felt like my body was submerged for longer than it would take to kill me from the crisp coldness, and when I broke through the glassy surface, I gasped for air as my body begged for me to jump out.

I ran out of the water and rubbed my skin until most of the water had dripped away; I let the sun do the rest, warming me up and drying my skin off. Sadi waited for me to slip my clothing back on and waved her hand for me to follow. "You helped me escape. It's the least I can do in return."

"Where am I supposed to go? Which way is home?" I asked.

Her big eyes met mine as I finished my question. "You will need to travel through the Dark Lands," she said. "It won't be easy. It will take about three days of travel…if you make it."

"If?" My eyebrow raised.

Sadi glanced away for a moment. "These lands were not meant to be explored by humans. It feeds off people like you. But if your magic truly is here, then maybe that will be your way out."

Sadi went to turn away, but I snaked out my hand and grabbed her arm. "Wait."

She looked down at my hand and then up at me. "Yes?"

"How will I know what magic I possess? You said you could smell it on me. What is it that I can do?"

"I don't know but whatever it is, it smells powerful. You have a connection to these lands. That I am certain of. Now, I need to get back into town. Good luck." And just like that, Sadi disappeared like smoke blowing in the breeze. She was gone and now I was alone again in the Dark Lands. Hopefully this time, they wouldn't try to kill me.

Chapter Seventeen: The Dark Lands

Lilah

It hadn't even been an hour of me walking through these forsaken lands and already I felt as if something were following me. I couldn't shake the feeling that I wasn't alone. Sadi's voice echoed in my mind, which was the only thing keeping me sane at this point. I tried to feel for my so-called magic and bring it to the surface. She had said that I had a connection to these lands. What did she mean by that?

I walked another hour or so, trying to make magic fly out of my hands, but nothing. The air was still, save for the few gusts of wind that would blow through. I was now far enough to where the sunlight was starting to fade away from the thick canopy above me. It felt like so long ago that I was here in these woods. When Nyx was forced to let the woods take him how they tried to take me. Did he burn while I was being held against my will?

I hated him for lying to me, for tricking me, but still, I didn't think I wanted him to burn to death. That seemed too cruel. My heart ached with the emptiness it was now feeling, missing the presence of him. I refused to let myself cry, and as badly as I wanted him to be alive, here with me, I knew that he was dead. There was no way he could have survived the sun by the way he was left tied up under the only open canopy in the woods. It was just me out here now, and I needed to be careful.

Suddenly, a crackling sound stole my attention, snapping me back to reality. "Who is there?" I shouted. No need to be quiet anymore if something was stalking me. There was a large stick lying on the ground, and so, I leaned forward and yanked it up and held it against my chest. If it were umbragores following me, maybe I could stab them in the eyes with this thing. My body stiffened and I slowly took a few steps backward as I peered around the darkness that surrounded me. I could tell that the day was now coming to an end by the way that the dark void of the forest grew with intensity, but there was this growing feeling inside of me that I could not explain, and the more time I spent out here in these woods, the clearer these feelings became. Was this my magic?

I shouldn't be able to see a thing, but for some reason, the land lit up like the starry night sky. The electric pulses in the roots of the trees, in the veins that curved through the leaves, and everywhere in between, glowed a soft blue, vibrating and pulsating as if it had a heartbeat of its own.

I sucked in a breath when it clicked. My magic. Was it finally starting to surface? The darkness brought out a whole new light, a whole new world for me to discover, and it was beautiful, but this new sight of mine was difficult to hold on to, like a stream of water slipping through my fingers.

A twig snapped behind me. No time was wasted for me to ponder on what it could be before I barreled my large stick through the air, swinging it with all my might. My eyes were closed, and I felt it hit something behind me, followed by the sound of a snarl.

"Shit!" I heard a male voice growl.

When I opened my eyes, my heart sank into my stomach. "Nyx?"

He was cupping his head and glaring at me with those evil eyes. "You got me right in the head," he growled.

"You were sneaking up on me." I stuck up my nose and crossed my arms. "How are you here? I thought you were…"

"Dead?" he finished. "Don't look so happy to see me now." His lips curled up in a devilish grin. The sight of him ignited something in me, a festering feeling deep from my core, and as I stared into his ice blue eyes, a wave of relief washed over me.

"How did you survive that? I thought you couldn't be in the direct sunlight."

"I can't," he said, stepping forward.

I took one step back, drawing in a shaky breath. "Then how?"

"It's magnificent. I never would have thought." He reached his hand for me, grazing his finger along my jaw. "It must have been your blood. When the sun hit me, and when I didn't burn, I knew that your blood offered me protection. I was able to wait out the day until the magical hold on me weakened enough to where I could break my way out."

The last moments I spent with Nyx were of his tongue down my throat and his fangs in my neck. I reached for the swollen puncture wounds where he sunk his fangs into me and touched them lightly. I thought that I was feeling something for him then, but I realized that he was just using his powers on me. To control me and trick me into feeling safe with him, all so he could hand me off to his father.

"You lied to me," I growled, ignoring the fact that he said my blood gave him superpowers. I took another step back but was met with the bark of a tree. He stepped closer. "You tricked me." Another foot took a step, followed by another, slowly closing the space between us. "You used me." Tears were now running down my cheek, as he was now standing so close that I could feel his chest pressed against mine. "I am no one's to be used," I seethed.

Nyx smiled softly at me, as if I weren't crying, and reached for my tears, wiping them away slowly. "I never lied to you," he said, his eyes set onto mine.

"Your father ordered you to find me, and to bring me to him."

Nyx smiled, flashing me his fangs and ran his tongue over the top of his lips. "I never said that wasn't true. I just simply didn't say it."

"Keeping things from me is still lying." Anger was now building inside me as this monster held me pinned against this tree, and all I wanted to do was to smack him in the head again with my large stick. Too bad I dropped it. "You were going to hand me over to your father."

"I had no choice but to bring you to him, but it killed me inside to think of putting you in any kind of danger. But there is a way to get what I want, what *you* want, and keep you safe. He thinks I will deliver you to him willingly. With his prized possession so close in his reach, his guard will be down, making it easy for me to take him out."

"What?"

"My father cast me out a long time ago. I tried to bargain my way back into the royal lands, but he said he would kill me if I ever tried to get close to him, regardless of the treaty. He said the only way to release me from my banishment was if I brought him the girl who bore the mark of the blessed. There was a rumor that spread among our lands that a woman who bore the same mark as the girl we sought for was spotted days ago on the outer parts of your lands. My king wasted no time on putting the bounty on your head."

"How do you know that I have the mark?"

Nyx's eyes flicked to the side of my head. He didn't have to speak for me to know what he was looking at.

My hand reached for the small spot behind my ear. My birthmark. Mother had one just like me. I had always pulled my hair back when training or when I was working on the farm, which would have exposed my mark. How could I have known? If I had, I would have hidden myself better. I wondered, had a vampire been scouting our land and seen it then? Nyx placed his hands on either side of my body, encasing me between them. "You were never going to be handed over to him. I just needed him to think you were going to be."

I shoved my way through him and began to pace. "What the fuck!" I threw my arms up in frustration. "You could have at least mentioned that to me. Is that what you had planned for me? Was that what was so secretive that you couldn't tell me?"

"Lilah, please."

"Don't," I hissed. "You were going to use me for your gain. How did you even know where to find me? It was as if you were waiting for me out there when those umbragores attacked us."

"I was."

My seething stopped at his words. "What?"

Nyx stepped forward some more. "I knew the bounty on you had been put out, and when he mentioned the mark of the Veyl bloodline, I knew I had seen it before when scouting. My father gave me the order to find you and I knew other vampires would be searching for you too. I waited in those woods because I knew that it would give me an opportunity to find you before anyone else did. You practically walked right into me."

I scoffed at his arrogance. "We were on a mission. I didn't just frolic into the Dark Lands like some ignorant girl." My hair was now stuck to my face as the sweat dripped from my head, regardless of the brisk nightly air.

"I am not going to hurt you. I was never going to hurt you," he said.

I didn't know what to do or who to believe. These monsters were masters at tricking their prey. It was how they survived. My mind couldn't help but wonder if this was just a sick game of his to trick me into falling into his trap.

"Lilah, please. You shouldn't be out here alone. You won't survive it."

"I was doing just fine!" I yelled.

"Then how did I find you so fast? Your magic, it has a scent, Lilah, and it is getting stronger. If I can smell you, then more vampires will be coming. You need to trust me, and we need to find somewhere safe for now."

Nyx held out his hand and looked at me with pleading eyes, begging me to take his hand with no words spoken. A part of me knew he was right, that if I tried to make it home alone, I would succumb to a terrible fate. I bit my tongue and reached out my hand and slipped my fingers into his, hating every second of it.

"Where are we going now?" I asked.

"If you want to evade the ones who seek you, we need to lie low and travel during the day."

Great, I thought. There wasn't anything else that I could do, so I nodded my head and tried to offer a smile the best that I could. "Okay then. You lead the way."

Nyx tightened his grip on my hand and pulled me forward as we both ran through the woods faster than I thought was possible.

Chapter Eighteen: Hidden Travels

Lilah

I felt his arm around my waist as he threw me into another one of his holes. We hit the ground as our bodies tumbled forward. I groaned and rolled onto my side as the pain slowly traveled down to my legs. "Ugh. Are you going to chain me up again like you did last time?" I asked through a cough.

Nyx offered me a sinful smirk and said, "Only if you want me to."

I rolled my eyes at his cockiness and pulled myself to my feet, swatting away his hands as he tried to help. "Whatever," I groaned. We walked down another cavern until it opened up into another "room". How many of these did he have? It must have taken him years to furnish all his hideouts.

"So, what's the plan? We wait out in your holes until daylight and then run as fast as we can back to my lands?" I was half joking, but by the way he looked at me I knew he was all serious.

"That is exactly what we are going to do."

My eyebrows arched. Did he just say that he was going to take me back to Eldoria? Had he changed his mind? A loose strand of hair twirled around my finger as I pondered. "But I thought you didn't have a choice but to take me to Dravian."

Nyx walked over to a small table and poured me a cup of water from a pitcher that looked like he had carved himself and handed it over to me. He ran his hands through his hair and sighed. "There are consequences for disobeying the King. His power over the land is strong. I might not be able to fully take you back, but I have to try. I will go as far as my body can until his magic takes hold of me."

I eyed the cup of water he handed me and glanced up at him. "You need to drink," he said. Nyx nodded his head to the corner of the room where a small bed lay, and said, "And rest. Go lay down and try to get some sleep." As much as I hated the idea of letting myself become so vulnerable, sleep was something that my body desperately needed, and if I was to run my way back home, I would need to get as much sleep as possible. I strode my way to the bed and let my body fall into the mattress as sleep almost instantly consumed my mind.

Nyx

My little flower lay beneath the dim glow of the dying embers of the fire next to her, her breath soft and steady, completely unaware of the storm raging inside me. I stood at the edge of her bed, watching. Always watching.

She was so fragile like this, stripped of the fire she wielded against me when she was awake. Her lashes fluttered slightly; lost in dreams she would never share with me. Something primal curled in my chest at the thought of her dreaming of another man. I've heard her whisper a name in her sleep, calling for him as if she needed saving from me. I wanted to own those dreams.

Wanted her to wake with *my* name on her lips, not in fear, but in surrender.

My fingers twitched at my sides, delicately playing with the hem of my pockets. I had no right to touch her, not like this, not while she was so peacefully in a slumber. But gods, the hunger in me was unbearable, the darkness in me begging to be released to calm that desire. The need to claim, to mark, to make sure no one else would ever dare look at her the way I did. *Mine.* She didn't know it yet, but she was mine.

A loose strand of hair had fallen across her face, and before I could stop myself, I reached down and brushed it back. I was so close to my little flower, hearing the little flutters of her heartbeat thrum against her chest. Her lips parted slightly, and my throat tightened. What would she do if she woke now, found me standing over her like a monster from the shadows? Would she recoil? Fight me? Or—would she let me continue to explore her body?

Oh, how I wanted another taste of that sweet blood of hers. Her delicious scent drifted through the air which almost sent me to my knees begging for more. It practically made my cock hard just thinking about it.

I exhaled slowly, forcing myself to step back. Not yet. Not while she was asleep. She needed to want this just as much as I did. Truth was, my heart was always broken. Shattered from the life that I lived—still live— and yet, here I was, feeling something spark within my dark soul. My little flower awoken something in me that I haven't fully accepted yet, but maybe it was time to let her in.

Lilah

A hand gently stroked my cheek, pulling my mind from the darkness of sleep and back to reality. I cracked my eyes open and shot forward, gasping, forgetting where I was for a moment. "What are you doing?" I growled.

"I was trying to wake you. It's time to move. Next time I can throw the water on your face if you'd prefer that?"

"No, I uh…you just startled me is all. I'm not used to being woken like that." I swung my feet over the edge of the bed and stood, my body feeling refreshed and rejuvenated. "What time is it?" I asked.

Nyx gathered a small leather pouch and slung it over his chest and pulled his cloak over his head. "If I had to guess, probably just after sunrise. Which means it is time for us to move. No one knows of my hideouts, but I am sure they will find them soon with your magic growing."

I rubbed my eyes and tried to comb my mangled hair with my fingers as best as I could. I could only imagine what my hair looked like right now. "Can you go out in the sunlight still?" I asked.

Nyx shrugged his shoulders. "I don't know. That is why I have this." He gestured to his cloak. I knew it would offer him some protection from the sun, but his movements would have to be slow, careful.

The daytime was so different compared to these woods at night, and with my growing magic, I could sense these woods shifting around me, as if it knew what I bore within my blood. My question was, did it want a taste for itself?

Golden rays of sun spilled through the cracks of the trees above us, gilding the pathway like a shower of golden stars. Nyx kept his cloak over his head for now and took careful steps through the forest. "Do you know who killed my father?" I asked, breaking the silene.

I heard Nyx suck in his breath and sigh. "I already told you that I don't know who they were."

"You must know something," I pressed. "For fuck's sake, Nyx, you are the literal Dark Prince. Shouldn't you know what goes on in your lands?"

A low growl reverberated from his chest as he swiveled around until his eyes burned into me.

"How long have you been cast from your lands?" I asked. My eyes searched his, desperate for answers, but they were nothing but black pits, consumed by his anger. I could feel the rage seeping from his pores and lingering out into the air. Maybe it was another part of my magic coming to the surface.

I've been getting a lot of weird sensations since I stepped into these woods. Slowly, the blackness faded away and then his eyes were ice blue again. "I've been out here alone for many years, Lilah. The men who killed your father were most likely part of his guard."

I stopped moving forward and inhaled. "So, if we were to get close to your father, I would meet the men who killed mine?"

Nyx looked confused at first, but then it dawned on him. "No, I am taking you home. That is what you wanted. You will be safer there. We are almost halfway." His body came close to mine, and I could feel his desire to reach out and touch me. Part of me wanted him to.

"I know what I wanted. But I want this more. I spent my entire life, since that night, trying to find a way to get to the vampires who killed him. I promised myself that I would avenge his death. Now, I might have a chance at that. You said you needed me to get close to your father. Well, maybe it will get me close to them also and we can take out your father and the men who destroyed my family."

"Lilah," he breathed.

"Nyx, stop. Maybe it was always meant to be this way. You were my missing piece, and I was yours."

I could tell that a million different scenarios were ravishing his mind right now, but I waited until his blue eyes met mine. "Are you sure? If we turn around now, we won't be able to come back for a while. Your scent will be too strong here."

I gave this a thought. It was all my mind could think of the past few hours. I knew what I needed to do and that was find those motherfuckers who killed my father and rip their damned heads off. "I'm sure."

A wicked smirk crossed his beautiful face as he said, "Well then. Let's go."

Lilah

We spent the rest of our day undoing all the travels that we had made, but veered more toward the right this time to evade anyone who might have been tracking my scent. "Velorim should be about another day's travel and then we can pretend you are my prisoner. I'll even tie you up with this rope," he said while holding up some rope, looking at me as if I were a piece of meat to be ravished.

I couldn't help but to enjoy the way he looked at me like that. The way he made me feel wanted. Desired.

I bit the corner of my lip as I imagined him tying me up and having his way with me. With his prisoner. A rush of warmth pooled in my center as I thought of his fangs taking one more bite of my flesh.

Stop that Lilah.

I shook my head, annoyed with myself for even letting those types of thoughts enter my brain. What the hell was I thinking? He was a vampire *and* my captor. I should hate him, but the more time I spent with him, the more my heart seemed to be opening up. Maybe I was wrong about his kind. Maybe not *all* of them were terrible monsters.

"Are you going to do that the entire time?" he asked.

I blinked for a second and wondered how he could tell what I was thinking. "What are you talking about?" I played dumb.

Nyx didn't so much as turn around, but his voice carried through the wind as he spoke. "Lilah, I can feel your eyes undressing me as we speak. And don't get me started on the smell."

Smell? I lifted my arms to my nose and sniffed. Did I smell that bad? Nyx must have sensed what I was doing because he started to chuckle. "Not that smell."

It took a moment but then it dawned on me that he was referring to my arousal. How embarrassing.

I still played dumb, not wanting to give him the satisfaction. "You must be imagining things then."

Nyx just grunted. At least he didn't want to argue with me about this. The forest was a vast, dark void of eerie whispering winds and looming shadows. Every time I heard a twig snap or a rustle of the leaves, my heart would skip a beat, but Nyx didn't seem fazed. Even during the day, there was a presence about this place that shook me to my core. This place was alive in a way that I couldn't understand. We had been walking for hours now, the sun now starting to cast a warm pink and orange sky above. I knew that night was coming soon and that we were getting closer to Velorim.

"Should we stop now?" I asked, pointing to the sky.

Nyx glanced up and turned toward me, staring at me with those piercing, glowing blue eyes. "One of my hideouts is just over that hill," he said as he strode toward me. Every step he took sent me taking one step back. Not because I was frightened, but because I was scared of what my body would want to do. I couldn't deny it anymore.

Nyx was the sexiest man I had ever seen and through my time with him, my heart had begun to open up to the Dark Prince. I trailed my fingers along my arms and then down my chest as he continued forward, not once breaking his gaze from me. My heart was racing, aching for his touch. My dark hair had fallen loosely around my neck, and so, I pulled it to the side so that it was spilling over just one shoulder, exposing my bare neck. The same neck that I let Nyx feed from. I wanted to feel his breath wash over me again. I wanted to feel his hands on me.

Why was I thinking like this? What about him has got me under this spell? It must be this damned forest causing me to think so irrationally. I had to stop thinking like this. Letting my hands fall to my side, I stepped forward and walked past him, needing to keep my mind focused on what mattered. "Come on. We better hurry before someone picks up my scent."

And as I pushed through him, it was almost as if I could see the look of defeat flash beneath his gaze, but he didn't speak. Nyx just turned and followed me to where he had pointed for us to go.

I did what he said, following the path up and over the hill that was about twenty feet away until I came over the bend. I could spot his hideouts now that I had been in them. He would cover the entrances with twigs and leaves to make it blend in with the ground, but now I could tell what that was. I reached down and shifted the door to the side so that I could jump in.

Nyx followed behind me and now it was just him and me. Before I could turn around, strong hands gripped my shoulders, and I felt his body press against me, his breath washing over me like a cresting wave as he inhaled my scent. "My gods, Lilah, you smell so good."

I drew in a shuddering breath as I let his hands explore my body; the tip of his fingers traced idle circles along my neck, and so, I tilted my head to give him better access. I shouldn't want his touch. I should run for the hills from this predator, but there was something about Nyx that pulled me in, something more than just desire.

His mouth was hovering over my exposed neck and then made its way slowly to my ear. "It has been driving me insane all day. Do you know how hard it is to resist something so sweet?"

Quietly, I shook my head. His breath washed over me again. "It's like drowning, your lungs begging for just one more breath of air, and you are so close to feeling that sweet release, yet it's just out of your touch."

"Sounds devastating," I breathed.

"You have no idea the strength it takes me to resist such a delicacy."

"Nyx…" I closed my eyes and let his mouth hover over my skin, inhaling the pleasure that lingered in the air. "If you don't want this, Lilah, you just have to tell me to stop."

How could I deny my body the release it has been craving? In this moment, I had no more self-control. My begging lips parted as I managed to plead, "Please."

I felt Nyx wrap his fingers into my hair and crane my head back as his tongue glided over the soft skin on my neck. A slight moan escaped my throat, and from him…well, it was clear there was a predator that I had just willingly released to do whatever he pleased with me, and I was totally fucking okay with that.

Nyx spun my body around until my eyes met his. Gone were his ice blue irises, now consumed by the black desire shrouding every inch. A faint curve of his lip twitched in a wicked smile as his eyes raked over my body, wanting, desirable. It felt as if my breath had been stolen from my lungs as Nyx took his other hand and grazed his fingers over my thigh in slow, tantalizing strokes. Heat pooled in my center, pleasure exploding through my body just from that one simple touch.

My breath hitched as his fingers finally found me, tracing slow, agonizing paths along my hips, my back, pulling me against him with a need that burned hotter than the flames crackling nearby. I should push him away, should remind myself of the danger wrapped in his touch, but all I could do was tilt my head back as his lips brushed my throat—soft at first, teasing, before trailing lower, hungrier.

I needed more. More of him. I had never been with a man, something about pleasing a male always turned me off to the idea of sharing my body, but with Nyx, I couldn't crave his touch more. My thighs clenched together, trying to hide the fact that I was soaking wet. There was no use in trying to dilute my urges with simple tactics. He would be able smell my arousal, nonetheless.

"You have no idea how long I have wanted to touch you like this." His voice was deep, smoothly toxic.

I drew in a breathy gasp for air, managing to slip only a simple phrase from my parted lips. "I want this too." I couldn't speak. Couldn't think. Not with this perfection of a man stroking my body in ways that I wouldn't think to touch myself.

I wrapped my fingers into his midnight hair and pulled his face closer to mine. "Take me," I begged. There was no more control left in either of us as we crashed together in a fiery passion, unable to withstand the tension any longer. Nyx flung my body onto the bed he had in the corner, my legs parting for him, begging for his lips to have a taste. I tilted my head back and moaned from the pleasure I knew he was about to cause me. I wanted to beg for him. To see the predator in his eyes narrow in on me like I was his prized kill.

A shiver rolled down my spine, not from fear, but from something far more dangerous. He had captured me, dragged me through these lands, broken down every wall I had built. I was utterly under his spell, his charm stealing every last breath from my lungs. And then I realized the most terrifying truth of all...

I wasn't giving in.

I had been his from the very start.

Nyx leaned over me, his tousled hair hanging softly around his features. My back arched for him, wanted to feel the closeness of our heat pool together. His hard cock grinded against my sensitive core, giving me a taste of what I so desperately desired. Nyx grasped my neck in a firm hold and I yelped as he smiled wickedly at me under his grip. "Want me to make you beg?" he teased, his breath washing over my neck.

Before I could answer, I felt him rip open the front of my blouse and let his tongue whip out and lick me from my breast, all the way up. My nipples hardened as the fabric of my blouse rubbed over them. The way his tongue stroked my soft skin, I could tell that he was just as hungry for this as I was. A deep groan rumbled from his throat as he ran his lips over my breasts.

The only noise that managed to escape my mouth was a pathetic whimper as I nodded my head, begging for him to ravish me. His hand softened its grip and then gently glided down to my chest. He squeezed the plushness of my peaked nipples and smiled. "This will have to go," he growled. Within a heartbeat, Nyx had ripped my clothing from my body, leaving me bare.

I should be scared to be so close to a beast like him, but my body didn't want to run. It wanted to soar with him and feel him inside me. His hand cupped my naked breast as I felt his tongue lick circles around my nipple, causing a moan to cry out. His other hand slid lower, first grazing the curve of my hips, the small of my back, slowly making its way to the spot that ached for his touch. His fingers delicately played with my center, rubbing in light circles, allowing me to get a taste for what he was going to devour.

"Fuck," he growled. "Lilah, you're soaking wet."

"Mmhm." I licked my lips and closed my eyes, not wanting his touch to falter. I felt him shove them inside me and that was when my breathing hitched, entangling with a gasp of pleasure. His lips were on my neck, sucking and licking all the sensitive spots, and as he played with me down below, he brought his mouth up just one more time, offering me a devastating kiss.

I swallowed his moan as our lips danced together, but the pleasure was so intense that I could barely manage keep my lips on his. I threw my head back, mouth agape as his fingers teased me. After what felt like a wonderful, agonizing few minutes, I felt his fingers slip away. When I opened my eyes again and brought my gaze to him, he was naked, kneeling before me on the bed, proud and wanting for me with a look in his eyes that promised all the dirty things he was going to do to me.

I had never seen a man so bare before. His length took my breath away. Every detailed ripple of muscle, every flex, made my pussy clench for him. *Fuck. He was gorgeous!* Slowly, he crawled to me, bringing his fingers to my entrance once more. I gasped as they shoved inside me, curling so deliciously on that sweet spot that made me cry out for him. "I like it when you scream like that. Hasn't anyone ever made you come before, Lilah?" His voice was so smooth, so addictive. I only shook my head because my words wouldn't form with the moans coming from me. His fingers slipped out of me again, dripping with my sweet wetness and he brought his finger to his mouth, licking them clean, giving me a devilish stare.

Nyx grabbed the shaft of his dick and began to stroke, as if he could somehow grow even bigger, and then took the tip and guided over my glistening skin. His tip teased me as I felt him run it over my wetness. I felt him shove himself inside me, stretching me to meet his size, and began slow and steady strokes at first. "Fuck, Lilah," he groaned. "It's better than I imagined." I cried out his name in pleasure as my body took his length. My fingers dug into his back as his strokes grew harder and faster, each time, hitting that sensitive spot that made my thighs tingle.

"Do you like my cock inside you? You take it like such a good girl. Moan for me, little flower." His strokes grew harder, slipping in deeper until I was screaming from the sensation he was gifting me.

Who knew that this was what it felt like to be touched by a man. Fucked by a man. He was groaning so loud that I thought someone might hear us down here, and when I looked into his eyes, that was when I saw the predator in him come to the surface. His fangs dropped, gleaming in the torchlight. I knew it was his instinct to want a taste. I think I wanted it too.

"Fuck," he groaned.

"Nyx." His name faded on my lips. I leaned my head to the side, offering him a glimpse of my racing heartbeat. I knew my vein was throbbing, just like my pussy was. His strokes grew harder; I felt his fingers dig into my thighs, pulling me closer into him to give him deeper access. I moaned as his cock went deeper. Harder.

Breathlessly, I managed to say, "Drink." His eyes flashed from blue to black, and he took no time to sink his fangs into my flesh. The sting mixed with pleasure exploded my senses the moment I felt him draw my blood into his mouth. I remembered he said that he could make the venom cause me pleasure instead of pain.

The sensations that I was feeling intensified, causing me to scream out in a pleading moan as my body tingled from his touch. I was soaking wet, dripping as his cock kept hitting that perfect spot.

"You are such a good girl," he rasped. "I want you to come for me, little flower. Scream my name while I give you that sweet release."

My fingers scratched down his back as my body took his length, slamming into my wet core. I cried out, unable to hold myself back any longer. "Gods!" Heat pooled to my center, a sensation started to build between my legs, like a fire that kept on growing. Before I knew it, I was screaming at the top of my lungs as my body was sent over the edge. Nyx thrust in a few more strokes and then I felt his body tighten against mine, and then his body sagged back onto the bed.

We both were panting, lying sprawled across the bed naked with our limbs entangled with each other's. Silence filled the room, the only sounds being our breathless gasps of air. Nyx was the first to break the silence. He rolled to his side, staring at me with those ice blue eyes again.

"Are you okay?" he asked. His hand was delicately placed on my bare thigh.

I rolled to meet his gaze and offered a soft smile. "I'm okay. Why wouldn't I be?"

Nyx looked away for a moment, as if shame had ahold of his emotions, but then he turned his eyes back to me. "I bit you. Again. Drank your blood. After a day's travel, and then this, I shouldn't have been so selfish. You could get weak."

"I'm fine," I groaned, rolling my eyes. I smoothed back his messy hair so that I could see into his eyes. "I feel fantastic actually."

His lips curled upward. "Oh really? Was my performance to your standards?" He huffed out a laugh, as did I.

"I wouldn't have anything to compare it to, but yes, you exceeded my expectations," I replied.

Nyx's expression softened as realization dawned on him that he had just taken my virginity. "I didn't know—"

"It's fine," I interrupted him. "I wanted you to. My body...there is something about you that feels like I'm drawn to. My body wants to be touched by you. It wants to be close to you. I can't explain it."

"I can touch you as much as you'd like then." I curled into his chest, feeling the warmth of his skin melt into mine and closed my eyes as his body tightened around mine. I had never felt safer. More wanted. My head curled up into his warmth; his arms tightened around me. One thing he said caught my attention and was playing in my mind. My body pulled away for a moment as I peered up, Nyx meeting my gaze. "What did you mean that you had been wanting this for a long time?" There was a pause of uncertainty, as if he was caught off guard and wasn't sure how to answer. My big eyes seared into him, waiting for his lips to release their secrets. The bed creaked beneath us as his body shifted more to face me, his hair now tousled around his temples.

"Do you remember the first time you found a red flower?" he asked so delicately.

My heart stopped. My mind raced. *It couldn't be.* "Yes," I nodded.

Nyx drew in a deep breath and said, "Those weren't accidents, blown in by the wind. You looked lonely sometimes, and so, I started planting red flowers along the border so that you would have something to look forward to."

Everything came crashing into me too fast. *He planted those flowers?* But it had been *years* since that day. *Years.* My glossy eyes met his. "That was you?" I didn't know if I should be creeped out or impressed at his perseverance. The Dark Prince has been watching me for years?

The gentle touch of his fingers found my hair and tucked it behind my ear. "Little flower, you have fascinated me since the moment I first saw you…" I watched his eyes trace over my features, as if trying to find what to say next. Silence grew until his lips parted, spilling more of his secrets. "It happened by accident. I was watching your kingdom, studying it. I wanted a way to bargain my title back in Velorim. I thought that if I watched long enough, something useful would have happened for me to report on, but what I didn't expect was to see you."

He slowly licked his lips. "You were so determined. So independent. Something about you drew me in. I had to know more about you. After watching you, I realized that behind that tough exterior was someone who was broken inside. Lonely. So, I decided to leave you things to find to brighten your days."

"I can't believe it," I breathed. Nyx's fingers found mine in desperate search for my touch. "So, that's how you were able to find me after I fell? You were already there, watching…"

I paused for a moment. "Why didn't you tell me from the beginning? Why did you treat me so—"

"So terrible?" A sea of guilt was drowning in his eyes. He glanced away as if unable to look at me now. His voice was deeper, hoarser. "It's dangerous to be with me. I thought that if you hated me, that it would be safer for you. It killed me knowing what my father was making me do. Bringing you to him. I hated myself for it, and because of that, I let it consume me."

At first, all I could feel was rage when I found out that Nyx was taking me to the Vampire King, but now, I understood that it wasn't his fault. But then, my mind refocused back to what he had said. If he was watching me that day I was attacked, then that meant that he was around when the others were being attacked too.

Then, something deeper burned within me. He could have saved those men. Saved Ryker. They didn't deserve to die out in those woods. My eyes hardened as I growled, "You let those men die." Nyx flinched at my harshness and pulled back.

"Lilah—"

"No." I held up my hands. "You could have warned them. Saved them. At least tried to help while those umbragores hunted us." My eyes were burning with fresh tears as the horrors of that day replayed in my mind. Ryker was my friend, and he didn't deserve to die.

As if being able to read my thoughts, Nyx interrupted, "Your little friend made it across the border. Half of those men did too. I couldn't risk letting myself be seen. They would have tried to kill me, and then you would have been out there alone. I couldn't let that happen. You are the one that I care about. It is you that haunts my dreams every day. If you had died out there in those woods Lilah, I wouldn't be able to live with myself anymore."

Nyx's breathing picked up, his fingers now holding onto me as if I was going to float away. The glimmer in his eyes was now replaced with another emotion that I hadn't seen before—fear. I exhaled and brought my palms up to cup his face, drawing his gaze back to me. "You are right. It all makes sense. I shouldn't put that on you."

"I would do anything for you, Lilah. I love you."

My breath hitched in my chest as those three words slipped from his mouth. Did he just admit that he loved me? The warm touch from his body intensified, his eyes pleading for me to answer, but the best that I could give him right now was a soft smile and kiss. My nose nestled deeper into him, and I placed a gentle kiss on his arm. "Thank you," I softly spoke.

As I let my body relax into his, the last thing that played in my mind before sleep consumed me was the thought that the Dark Prince just admitted that he loved me.

Chapter Nineteen: Fuel to the Fire

Lilah

"Lilah!"

My brain was still halfway in dream mode. *Did I just hear someone yell my name?* As I let my mind leave the grasps of my subconscious, more of my senses started to heighten. There was a sharp acrid scent in the air and when I tried to inhale, it felt as if someone had shoved a torch into my lungs. My eyes shot open, and I jumped forward to see Nyx over me with a wild look in his eyes.

"Lilah, thank gods. You wouldn't wake up. We need to get out of here. *Now*." Nyx shuffled his body off me and that was when I noticed that the room had filled with smoke. Thick and suffocating plumes of dark ash consumed the air like the scorching sun sucking up any ounce of moisture.

I coughed into my arms and began to panic. "What happened?" I asked while slipping my clothes back over my body.

Nyx had already crossed the room and grabbed a small satchel and threw it over his chest. His cloak slung around his body as he secured the hood on his head. I reached for his hand and then he pulled me to my feet. "There's a fire. All these tunnels are connected. Someone must have found one of my hideouts and is trying to smoke us out. We need to get out of here, now." I took no time to follow Nyx to the opening of our hideout and let his arms wrap around my waist. His fingers dug into my side to hold me tight as we climbed from the ground. As my feet hit the ground in the forest, it was like being transported into another realm. A sharp gasp forced its way into my lungs as I peered at the horror.

The heat was intense. Overwhelming. All-consuming. Walls of flames towered above the trees, licking the sky fiercely. "Nyx! How do we get out of this?" I felt his hand let go of me for a moment as he tried to think of where we could go. We were surrounded. Trapped.

There was a harsh mix of dry leaves, burning wood, and a sickly, sweet scent undertone of scorched vegetation. Screeches and howls echoed into the air, sounding like calls for help from gods knew what beasts. I inhaled sharply. "Did you hear that?" I asked.

Nyx broke his focus for a moment to look at my trembling face. He ran over to me and brought my cheeks between his hands. "Lilah, you are going to be okay. Don't worry about those. They are just escaping the fire. I think I know which way we can go."

I nodded my head, licking the salty stream of tears that had gathered at my mouth and tucked my fingers into his hand. "Stay close," he yelled as he pulled me into the burning inferno.

There was only one spot that was not overcome by the crackling flames, and yet, as we ran for this opening, I still could feel the heat exploding all around me. I screamed as we ran; my skin felt as if it were melting from my bones. "Almost there!" Nyx yelled. I could barely hear him over the roar of the chaos and the pain that now throbbed in my head. Just a few more feet and we would be out.

As my body broke through the threshold, I immediately collapsed onto the ground, hacking up ash and gunk that clung to my lungs. My fingers dug into the dirt beneath me. "Who did that?" I asked, breaking the silence. Nyx was lying on the ground too, seemingly winded just as I was, and then that got me thinking. Why didn't he just run us out of there with his vampire speed? Why did he seem winded as if he were *human*…

Then it hit me. My blood. He drank from me. Did that mean that my blood temporarily diluted his abilities? Did he know this? "Nyx," I said through a cough.

His blue eyes met mine, dazed. "Yes?"

"You're not burning," I stated. I think we were too busy trying to escape death that we didn't notice that Nyx's hood fell off his face, and yet, the sun wasn't scorching him.

He lifted his hands and grazed his cheek. "My little flower saved me again." Even in the middle of a damned fire, Nyx would be the only guy to offer me such a devilish grin.

"I think my blood does more than just protect you from the sun. I think it almost makes you more human. Weren't you wondering why you didn't just run us out of there? Or why you seem so winded now?"

Nyx cocked his head to the side as realization set in. My blood wasn't just a protector. It was a way to mask his vampire abilities, and I wasn't sure if this was a good thing or a bad thing. "Whatever your blood does to me, I don't care. It saved me, Lilah." Nyx stood and tried to help me up, but as I tried to lift myself to stand, that was when the real pain started to set in. I screamed and dropped to the ground, but Nyx had already caught me in his arms. "What is it? What's wrong?" His eyes grazed over me like a mother coddling her wounded child.

I whimpered. "My leg. It burns."

His hands found the edge of my ripped pants and peeled back the cloth, exposing my skin. When I said that it felt like my skin was melting from my bone, I didn't think that it actually was. "Lilah, my gods. This isn't good. You need a healer."

"What about your blood?"

"It's too risky. When a human drinks our blood when they are injured, their body will have a harder time fighting off the change that can happen to them. It could turn you."

"Fuck." I threw my head back into his arms and cried as the pain rushed through me like lightning.

"Who would do this?" But as those words left my lips, it dawned on me. I knew who did this. Who else would want to burn me to a crisp?

"Alerice," Nyx growled.

"You think she did this?" I clenched my teeth to handle the pain.

His fingers gently grazed over my cheek, wiping away the steady stream of tears. "I know it was her. She and her rebel gang won't stop until they get what they want. Even if that means burning the whole fucking forest down. Gods!" he cursed.

"It's okay—"

"No! It's not. She fucking hurt you. I should have killed her when I had the chance. This is my fault. But first, we need to get you to a healer."

"What? Where?" Where the hell was he going to take me to help me get better? "I thought you had those herbs. Can't you just make me some more tea?" Nyx's eyes softened until they drifted over me, analyzing me. He sighed before dropping his fangs and puncturing a small hole in his wrist.

"We can try this, but I have to be careful about how much I give you. Especially when you are in this condition." Blood dribbled from his wrist and slowly began to drip over the ground as he brought it closer to me. "Open your mouth." Even though I risked being changed, I did what he said, parting my lips for him as I let his blood hit my tongue. It was sweet and coppery, but the taste was drowned out by the pain flooding my system. He pulled me in closer, placing gentle kisses along my forehead. "Just give it a minute," he whispered against my skin.

It should have worked. Should have taken the pain away, but something wasn't working, and the pain was growing worse. Maybe it was because part of my magic was dulling his abilities. I whimpered and let out a small cry. "I don't think it's working. You can't get more of that tea?" I heard Nyx curse under his breath as my whimpers grew into cries.

He scooped me into his arms, his taut muscles flexing to hold my weight, and glanced down at me, offering a soft smile. "My little flower, this is beyond what I know how to heal, and besides, the herbs that I used before are probably burnt away by now. But don't worry. I have a friend. I know where we can go."

Nyx carried me for miles as the fire chased us, burning away even more of the Dark Lands. It was unfathomable, the amount of death and damage done to the woods that neighbored our lands. Now, it looked like a scene plucked right from a nightmare. It looked like death.

My mind swirled down into darkness as the pain kept knocking me out. Probably for my own good not to feel every bump and step Nyx took. I couldn't tell how long we had traveled, but judging by the sun in the sky, I knew that it must now be midafternoon. Nyx had his hood up now and his face was etched with lines; a discomfort lingered in his eyes.

"What's wrong?" I managed to groan. I could tell by the hard line his jaw was set in that something was off. His blue eyes looked down at me and he smiled, yet the smile did not reach his eyes. "Everything is fine."

I knew he was lying. Reaching my hand up to his face, I asked again. "What is it?" This time, he didn't meet my gaze.

I heard him sigh. "I think your blood is wearing off. I can feel the sun now." He winced for a second and then I noticed that his hands were exposed to the sun. They were bright red, as if he had been sunburnt, but I knew that eventually he would suffer a terrible pain if he didn't get somewhere safe soon. Even with their cloaks, vampires couldn't be out for too long. It only offered a slight shield for short distances. But Nyx had been travelling for hours under the blazing rays.

"Where can we go?" I glanced around but every tree now had crumbled to ash. Embers now drifted to the air, decorating the sky like tiny glowing stars.

"We are almost there." Nyx's gaze was straight ahead and that was when a familiar scent in the air drifted to my nose. It smelled like flowers, like freshly prepared food, and now, I could see where it was coming from.

"You're taking me to Velorim? Like this? Nyx, I won't be able to walk around and hide myself. Plus, you only have one cloak, so how are you going to hide me?" Was he crazy? I needed to be healed before walking into the viper's den. This was going to be a death sentence for me. The town looked just the same as it did before; beautiful stone arched pillars snaked around some of the streets; cobblestone houses and storefronts lined the outer parts of the city.

As my head threw back in an agonizing sob, I felt Nyx's clutch on me tighten. He stopped walking for a moment as if analyzing the area. "Since it is daytime, most of my people will be in their homes resting. If we take the back alleys, we can avoid being seen."

I winced from the pain as my leg started to throb. "It's getting worse," I cried.

He pulled me closer. "Don't worry, little flower. We will be there soon." And here it came again. The black wave washing though my mind. I knew I was being pulled back into the dream realm, and maybe right now, that was where I wanted to be.

Lilah

"Here. Let me take care of your hands—"

"No. Her first."

"What happened to her?"

"Someone burned the whole damned woods down."

"Nyx, this is too dangerous. You haven't been around, but the King has now set out a new bounty for her. He doesn't care if she is hurt or even barely alive when delivered to him."

"Why the fuck would he want her nearly dead if he wanted to use her?"

"Has she not told you anything? She killed one of us. Chopped her head right off and burned two others. Word has been spreading about her, and every vampire in this city wants to kill her. Dravian is offering a royal pardon of duties and a discretionary pay for whoever brings her to him."

There were voices trickling around me like a fading song in the wind. I could hear them talking and yet they sounded so distant. In my mind, there was only blackness, but as I grasped for the surface, I began to see light. I cracked my eyes open and groaned. "What happened?"

I heard Nyx gasp and then shuffle before reaching my side. His hands delicately rubbed my head as he leaned closer to me. "Lilah don't worry. You are safe. I'm right here little flower." My vision slowly focused and the first thing I saw was Nyx's blue eyes staring right at me, followed by a slight smile tugging at the corner of his mouth.

"Nyx. Did I pass out again?"

He nodded his head. "Yes, but you should be feeling better soon. I was able to bring you to my friend. Don't worry, she won't hurt you." The moment his words faded, I shifted my gaze to the far side of the room, taking in the details of the place: a small fireplace, a sitting area, a kitchen, a...

My eyes went wide when I saw who his friend was. Out of all the vampires that lived in Velorim, *she* was his friend? "Sadi?"

"You know her?" Confusion spread all over his face as me and his vampire friend stared into each other's eyes. Sadi's hair was still a beautiful orange color, draping over her body like a silken scarf, and her eyes reminded me of a wolf's eyes.

"Lilah," she said, stepping forward. "I am here to help you." She glanced at Nyx and while she continued to apply a cool paste to my burn she said, "I met Lilah back in Eldoria. She was the human who helped me escape."

"That was you?" his tone went up an octave. "Sadi is my only contact here in Velorim. She told me about a human girl helping her, but didn't say who it was."

I still felt an uneasy feeling festering in my chest. As Sadi wrapped my leg up in cloth I asked, "But I thought you were sent to spy on us. On my people. Aren't your people trying to break our barrier?"

Sadi gently finished securing the bandage and sighed. When her yellow eyes met mine, there was a shift in her energy that flashed through her. "I had no other choice. Dravian wanted to know about your land's borders and for me to find weak points. For what? I don't know. All I know is that he ordered me to do so."

"Why did he send you? Why not his guards?"

Sadi flinched before she answered, "Part of my duties here in Velorim is bringing the royals essentials from our nearby herb garden. I make healing pastes, teas, medicines…" she finished wrapping the bandage around my leg and continued. "I keep his grounds stocked, but I assume that he sent me, because I am…expendable. I assumed it was because he didn't want to waste any of his guards for such a task. He wanted to keep them close where he could control them better. When the vampire King orders us to do something, it is more than just following orders. There is magic within his words that makes it very difficult to disobey."

So many questions danced dangerously in my mind. I pressed Sadi with a stare before asking, "Well, did you?"

"Did I what?" Sadi asked.

"Did you find any weak points? Does Dravian know about them?" Sadi glanced away for a moment as if afraid to answer my prying question.

I shot a look at Nyx, and he grunted. "Sadi, you can tell her."

"Tell me what?"

"After I got back to Velorim, I reported to him what I saw, but also, I told him that you let me go. He asked me so many questions when I got back. Mostly about what I saw, *who* I saw, and when I mentioned a girl, he made me describe every detail." Her eyes flicked to the side of my head, and I touched where my birthmark was. I must have brushed my hair back when talking to her that night.

Sadi continued. "I didn't think anything of it, but then I overheard that he was sending more to your borders. Now it makes sense. He wanted you. All this time, trying to break onto your land, it was because he has needed *you*. He wants your blood, Lilah."

My palms were clammy and sweaty now, and my chest felt heavy every time I tried to take a breath in.

"How did he know who I was?"

Sadi reached her hand up to my face and pulled back my hair, revealing the small spot of skin behind my ear. "With this. It's the mark of the Veyl."

Mother had one just like me. A swirling storm of realization set in as my mind focused back to what Sadi said. She said that Dravian sent more vampires to the border, but when we were attacked by the umbragores, only Nyx was around. My eyes opened wide. "Wait.

When did his vampires arrive to Eldoria?" Sadi and Nyx shared a shy glance and then both focused their attention back on me. "After Nyx found you, Dravian's men stormed your barriers and from what I heard, there has been a battle brewing between them."

"Nyx! You didn't tell me?"

"Liliah, I didn't know about that part." Nyx stepped forward to reach for my arm, but I pulled it away, searing him with a fuming glare. Fear weighed heavily on my heart as I listened to Sadi and Nyx speak of my home.

"How could you not know? You must have seen them out there while stalking me." I threw my hands up and scoffed. "My friends, my people, are probably having to defend the barriers right now, and I am not there to help them."

"Lilah, please." Nyx reached for my hands, pinning me with pleading eyes. The softness to his gaze softened my rage, causing me to sigh.

"Ryker—"

Nyx growled at the mentioning of Ryker; his eyes were consumed by the blackness of his dilated pupils. I continued. "If Ryker and the others truly did survive, then they need me. We need to go help them." Sadi looked as if she were still holding back from telling me something, her eyes wavering. I pressed my glare into her and asked, "What is it? What is it that you aren't telling me?"

For a moment I didn't think she was going to answer me, but when she did, I was not prepared for the bomb that she just dropped on me. "Lilah, I know that you want to help your people, but have you ever considered who and what you are trying to defend? Do your people not know the truth about your Queen?" Sadi started cleaning up her supplies, all the while pinning me with her yellow eyes.

What was she talking about? My Queen? "What do you mean?" Fear trickled its way over my spine as I dared to ask.

She looked at Nyx and they both shared the same expression and sighed. "Okay, should I tell her or you?"

"I'll tell her," Nyx said. I was shaking now. What the hell did he have to tell me that was so serious? My gut was telling me that whatever it was, I was not going to like it. Nyx pulled a chair over to my side and took a seat, placing his hands over mine gently. He drew in a deep breath. "Have you ever questioned where your Queen's magic comes from?"

"Yes. No. I mean, I've thought about it but never asked enough to get answers."

"She doesn't have the bloodline like you. You, in theory, should be able to draw your powers from the forest itself, but Margarethe, she must offer something to the Dark Lands in return for her power." My eyes were locked onto his searing stare. In my chest, my heart was now beating like fluttering wings.

"What are you talking about?" I dared to ask.

"Your Queen has been sacrificing her people in order to feed her magic. Without that, the magic will die out."

I shot up from my seat so fast, shaking my head uncontrollably. "What? But I would have heard of this if this were true."

"She has a way of covering it up. The last that I heard, she had cast a sickness upon your people, making them believe they were on death's bed, and then in an attempt to "save" them, she would bring them to her castle and sacrifice them to the Dark Lands."

His words danced in my mind, swirling around like a raging storm, and as my brain put the pieces together, it dawned on me that the Queen that I had served and protected was the one who killed my mother. I shook my head. It couldn't be true. "Why should I believe this to be true? She wouldn't do that."

But as my words faded, something deep inside me knew that they were telling the truth. Burning tears gathered in my eyes and I looked up at Nyx, begging for this not to be true. "But my mom…"

"Did your mother have the sickness?" he asked.

I nodded my head, too consumed with rage and sadness to answer. All this time, I thought my enemy lived among the Dark Lands, but it turned out, I now had two enemies, both responsible for ripping my world apart. The tips of my fingers clenched into my fist as I tried to control the burning rage that now ravished me. I was going to kill the vampire King and when I was done with him, I was going to bring Margarethe to her knees and make her beg for her life before I slit her throat.

Rage burned through my mind like a wildfire as the night passed over me. No matter how hard I tried to sleep, it was impossible to let my mind drift away. I couldn't. Not when I just found out that the Queen that I had been serving was the one responsible for my mother's death. All I thought about were the ways that I could kill her. Make her suffer. I wanted to hear her pleading cries for mercy before I brought my sword down on her, and even then, I would not feel satisfied. Nothing would complete me without my mother and father. Nyx didn't know it yet, but after we killed Dravian, I was going to bring down my wrath upon Eldoria and anyone who got in my way.

I felt a shift in the bed next to me. Thankfully, Nyx had gotten some sleep after taking care of me out in the forest. We didn't rest much out there, and after barely escaping the wildfire, I knew his body must have been tired. Sadi slept in her sitting room, on one of her plush chairs. Once they woke up, I would be their prisoner, and we would march our way to the vengeful King himself. The heat from Nyx's body pressed against mine made my heart flutter in ways that I couldn't describe.

He stirred and then groaned as he rolled his body out of bed. "Hey little flower," he said, his voice like silk.

"Hey, did you get some sleep?" I asked.

Nyx ran his fingers through his tousled hair and nodded, his eyes glimmering with a freshness. "What about you?"

"Yes," I lied. It would do him no good for him to know that I didn't sleep last night. He needed to believe that I was ready for this fight. Sadi was in her kitchen cooking something over her stovetop. As she glanced over her shoulder toward me, she smiled. "I have some tea ready for you, as well as some breakfast. Do you want some?"

My lips practically begged for that cup of tea as the aroma of the ground herbs drifted through the air. It felt as if sandpaper coated my mouth when I tried to swallow. Sadi brought me a cup, the warm steam tickling my nose as I inhaled the sweet, musky scent. "Thank you." I let the warm liquid run down my throat, drowning out the dryness that once was, and then set my cup down. She placed a small plate of fruit in my lap and smiled. I can't even remember the last time I had eaten something. Grabbing a handful of berries, I popped them in my mouth and finished the entire plate before bringing my focus back to them. "Are we leaving soon?" I asked.

Sadi was throwing on some clothes: black pants, a dark crimson red corset top, and a black cloak. Her bright orange hair had a vibrant contrast to the nightly color palette. As she fastened a few throwing knives in her beltloop she said, "Yes. We should get moving now. Here, put on these clothes and take some of these knives too. Hide them in your belt."

Nyx and I shared a glance as Sadi handed me her wardrobe and weapons. I could practically hear Nyx's mouth salivating as he imagined my body in one of her tight corsets. My eyes rolled at him. "You should get ready too," I said to Nyx.

He chuckled and nodded his head. "As you wish, little flower."

It didn't take long. Before I knew it, the three of us stood at Sadi's front door, dressed, cloaked, and weapons fastened, ready to march me as their "prisoner" to Dravian. I gulped as the fear began to trickle its way onto my nerves. Nyx reached out his fingers and laced them into mine. "It will be okay. I won't let him hurt you."

I smiled and nodded. His words should offer me comfort, but truthfully, I had no idea what I was about to walk myself into, but my gut was telling me that this mission was going to be harder than I thought. Sadi cracked open her door, letting the sunlight spill onto our feet. With their heads down and covered by the cloaks, they both stepped outside and tugged on the chains that now shackled around my wrists. If I was going to be their prisoner, we had to make it believable. "Here we go," Sadi called back.

Lilah

Even though sunlight scorched their skin, during the day, some vampires would still make small trips among their city, as long as they had their cloaks on. Sadi thought it would be best to escort me through the back parts of the city and cut through part of the Dark Lands to avoid being spotted. Velorim was a massive city with hundreds of acres of land that surrounded us. As my boots hit the ground, I listened to the crunch of the Fall leaves. Anything to calm my nerves at this point.

Nyx kept his hand on the chain that connected to my wrists, gently pulling me forward with his pace, and Sadi, she led the way. If I would have told myself that I would have given myself up to a vampire, befriended another one, and willingly let them chain me and walk me to the one man who sought to kill me, I would have laughed in my face. My eyes traced over Nyx's silhouette, taking in his smooth stride, the way he walked, the way his hair would gently dance with the wind. What was it about him?

My mind and my heart were battling silently. My entire life, I swore to get vengeance on the vampires; I swore to myself that I would kill any vampire that came close to me, and yet here I was, falling for the very thing I vowed to hate.

What was it about Nyx that drew me in? I tilted my head to the side as I watched him take a steady stride forward, as I trailed slightly behind him. I couldn't deny the attraction that pulled me in like the sun's gravity, but truthfully, I believed it was because of that fact that despite it all, he kept showing up for me. I never had someone who dedicated their loyalty to me, and even if he had an agenda at first, I believe that Nyx's heart was feeling the same thing too.

"We're getting close," he said, breaking the silence. His voice was like honey. Sweet and delicate. I couldn't get enough of it. He stopped and turned around and smiled at me. "Are you sure you want to go through with this, Lilah?" his eyes were pleading for me to say *no*. To turn around and run back home, but I couldn't. I was so close to answers. So close to finally getting my vengeance. *For Father*, I kept telling myself.

I nodded my head and stepped forward. "We traveled so far. I can't turn back now." I slipped my fingers into his and leaned against his shoulder as I drew in a large breath. Nyx glanced down at me, a hint of worry glinting in his eyes. "This will be dangerous, you know."

"Is that why you were going to change your mind and take me back home?"

The silence said enough. "I couldn't put you in danger's way. I didn't expect—" Nyx stopped, silence consuming him.

"Expect what? To fall for a human?" I was only half joking but by the way his eyes met mine, I knew that I wasn't far from the truth. My heart beat faster in his presence, a sensation I never thought I would ever feel, and I knew by the look in his eyes that he was consumed with the same sensation.

Nyx changed the direction of the conversation and said, "My father stays in the east wing of his castle. His guards are positioned around every entry point at all hours of the day. He will almost always have someone watching his back, which will make getting him alone very difficult."

It dawned on me that we hadn't fully spoken about the details of the plan, but I was sure that Nyx had every finite possibility etched into his mind. I blinked. "How do we get past the guards?"

Nyx sighed and ran his hand over his face, as if ridding himself of his stress. "I've gone over this countless times in my head and every single time, the only way I truly think we can get by is if he thinks you are my prisoner. Which means that you will be treated as such."

"Okay," I softly spoke. My eyes darted down, watching the chains rattle under my trembling hands. Sadi offered a soft smile as she stood off in the distance. Nyx shifted his energy, something clearly bothering him that he wasn't speaking out loud. He turned his face away, as if hiding his true emotions and sighed.

"No, this plan is going to get you hurt. I don't need my father to lift my banishment. I can try to fight his hold on me. We can just run far away somewhere where he will never find us. You don't have to get vengeance on the men who hurt your father." His voice wavered in a pleading tone.

"Killed my father," I corrected. "And I know it's dangerous. I've done a lot of thinking with my time being out here, and I need to do this. I have trained for years just so that I could take my vengeance on the men who destroyed my family. I want to do this."

His silence struck me like a whip, making me want to curl into myself for putting him through this. Us through this. I could tell that guilt raged inside him at the thought of this plan going bad and me getting hurt, but...Nyx didn't argue. "Do you remember anything about that night? About the vampires who did that to him?"

How could I forget? Every second, every detail of the night was scorched into my brain, no matter how hard I tried to rid myself of the painful memory. I will never forget the way their voices snarled orders at my father, or the way their towering bodies tumbled through my home searching for me. But there was one detail that stood out the most, and in a shaky breath, I spoke, "A tattoo."

Nyx growled. "What kind?" His voice was clipped with anger now. I glanced into his eyes which were now the color of death. Him and Sadi shared a stare before his attention was back onto me.

My voice choked in the presence of him as I spoke, "A snake. It wraps around his wrist. That was all that I could see through the blood that was dripping down his arm." I had to blink away the memory of my father's pulsating throat hanging in the clutches of that monster.

The air crackled in his presence, electrifying the eerie silence with his low snarl. My body shook as a river of chills spread across my skin like wildfire, causing me to hug my arms into my chest and shiver. By the look in his eyes, I knew that he knew who I was talking about. My ears buzzed, my pupils constricted, rage and excitement thrashed around me like an unrelenting storm.

He knows who killed my father.

I let go of his hand and stepped back, giving him some space. The wind blew furiously around as if matching his anger that seemed to be pouring off from him, and before I let the silence go on too long, he turned toward me and said, "His name is Keiran," as if that name was poison to his tongue.

"You know him?"

Nyx's eyes were consumed by the blackness of his rage as he turned to me and said, "He is the reason I was banished from my kingdom. My father's second in command, and so, naturally he would believe whatever Keiran would tell him. My father believed I was conspiring against his throne. Keiran planted that seed into his mind, and there was no stopping it once that poison started to grow." Nyx narrowed his eyebrows and continued. "If it's Keiran you want to kill, I will go to the ends of the world to help you achieve your vengeance."

It wasn't just Keiran I wanted to be lying in his own pool of blood. Nyx's father was just as much to blame. I lifted my chin high. "I want all of them dead, Nyx.

Every last one of them who was there that night, including your father."

There was a twinkle in his eye, a shift of something dark lingering beneath that ice blue color of his. His mouth corked up into a wicked smile. "My little flower, I will do whatever it takes to make you happy. I will spill the blood of the royals, I will march in there and rip their throats out for what they did to you, and when I am done, I will have you right there on the floor moaning my name while their bodies drain of their own blood."

My heart skipped a beat, imagining Nyx killing for me, ravishing my body like a prize at the end. I bit the bottom of my lip and smiled. "Then let's go kill these motherfuckers."

Chapter Twenty-One: Prisoner

Lilah

A sensation was festering beneath the surface of my flesh, an energy that seemed to buzz through me with a newfound power. My body, my soul, felt electrified, and the closer we got to Dravian's castle, the more this magic inside me seemed to surface. The forest was alive. White and blue electric bolts weaved through the ground and trees, shifting with the gentle movements of the land. This vision would come in waves, crashing into me and then dissipating just as quickly. I was almost certain that only I could see this, and I knew that whatever magical bloodline I had was now showing me the potential of what it could do.

Nyx and Sadi guided me forward, my arms shackled to the cold, heavy chains that kept me prisoner, and as I followed, I let myself soak in this new experience. Every vibration from the animals scurrying through the ground, I could hear as if their little mouths were rustling in my ear. Every howl of wind blowing through the treetops, sent a shivering cold throughout my body. I could feel it now. My soul was connecting to the Dark Lands, and it was connecting to me.

"We're getting close," Sadi spoke. Her pace slowed as we began to approach the edge of the forest. To our left, the city of Velorim nestled beneath the rocky canyon, and to our right, the Dark Lands stretched for miles before reaching Eldoria, and forward, there stood the place that my people had sought to find for over a hundred years.

Tall spires jutted upward, piercing the dark clouds that loomed above the castle. Through the dark clouds, beams of sunlight spilled through. Nyx and Sadi kept their hoods over their heads as they took in the castle before us. "Remember, you are our prisoner. We just need to get close enough to my father, and when I have the chance, I will kill him."

"How will you kill him?" I asked. I wondered if he was going to tear his head off the way he did with Viktor. "Besides, I thought you were already dead. Immortal."

I heard Nyx expel a laugh mixed with a choke as he slipped a side glance to Sadi. "We are not dead; however, we age very slowly. And you can kill us. There are ways to do so."

"Oh?" I inquired. "Besides ripping their heads off?"

"I have a plan, Lilah. I will kill him once I am close enough. And when he is dead, it will be me who commands his army."

My lip curled up. After all these years of yearning for revenge, I finally was going to get close enough to kill Dravian. "Are you sure he won't suspect what we are planning?"

Nyx turned to face me, his eyes flashing from blue to black. "My father ordered me to bring you to him in exchange to lift my banishment. He still thinks that I am going to bring you to him for that reason. When we get there, you will be taken from me and brought to his dungeon for holding. I will have Sadi keep an eye on you while I figure out a way to get him alone."

I sucked in my breath as a rush of fear coursed through me. I was about to willingly give myself to the Vampire King, who has put a bounty on my head. "And you will kill him?" I had to be sure. The moment Dravian's cursed heart stops beating, and the moment the men who killed my father take their last dying breaths, I will need to figure out the extent of this Veyl bloodline of mine. If I had some connection over this land, over this curse, then maybe it would be smart to take control before more enemies of mine come hunting for my head.

A river of chills ran over my sweat-slicked skin as my eyes drank in the horror of this castle before me. I gulped down whatever spit my mouth could produce to coat my dry throat, which wasn't much. The iron bars—bearing intricate twisting designs—pierced the sky, towering over my petite body. Nyx glanced back at me, as if speaking to me through an unspoken language. I knew what his eyes were asking. *'Are you sure?'*

I parted my lips to speak, but before any words left my mouth, the gate opened. I sucked in a breath, realizing that there was no turning back now. In my mind, I counted the hidden daggers in my belt, hoping that they wouldn't find them all. I could tell that Sadi and Nyx were yearning for darkness, having spent too many hours cloaked under the relenting sun, and as the gates opened, they were gifted what their bodies craved—shade. There was a dirt pathway that led on for a good mile, covered by a canopy of trees that seemed to have no effect from the Fall weather. I could practically hear the exhale of relief as we stepped through the threshold. As for me, only doom and fear eclipsed my senses.

Ahead, there were three men—vampires—guarding the castle doors. None holding any weapon that I could see. Not that they would need one anyway. *They* were the weapons, their bodies gifted the magical gift of strength and speed. Thankfully that curse still haunted them though. If I needed to escape, at least I had the sun on my side.

"Nyx," the one on the right said, straightening his posture.

Nyx only nodded his head and kept moving forward. "I have come to offer my father what he has been searching for in exchange for a lift on my banishment." Nyx practically growled at the three men standing before him. Sadi kept quiet, but her eyes burned with a predator's stare. The rapid fluttering of my heart beating in my chest thrummed in my ears, drowned out the world around me as fear ravished me from the inside out. I was a Huntress. I shouldn't be scared, but being so close to such evil did something to me that I couldn't control. My head stayed down, playing into the whole prisoner role.

One of the guards clicked his tongue and then said, "Let them through. Tell the King his package is here." Nyx pulled on the chains that clamped onto my wrists and yanked me forward, Sadi right beside me keeping a death stare on me. I guess we were in full character now. The moment we stepped inside, I gasped as I peered around the vast, open inside. This was my first time inside a castle. Even back in Eldoria, I hadn't seen the inside of the Queen's castle. Only her special Hunters were permitted to do so. It took my breath away at how massive everything was. Towering stained-glass windows stretched from the floor to ceiling, allowing fractals of colored light spill onto the sides of the room. But in the center, it was dark as night, along a crimson velvet rug stretching on for as far as my eyes could see until it disappeared into the darkness.

Nyx was following one of the guards into the shadowed veil. I would be lying if I said that fear didn't have a death grip on me. My throat constricted in a swallow as I let the darkness swallow me with it. Vampires could see perfectly clear in the middle of the night if they chose to, but for me, I couldn't see shit, save for my chained hands right in front of my face. His breathing began to pick up. The heat from Sadi's body warmed my side as we kept moving, so I knew that my friends were still with me.

"The King is through here. Move," one of the guards growled. I felt the chains yank me forward again and then before I knew it, I collapsed onto the floor of another room. On my knees, I peered through my tangled hair, only to see bright, yellow glowing eyes staring right back at me, and as I traced my gaze down the face of the Vampire King, I stopped right on his crooked smile.

"Hello," his voice purred. "Bring her forward." Dravian motioned for Nyx to bring me forward, but I could tell that he was hesitant. We had to make this believable if this was going to work. Once Nyx got Dravian alone, he could strike, and then Sadi would break me out of the dungeon. Nyx stepped forward and guided me to his father as I followed on shaky legs. I did a quick glance over my shoulder and met the eyes of Sadi softly staring at me. Her eyes flickered with something I hadn't seen in her yet. Fear?

Nyx got straight to business. "The girl in exchange to lift my banishment," his voice boomed.

Dravian flashed us a devilish grin, playing with the tips of his fingers. "So quick to jump to business I see. Tell me, son, how did you capture this one? I have been searching for her for quite some time and yet here you are, dangling her in front of me as if she was caught fresh from the stream."

I kept still but my eyes darted to Nyx. If he said the wrong thing, we'd all be dead. Only a few seconds passed before he spoke. "Maybe you just were looking in all the wrong places, Father."

Dravian sat in silence for a moment, pinning Nyx with a searing glare before belting out a chuckle so loud that it echoed into my ears. "Well son, whatever means you used to capture this delicacy, bravo. Come, bring her to me. I want to see my prize up close."

His eyes were pleading for me to stay, not to go to his father as he looked back at me, but what else was I supposed to do? Again, I silently counted the sharpened daggers on my hip. *One. Two. Three—*

"Come!" Dravian demanded. I sucked in my breath and shuffled forward, remembering to keep my head down. His long, pointed finger grazed through my hair and I practically had to hold down the vomit as the repulsion from his touch set in. Most vampires were beautiful. Charming. But Dravian, everything about him screamed evil, from his twisted eyes down to his pointed fingertips. His lip curled up slightly, reminding me of what dangers lurked underneath his mouth. He could kill me in less than a heartbeat if I said the wrong thing.

Play cool, I told myself.

A river of shivers extended from my neck down to my toes. As I brought myself closer to this monster, his hot breath violated my senses. There was a glimmer of desire in his eyes, but this desire was not the kind I would see in Nyx's. This look was the look of pure and utter bloodlust. He wanted to torment me. Tear me apart. And when he was done, he wanted to feast on my blood.

"You're a hard one to find," he purred. I gulped and stared in silence. "Tell me how you did it? Did you use your magic to hide yourself?"

"I—uh…" I couldn't speak. My eyes darted to Nyx, but he wouldn't look at me and neither would Sadi. It would draw too much attention.

"No need to speak. I'll have my answers soon enough. Let me get a good look at you." Dravian reached out his fingers and grazed his pointed nails over my skin, analyzing every inch of my body before stopping at the spot behind my ear.

"Ah, there it is."

"What?" I managed to ask.

"The mark of the Veyl. Your mother had the same mark." Dravian turned his gaze to Nyx and flashed a devilish grin, but the only thing my mind was set on was that he mentioned my mother.

"How do you know what my mother looked like?" Slowly, anger began to fester inside me.

Dravian chuckled. "My darling, you have no idea, do you?"

"Know what?"

His nose tilted ever so slightly that I could see the tiny hairs that protruded from his nostrils, his mouth curling dangerously wicked. "Your Queen sent your mother to her death. Did you know that? Her mysterious flu that swept across your pathetic lands wasn't a force of nature but in fact, her doing. How else do you think she keeps her magic alive?" Dravian stepped closer to me, analyzing me, toying with me, and then he pressed his lips against my ear as his voice slithered into my skull. "She was practically dead when I found her. Once a Veyl bloodline reaches our lands, a shift happens, a rip in the magical energy of my kingdom. I knew my chances of breaking the curse over my kingdom was slim, and so, I sent my people to retrieve her body after your Queen thought she disposed of her. All we needed was her blood anyway. Dead or alive, and then we could try to activate the Dawnstone and set my people free." Dravian clicked his tongue and scoffed. "Your mother was weak. She died too quickly. Her body barely had a drop left of that precious blood by the time we brought her back here."

My heart slammed against my chest. My ears rung out in a desperate attempt to control the anger that was exploding through me. My Queen, my leader, my kingdom had betrayed me and killed my mother. How the fuck did I not find out about this back then? How did *no one* find out about this?

I felt like I was going to collapse and so I shifted my weight to keep my body upright. "I think I am going to be sick." My fingers curled into my stomach as I felt the bile rise into my throat. Nyx shifted his body toward me, but I held out my hand to keep him away. We still needed to make Dravian believe that I was his prisoner, but I would be lying to myself if I said that I didn't want this all to end now. I had no one anymore. I couldn't trust my own godsdamned kingdom or Dravian's.

Then I thought about the people I had met in my life. Ryker, Damon, Kanen, and Eldrich. Did they know what our Queen was up to? Casting a sickness upon our people so that she could sacrifice them to feed her magic? I spat on the marbled floor and seethed from my clenched teeth.

Dravian's wicked voice sliced through the moment of silence. "And now, here we are. I have finally found you. The last of the Veyl bloodline. My last hope at shattering this curse." Dravian's arms rose high above his head, as if letting his imagination soak his body in the warmth of the sunlight, he so desperately desired.

"I don't even know what a Veyl is. I don't have what you think I have," I cried. Truth was, I could feel something inside me growing. Something ignited in me the moment I stepped into the Dark Lands. Who was my mother? Where did she come from? So many questions crowded my mind but all I could do to keep myself from going insane was cry.

"Don't cry. Not yet anyway." Dravian nodded his head and yelled for the guards to take me to the dungeon. As their fingers gripped around my arms, I couldn't help but to yank myself away, wanting a taste of my freedom back. Sadi's eyes never left me as I was pulled away, and the last thing that I saw as darkness swallowed me was Nyx's face, stone cold and emotionless as his father watched.

Cold, damp air chilled me deep within my bones as I sat there on the floor of the dungeon cell. One single lantern dangled from the ceiling a few feet down the hall, which offered me the tiniest bit of light. I was one flicker away from being consumed by total darkness. Dravian's guards left me alone to my thoughts, and at first, I was drowning in my own pity and sorrow, but suddenly, something dawned on me. Dawnstone.

What was a Dawnstone? Dravian mentioned it so passively, as if I should know what the fuck he was talking about. If I could truly break the curse that kept the vampires prisoner to the night, then it must somehow be with that stone. If I could get my hands on it, maybe I could use it as leverage over the vampires. There was no doubt there would be total chaos after we killed Dravian, and if I had the power of the curse to dangle over them, maybe they wouldn't try to kill me.

The dungeon was silent, save for the constant dripping of water from the stone wall behind me, and the wild beating of my racing heart. Down here, I had no idea if our plan was working or not. How long would it take? I was so set on this plan that I forgot the minor details. Would I be down here for hours? Days?

I sighed and leaned my back into the wall behind me, letting my heavy arms fall into my lap. My mind played out my entire life to drown out the silence. How could I not see the evil of my kingdom when I was little? The flu had ravished my town, my mother included, so abruptly, killing hundreds of people within a few years. Back then, I was too close to see the mistakes trailing behind like crumbs. Mother never got sick. Hell, we even lived on the outer parts of the castle grounds on our own farm, away from people, so it would have been nearly impossible for Mother to catch it. Everything was all making sense now.

I could practically hear the reminiscences of the Sunfire Court guards banging on our door to take Mother away. To "save her". I scoffed. How fucking stupid. A single tear ran down my cheek, realizing that I was so close to being able to save her, and I had let her slip through my grasp.

Then, that night Father was murdered slithered into my mind like a vile predator wanting to cripple me to my knees. A sob ripped from my chest as flashes of his blood came flooding back into me. The quiver in his voice as he tried to protect me. He didn't deserve that fate, and neither did Mother. Both were murdered by my own kingdom and Dravian's.

Who did I belong to now? After this was over, after Dravian's body was finally lying in his own pool of blood, I would kill Margarethe for what she did to my mother and her people, I would expose her to everyone and bring down my fury on those who helped her—

"Lilah," a deep voice echoed, snapping my mind back to the real world. I gulped and straightened my back. There was a heinous chuckle that reverberated down the stone hallway, dancing around my head, taunting me.

"Come here to kill me so soon?" I barked. Dravian approached in his tailored cloak and suit, striding toward me like some godsdamned businessman. His pale face pressed against the metal bars in front of me and a wicked smile stretched across his face. The sharp canines gleamed under the flickering torchlight, reminding me of how much of a predator he was.

So, I guess Nyx hadn't killed him yet…

"I've been searching for you for nearly ten years. Why kill you so fast when I can play with you first?" The way he spoke to me sent an uneasy feeling into my core. What did he mean by play with me? My imagination ran wild with all the horrible things a vampire could do with their prey. They were predators after all.

I wouldn't show him that I was scared. That's what he wanted. I stuck up my nose and replied in a seething voice, "Play all you want. I'm not scared of you." Hopefully, he won't be able to smell the lies seeping from my lips. I was fucking terrified, but I'd be damned if I let him know that.

His deathly glare pressed into me as silence fell upon us, drowning me. "You will be scared," was all he said before he turned and stormed off. Before I had time to process what happened, one of his guards rushed in and opened the metal door and reached for me. Instinctively, I thrust myself backwards, trying to avoid his grip, but he snatched my arm up so fast that I barely had time to yelp from the pain before he sauntered off with me.

"Where are we going?" I asked. My eyes were wide with fear. Nyx should have killed him by now. What was he waiting for? And where the hell was Sadi? The guard squeezed my arm harder, causing me to wince from the sharp pain of his nails digging into my skin.

"Shut up and keep walking."

I noticed that he wasn't wearing a cloak. Was it nighttime now? That would make escaping a lot more complicated since they would be able to follow me easily into the night.

As he dragged me through the castle all I could see was the massive army that Dravian commanded as they all lined up along a dark velvet carpet, watching me, smiling at me with those predatory eyes. What the fuck was going on? I desperately searched for Sadi and Nyx, hoping that they were somewhere close so that they could get me out of whatever was about to happen. My gut told me that this wasn't good. Something was wrong.

Another vampire took my other arm, my body now being dragged off by two of Dravian's guards. Their sharp nails dug into my flesh so deep that I could feel small trails of blood running down to my fingers. The slightest movement of their nostrils flaring told me that they could smell it too.

"This is going to be a fun one," one of the guards spoke.

"You think it will work?" the other asked.

"Hard to tell. I was told that she will have to endure the forest before she can unlock her true power."

The other one grunted and they kept moving. What did they mean endure the forest? Before I knew it, we were outside, the bright full moon shining high in the sky. Father always cautioned me during the full moon nights. He said that it was the one night a year that the creatures of the Dark Lands could break through the thresholds of magical barriers. Back then, I didn't believe him or the stories he told. I had never seen a monster in the flesh, but Father just did a good job at protecting me from the horrors that lurked beyond.

"Lilah!" I heard Nyx's voice cry out in desperation. My head shot to my left and that was when I saw him, on his knees, chained like an animal.

No. Please no.

Dread filled every empty space inside my heart as realization started to set in. My hazed eyes traced the ground, over Nyx, and now it was on Sadi who was kneeling in the same position. I sucked in my breath.

"What—"

"I'm sorry!" was all he could yell before one of the guards took the backend of his sword and knocked him in the back of the head with it. Nyx dropped like rock. Sadi cried out, crying a stream of tears for him, and then fixed her gaze onto me. No words came from her mouth, but they didn't have to for me to understand what was happening.

Somehow, Dravian found out. They were just as much of a prisoner as I was now. *Fuck!* A sea of guards parted ways for me to be pulled through. My captor yanked me forward until I was standing upon the edge of the forest and Dravian was right there with me.

He smiled. "Did you think I would be that stupid? I could smell the lie on you as you stepped into my castle. I know my son, and he would never be so willing to please me after what I have done to him. Tell me, what was it that you were planning to do with me? Kill me? Take over my throne? You stupid girl. I am the ancient Vampire King, the most powerful creature in these lands, so don't you for one second think that you'll be able to defeat me." Dravian flicked his wrist so that his sharpened nails grew even longer, like tiny daggers protruding from his fingers before he snatched my hair up into his grip.

I yelped out in pain as he pulled my head back, exposing my neck. "You have no idea what real fear is, darling. But you will…" his voice growled. There was something about the promises that he spoke to me that made me want to drop to my knees. Before I knew it,

Dravian took his nails and sliced me down my neck until I was left a shredded mess, warm blood trickling down my shoulder and down to my hip. I cried out. Before I could ask what he was going to do, his voice sliced through the silence. "The blood will call the creatures of the night to you. The forest will hunt you. And the moon will activate the power in your blood. Survive the night, and I might consider keeping you alive for fun. Either way, Lilah, you're going to be mine. Your blood will be *mine.*"

"I can't—"

"You will do what I say! Try to run back here before the night is up, and my guards will make sure you wish you were dead. Better hurry up before they catch up to you." Dravian shoved me into the forest. I glanced back at him, a glimmer of pure evil lurking within those eyes. I gave one last look at Nyx and Sadi and nodded my head. I had to be strong. I had to be the Huntress that I knew I was.

With a swift motion of his hands, Dravian and the rest of his army vanished, and I was now somewhere entirely different.

A full moon towered in the night star-splattered sky, illuminating the Dark Land's forest floor. Fear gripped my throat as I tried to call out, but no words could escape my clenched mouth.

My neck throbbed and ached from where Dravian sliced me open, blood trickling down my body in a constant stream. The metallic tangy scent hung in the air as I bled onto the ground. Surely the umbragores would smell me. What other creatures lived out here? Hunted out here…

I had to survive the night, Dravian mentioned. The forest would hunt me. The moon would activate my magic somehow. My hands reached for my hip, touching the cold metal that I had hidden in my belt. My eyes went wide. I had forgotten that I had my daggers. Gently, I slipped one from my belt loop and held it firmly in my hand as I strode forward. Direction was an illusion, my senses distorting more aggressively the longer I spent out here. The forest was shifting around me, taunting me, trapping me.

I was lost with no way out. Suddenly, a shrilling howl ripped through the air, and immediately my mouth went dry. I knew that sound.

"Umbragores…"

The heavy thuds of their footsteps rumbled through the ground, indicating that their bodies were headed right for me. There was no time to think, let alone plan a way out. Instinctively, I ran for the largest tree and kicked my foot up until I slipped it onto a small notch on the trunk. I reached for a low hanging branch and pulled my body up until I could reach the next branch. It was seconds before the large jaws of the umbragores were snapping at my feet, just barely missing me.

I screamed from the pain in my arms and legs as fear tore through me. My dagger was still in my palm, and as I perched my body against the tree, I twirled it in my fingers, letting my imagination play out how I was going to kill this thing. My chest heaved as I struggled to catch my breath.

The umbragore scratched and chewed away at the base of the tree as if trying to eat its way to me, while the others huddled around like a swarm of insects. As I peered over the edge to get a better look, a small droplet of my blood fell down, coating the umbragore's tongue. Its eyes rolled back in its head, its screeching halted, and for a moment it was silent, but as I watched this creature savor my one drop of blood, my heart sank when I realized that now it has had a taste of me. A taste of what it has been after.

A moment later, its eyes turned black, and it curled its mouth back in a snarl as it bellowed a yelp of fury. It took its claws and one by one dug them into the trunk of the tree, pulling its body up until it was lifted partially off the ground. I gasped.

Next, its legs clawed at the tree for a grip and slowly, the umbragore began to climb.

"Fuck."

It was climbing the fucking tree. My hands began to shake but still, I held out my dagger, preparing to kill this thing or die trying. In only a few seconds, its mouth was now merely a few inches away from the branch that I was sitting on. I had to think fast. My legs steadied as best as they could, my arm closest to the tree clung on for support and with my free hand I took my dagger and jabbed at the beast.

I barely nicked it, and so, I only seemed to piss it off more. The umbragore pulled itself higher and then snapped its teeth at my legs. I had to jump back to avoid being bitten. My foot slipped and before I knew it, I was tumbling down the tree, but before I fell into the sea of beasts below me, I felt a hard whack in my back. For a moment, everything went fuzzy, pain shot through my body like lightning and my hearing felt as if it were under water.

Then, I realized that my body hit another branch on my fall down, saving me. When my mind came to, I scrambled to my feet again and peered over the branch. Now, I was right above the ground. Right above these bloodthirsty monsters. If I was down here, then that meant the other umbragore was…

Slowly, my gaze shifted up as I drew in a ragged breath of air. Looking down upon me were those coal-black eyes, its teeth dripping with saliva It leapt from the branch and hurtled itself toward me, crashing into the branch I was on and snapping it right from the tree. I belted out a scream of terror before I felt myself falling with the beast, our bodies entangling in the air. Everything happened so fast that I didn't have time to react.

The wind expelled from my lungs, my bones ached, my head throbbed, and my ears were ringing with pain as I pulled myself to my feet. I held my dagger in my hand and stood on shaky legs, and as I spun around, I realized that I was surrounded by the jaws of these bloodthirsty beasts. Now was the time to use my skills as a Huntress. Life or death.

I sidestepped just before one of them barreled toward me, trying to take a bite out of my leg, and in the process, I took my dagger and sliced into its eye. It hissed in pain, but that didn't seem to stop it. Another one rammed into me, and I almost fell over but I ducked and rolled out of the middle of the creatures and was now face to face with them. The air crackled with their hunger, their lingering hissing slithering around me like an invisible chain. The one with the busted eye had it out for me. It charged forward, slamming its tree trunk claws onto the ground, but I twirled around the beast and jammed my dagger into the back of its neck. The umbragore fell to the ground in a growling rage, and that was when I turned my attention to the others. Two more came for me with their mouths curled back in a snarl. I took another dagger and chucked it forward, watching the blade spin in the air until it sunk into one of the creature's eyes. Black oozing blood leaked from the socket; it dropped to the ground.

Two down. Three more to go. I only had two daggers left, and so, pulling them from my belt, one in each hand, I danced around their movements, keeping them moving in a circle, disorienting their senses. The umbragore to my left seemed to be getting tired and slowed its pace a bit while the other one kept its glaring stare right at me. I readied my arm and flung my dagger toward the beast, watching as the tip pierced its eye socket. This one curled into itself and yelped out a hissing screech.

"Okay, just you and me now," I huffed out. My dagger gleamed under the moonlit sky, begging to spill the blood of these vile creatures. While most of them were injured and not pursuing me, I decided to take off running away from the group of bloodthirsty monsters, to lead the last one away and tire it out and save my last dagger just in case. My feet hit the mossy terrain heavily, with determination, and equally behind me, the umbragore followed my path. I could feel its hot breath caressing the back of my bare arms and neck as it began to close in.

There was a ledge coming up ahead. A cliff with a sheer drop at the end. I remembered seeing this part of the forest during our travels to Dravian's castle. My breathing picked up, a fluttering pulse vibrating through my veins as I ran for my life from this creature. As my body approached the cliff's edge, I dug my toes into the ground and slid through the dirt, ducking as the umbragore leapt to take a bite from me, but as its body came crashing toward me, I rolled just in time before being taken over the edge with it. My arms lay flat across my chest, the rise and fall of my breathing heavy and tired. I knew that the others weren't fully dead and that once they regained some of their energy, they would be hunting me again.

The full moon had a plan for me, the forest seemed to have a personal vengeance against me, and whether I liked it or not, I had to play by its rules. My sweaty hair fell loose around my face, my clothes were torn and dirty, and my body was scraped up, but I was alive. Dravian said that surviving the night would activate my magic and I would be able to break his curse, and honestly, out of everything, that terrified me the most.

Chapter Twenty-Four: Darkness

Lilah

Darkness swept over the forest like a blanket of heavy mist. All-consuming. Suffocating. Wherever I was, I could tell that I was in a dangerous territory. The wind wisped through the forest, my loose hair slicing through the air like whips. That weird feeling inside me was festering again; my body trembled with energy, my vision now heightened to another level. It was as if I could see the energy of the forest, the veins of magic that sprawled through the dirt.

It pulsated, like a beating heart, thrumming faster the deeper I walked into the darkness. The ground began to shift under my feet and when I went to take another step, my foot sank into the mud, getting stuck.

"Shit!"

I had no time to process before a loud creaking sound echoed through the forest, startling me. A large branch from the tree next to me came barreling toward me at full speed, slamming into my chest, and knocking onto my back. As I lay there, my lungs gasped for the air that had been ejected, a burning ache now radiating through my chest. As I went to turn over, a root snaked through the dirt and wrapped itself around my ankle.

"No…not this again…"

I knew what was coming next. If I didn't hurry, my body would be pulled apart by these trees. I took my last dagger and began slicing through the root as fast as my hands could, trying to escape the inevitable attack. Just as I freed myself from the grips of this tree, another root snatched up my wrist, causing me to drop my dagger.

Fuck! I needed to get out of this. Now! I quickly scrambled to my feet with my wrist still held prisoner by the angry tree, but now I could see what was coming for me: a wall of branches and roots hurtling themselves for my body as if I was their last meal before their death. My free hand clutched onto the root on my wrist and held tight as I spun my body around the tree and pulled hard. I kept twisting and yanking until I heard a snap. A piece of the root still clung to my wrist but now that I was free, my body took off running as fast as it could away from this place.

Tiny twigs and leaves sliced through my cheeks as I ran through the vegetation, but I paid no attention to the sting of the cuts. My mind was on getting myself somewhere safe for the night. But was there anywhere that I would be safe out here? Dangerously, my mind went to a dark place, thinking about all the fucked-up things that have happened in my life.

My Queen killed my mother, Dravian tried to use her blood to break his curse, and ever since he had been searching for me, which led to my father's death. Even after surviving that horrible night, my life as a Drifter was rough. It wasn't until Eldrich took me in that I started to feel a sliver of happiness, but now, here I was, stuck in a living nightmare again.

My mind taunted me with worries and regrets, and my heart bled for Nyx. I wanted his touch so bad. I wanted to feel his breath wash over my skin before pressing his silk lips to mine. My body craved him like it craved water. Was he okay? Was Dravian hurting him right now? Anger fumed inside me at the thought of that monster touching a single hair on my man.

I cried out in a desperate plea for help, not really sure who I was talking to. My voice wavered with pain and fury, regret, and sorrow, and when I was done, a single tear dropped onto the ground beneath my knees and soaked into the soil. I almost gave up. I almost let the trees take me, but then, something happened. All sound stopped. Silence shrouded the noise of the forest, and the energy of the forest shifted as if it were all leading back to me.

As I kneeled on the ground, the magical veins of the forest pulsated in my direction, as if connecting to me somehow. My hand searched for a connection; I placed my hand in the dirt and closed my eyes, letting the energy flow into my soul. "I don't know what I am supposed to do or what I should say, but I am not your enemy."

I felt it. Heard it. Whispers of the Dark Lands, as if it was a collection of thousands of forgotten souls, their voices trickling into my mind, and the closer I listened to their anguished cries, I noticed the anger that echoed into my mind. The forest was angry with me, with my bloodline. The curse put upon the vampires not only affected them but also everything in these lands.

No wonder the trees were trying to kill me. I shifted my knees and dug my fingers in more. "How do I help you?" I called out. The voices grew angrier, louder, until my head was buzzing with their furious whispers.

Suddenly, a large gust of wind raged through the woods like a crashing wave and behind it followed a beast I had never seen before. My heart dropped to my stomach as I stood before this massive creature. Black shadowy skin shifted among the trees, glowing white eyes glared right at me, and as it drifted closer to me, I shrunk into myself.

"What the fuck is that?"

I could hear the snarling coming from every exhale. I could feel the hatred pouring from its essence like spilled blood. It coated everything around me, suffocating me until I felt like I was drowning. The only thing I could think of at this moment was to run. My body reacted before my mind could keep up, and before I could snap back to reality, my body was sprinting away from whatever that thing was. The forest's energy pulsated around me like a beating heart and the whispers of its souls screamed louder into my mind.

'Evil!'

'The Suppressor!'

'Kill. Kill. Kill!'

I shook my head at their insults, a stream of tears now running down my face. It got my mind falling into a deep thought of what my blood meant to this land. To the creatures here. A river of chills ran up my arms as I ran forward. Trees passed by, branches slapped me in the face and body any chance they got, and my mind wanted to explode from the hatred that was being chanted to me. I must have been running for a few miles now, but I could still hear the darkness creeping up on me. That beast was coming for me.

Then Nyx drifted into my mind again. I missed him. I feared for him, but then I remembered that he had hidden hideouts all along the floors of these woods. If I could just find one, maybe I could wait out the night. My eyes searched for the discoloration of leaves, for the off-centered vegetation. He said that he had them everywhere, so maybe they were here too, wherever *here* was.

My heartrate thrummed in my chest with fear and excitement, and as my eyes searched tirelessly, I finally saw what I was looking for. I gasped and shifted my direction and ran so fast that I almost tripped on my own feet as I slid my body into the hole and closed the opening. My body dropped to the ground with a heavy thud, expelling the air in my lungs. My chest gasped and heaved to take in a breath as I lay there on the dirt floor, tired, sore, and mentally exhausted. A sob began to rip through me, but I had to be quiet. I forced my hands over my mouth to muffle the cries that poured from my mouth. Above me, there was a weird sound coming from outside the hatch: a rustling of leaves, a creaking of branches. Immediately, I knew what it was.

It had to be that beast searching for me. Maybe even the umbragores were still hunting me too.

I didn't dare move, let alone breathe, until I felt the presence of the darkness drift away. The moment I felt it leave the area; I sat up and ran my hands through my hair. It was dark here, but for some weird reason, I could almost see perfectly clearly now. Just like how I could see in the forest. Maybe it was my magical vision being activated. This hideout seemed untouched for years. My eyes traced the edges of the hallway that led down to the single room, taking notes of what was in here: a small, wooden table, a small cot, one blanket. No food or water.

Relief washed over me knowing that I at least had a place to lay my head and a blanket to warm myself up. My body ached so bad, desperately craving the sweet relief of comfort. I took no time to walk myself over to the small bed in the corner and lay down, pulling the blanket over my trembling body. Warmth coated me, and a heaviness began to weigh on my eyes. I was so exhausted, so tired from running and fighting, so done with feeling this rage burn through me. If I was going to survive this night and kill Dravian, I needed energy to do so, and so, I closed my eyes, falling into the desperate need for sleep. My mind was pulled into the darkness as I let it consume me.

Lilah

"I knew we would find her."

My eyes shot open, and I gasped as I sat up from the bed. Horror consumed me as I realized whose voice I had just heard.

"Alerice," I breathed.

Her wicked smile just taunted me as she stood before me, twirling her hair around her boney finger. And next to her stood Zev, his massive muscles rippling under his skin as if he were holding back attacking me like his hunted prey. Zev growled and kept his deathly glare on me.

"How did you—"

"Find you?" Alerice cocked her head to the side.

I sucked in my breath and scooted back farther against the wall. Nodding my head, I croaked out, "Yes."

"You stupid girl. Look at you. You are covered in cuts and gashes. I can see your blood dripping down your face and arms. What? Did you think that we wouldn't be able to smell you? I've been searching for you ever since you slipped through my fingers and I will be damned if I let that happen again," she growled.

Alerice took a step forward. "You are coming with me. Now." Anger poured from her voice. It seethed from her lips and bled from her eyes. I had killed her friend and threw boiling water on her the last time that I saw her, so I knew that she probably wanted nothing more than to make me suffer for what I did to her.

I shook my head and straightened. "No. I'm not going anywhere with you. There is no point in taking me to Dravian now. I already turned myself in, and he has sent me out here for some kind of trial. If you bring me back to him, it will ruin his plan for me."

I could see the gears turning in her head, the fire burning deep beneath her eyes. She was *pissed*. A tug at the corner of her lip pulled her mouth back in a devilish smile before she spoke. "It's funny that you still think that is what I want. You murdered my friend. Chopped her head off. You threw boiling water in my face. Do you think that I was just going to let that go?" Alerice laughed. "I couldn't care less about Dravian. I want you to suffer for what you did to me, and I am going to start by doing this…"

Before I had a chance to react, Alerice slammed forward into me and clutched her fingers around my throat, slamming me into the wall behind me. I choked out a cry of pain as my body went slamming into the wall. Her other hand pressed my arm back against the wall as her mouth hovered over my skin, right above my pulsating jugular. "You smell so fucking good. I can't wait to get a taste."

A sharp sting sunk into my flesh, her fangs sinking deep, her venom seeping into my bloodstream. She pulled back for a moment and whispered, "I'm going to make this hurt," before pulling me into her again. Pain radiated through me, through my entire body as she made the venom cause me agony. Every nerve in my body screamed for mercy, begging for it to stop. My body crumbled into her, a reaction I had no control over, and shook as she drained me. I could feel the blood loss taking effect.

She was going to kill me if I didn't do something. All my weapons were lost out in the forest, Nyx was being held prisoner in the castle, Ryker probably thought I was dead, and so, it was me who had to do something. There was a buzzing feeling in my head, almost as if those whispers from the forest were coming back, and at first, I tried to drown them out, but something deep within me told me to let the voices in.

It was a floodgate of chants, screams, pleas, and insults, all swirling around my mind, clouding me with their words. I focused on channeling it, sorting it. Controlling it. Then I heard something that made my heart skip a beat. A small voice that my body seemed to recognize.

'Darling…'

My eyes fluttered open. I knew that voice. A sob began to well in the back of my throat, but I held it back. The only words that I had the energy to form on my own lips were, "Mother…"

It was her. My ears picked up the sweet tone of her voice, the way it went down an octave when she spoke. Her soul was trapped here, among the thousands that had flooded my head. If she were trapped here, then maybe that meant breaking this curse on Dravian and his kingdom would ultimately free my mother's soul, along with the thousands of others that were trapped here.

She spoke again. *'Use your magic. You must fight.'*

It hadn't occurred to me to use my magic. I had no clue what flowed through my body, nor did I know how to use it, but if I did nothing, Alerice was going to drain me dry, leaving my body dead. I cracked my eye open to see Zev hovering over us like a hungry animal. The black of his pupils consumed his eyes in a rage, his mouth salivating at my blood that was being spilled.

"My turn," he growled. Zev reached for Alerice and yanked her shoulder back and I gasped a sigh of relief when her fangs finally left my body. Alerice hissed at Zev, looking like a wild beast with blood running down her chin and neck.

"Don't fucking touch me!"

"Enough! It's my turn."

Zev shoved Alerice away and groaned as he slid his massive hands under my neck and firmly grasped a chunk of my hair. I whimpered, knowing that the pain was imminent, but my mother's voice rang in my head again. *'Magic.'* Just one word, but it was that one word that sparked a flame of hope within me. I shoved my palms forward into his chest and with all the energy I had left in my frail body, I summoned my magic to the surface.

I had no clue how to, but it was as if my soul already knew what to do. Vibration rang through my toes and legs, traveling up my torso, until it left my lips feeling electrified. When I opened my eyes again, I could see the energy running through the soil of the ground, through the walls of the hideout, and now, it was running through *me*.

One word came out of my mouth. One word and Zev slammed backward into Alerice. "No!" I screamed. White energy came flying from my palms like a furious storm that had been building, begging to be released.

Regardless of my blood loss, my body felt recharged. Powerful. Unstoppable. Was this what Dravian was waiting for? For one of the creatures of the night to force me into a point of life and death, to activate what was hidden within me?

Zev groaned as he tried to lift himself from the ground, Alerice stumbling forward to help him, but I lifted my hand and with an invisible grip, I lifted him into the air, my eyes burning him with a seething glare. "I am no one's prey. I am sick and tired of dealing with you. The one mistake Nyx made was not finishing you off when he had the chance. I won't make that mistake."

His lips parted, but before he could croak out a desperate plea for mercy, I clenched my fists tight, snapping his neck. His body dropped to the ground like a rock and now my focus was on Alerice. She screamed, tears running down her porcelain skin, and now true fear was etched into her eyes.

"You fucking monster!" She leapt for me, but I dodged her attack and snatched her up by the back of her head and pulled her ear close to me.

My breath washed over her as I spoke the promises I was going to do to her. "You are lucky I haven't already done the same to you. I could kill you with the twitch of my finger, but I am going to use you for something instead."

And just like that, the roles have reversed. *I* was the powerful one now. I was the one who should be feared, because it was pure fury and rage that consumed me at this moment, and now, I was the predator. Alerice whimpered in my grip. She was lucky she drank my blood or else I would have let her burn on our walk back to the castle. Sunlight began to peak its way into the hideout, which told me that I had survived the night out here. I tightened my grip on her hair and softly spoke, "You're coming with me."

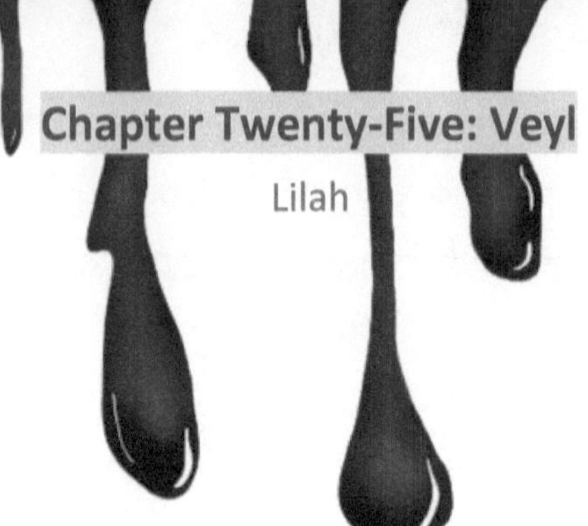

Chapter Twenty-Five: Veyl

Lilah

We exited the hideout, and now that I could see my surroundings, I knew just how far away from Nyx and Sadi I was. My new sight showed me the energy beneath my feet, the soul of the forest calling out for mercy. It was angry. The pulsating electric veins that only I could see stretched for miles until they abruptly stopped. When my eyes traced the area, my heart sank.

The forest was scorched to ash, a thick, black coat blanketing the dead vegetation. My eyes narrowed and I snapped my neck in Alerice's direction. "Was this you?" I demanded. My grip on her hair tightened and she whimpered from the pain. Alerice was stubborn. She didn't want to give me the satisfaction, but I persisted. This time I wrapped my hands around her throat and squeezed tight until I could hear her choking from my fingers digging into her skin. I leaned in closer now, a seething glare burning her as I asked again. "Was. This. You?"

Through teary eyes, she nodded and croaked out a whimpering, "Yes." I let go but yanked her head back into my grip. Alerice had burned down nearly the entire Dark Lands just to find me. Memories of that day flooded my mind just as harshly as the rage that coursed through me. The smoke practically lingered in my lungs still. These lands may be the lands of the dark creatures of the night, but this was my forest now. I was connected in a way that I didn't think was possible, and now, I wanted to get my vengeance.

As we trudged through the charred land, stepping over half-fallen trees, broken roots, and piles of dust, I broke the silence. "So, how does it feel to lose, Alerice? I bet you never thought you would become my prisoner now. Huh?" I corked up a half-smile, solely to piss her off more. She writhed under my fingertips, but I clutched my grip down harder, causing her to whimper some more.

Through barred teeth, she growled, "You won't win this war. The moment Dravian sees you, he will unleash his army against you for what you have done to me." Alerice spat.

I rolled my eyes. "Really, because if I remember correctly, you are considered a rebel in your kingdom.

I don't think Dravian will be so quick to help a rebel. He might even do me a favor for getting rid of your kind."

"Don't fool yourself. Dravian has been searching for you for over a hundred years. The mysterious Veyl bloodline. The last of its kind. After your mother died on his lands, after he came so close to that magical blood of yours, it's all our kingdom has ever heard about. His troops would be sent all over the Dark Lands to search for you." Alerice scoffed. "We would have found you sooner if it weren't for your Queen keeping that magical barrier up. It must have hidden your scent somehow."

It was as if a dagger had sunk right into my heart at then mentioning my Queen, a new hatred for her pooled inside me, just waiting to burst through. That magic barrier, the one I was never sure truly existed, only worked because she kept her own people sick, thinking they had some mysterious flu, and when she came to their door to "save them," she sacrificed them. Used their blood to keep her magic alive. I heard rumors of her having some kind of artifact that held magic, but I never believed it. And up until Ryker had shown me the dagger, I always wondered what that artifact was. I just never knew the price she had to pay for it.

We had walked miles now of the forest and now I could see where the fire had stopped burning. Spots of green burst through parts of the black-gray ash, and as I continued forward, I now saw the life again. The energy pulsated beneath my feet again. Electric. I closed my eyes and inhaled, letting my skin bathe in the warming sunrays, but Alerice's voice shattered my moment of serenity.

"This won't last, you know. Whatever power you think you have."

A low growl rumbled from me. "Neither will my blood's protection on you. You'll start burning soon once my blood wears off." Alerice gulped, her throat bobbing. I loved watching her eyes fill with fear. She wasn't used to being the prey, I could see that, which made this even more enjoyable for me. I let her drown in those fears for a moment before my voice ripped through the silence again. "Don't worry. I need you for something, and for now, that requires you to be alive."

Lilah

Hours slipped by, time seemingly running like a river flowing free. The sun was now high in the sky, and I could tell that my blood was starting to wear off on Alerice from the quiet groans of pain that kept slipping from her mouth.

"Does it burn yet?" I asked, a half-smile playing on my lips. I tugged Alerice forward and enjoyed the noises I caused to escape from her. She didn't answer, but by the way she pursed her lips, I would say that I was right. Her skin looked red, hot to the touch. I knew that if she didn't find shade soon, she would be just like the Dark Lands—scorched.

"You think you are all powerful now. Now that you have whatever magic blood running through your veins. Well, you must forget that us vampires are magic ourselves. You cannot match our speed. Our endurance. Our strength. Your power will run out..." Alerice coughed, heaving deep struggling breaths as she continued to walk under to tormenting sunlight.

"Don't worry. We are almost back to the castle. I can feel that we are close. You'll get your shade then." Ahead, among the horizon, through the trees, I could make out the silhouette of the castle. Like a snake preying on its food, fear crept over my body so slowly that I wanted to curl into myself. I was about to willingly go back to Dravian's castle. For vengeance and for love. I couldn't ignore my desire to have blood for blood, to kill the vampire who tore my father's throat out while I watched. Father deserved vengeance for what happened to him, and Nyx...

My heart was a shattered mess before he picked me up and put me back together. Now, I would go to the ends of the world for him. My body craved his touch, the way his muscles flexed when he would hold me tight. My fingers found their way to my throat as I found myself missing more than just him. I missed being *his*. Alerice stepping on a twig snatched me from my thoughts. I glanced down and noticed that the path we were walking on now was covered with broken tree branches. As if some massive creature had smashed through the entire forest along this area.

I gasped at the sight, knowing that something that big lived out here and Alerice chuckled at my amusement. "The whole damned forest has been hunting you. You got lucky that this monster didn't find you out there." My heart sped up, thrumming like a wild drum inside my chest as anger rolled through me.

"You don't know what you are talking about," I lied. But the truth was, Alerice was right. Ever since stepping foot over Eldoria's barrier, into the Dark Lands, everything seemed to be after me. I could hear the furious whispers of the souls of the forest screaming in my head. I could sense the shift of energy as I walked through the lands. My presence has disrupted the balance of energy, and now that I was here, it wanted to restore what had been lost.

"You are lying to yourself. I can see it in your eyes that you know what I am saying is true."

I kept my hand on Alerice as we walked. Even though I hated this vampire with every ounce of my being, she might be useful. Before we got too close to the castle, I decided to try to get more information out of her.

"Tell me what you know about the Dawnstone," I said. Alerice scoffed; I wasn't surprised. My rage and magic swarmed me, consumed me until I found myself slamming her against a tree with my hands around her throat. She choked and coughed, barely enough air escaping my grip to allow her to whimper. I demanded again, "Tell me about the Dawnstone. Now."

A single tear shed from her pathetic yellow eyes and so, I let go and pushed her forward onto the path again. This time, her voice quivered with fear. "All I know is that it is a very rare ancient item that is said to be magic. It was forged by a sorcerer. Dravian has it now. It's how he can control most of the Dark Lands and the creatures in it. They are bound to the magic in the stone."

My chin tilted up slightly. "If I were to get the stone from him, would I control the forest?"

"You?" Alerice choked out a laugh. "You aren't cursed like us. Like the forest. It is *your* bloodline that put this damned curse on us in the first place. What makes you think that you would just be able to make that go away? If you want control, you must break the curse on all of us."

Her words rang in my head with warning. Break the curse. But if I were to break the curse, I could potentially create another problem—an army of day walking vampires. It could be total chaos. I shook my head. "No, I can't break the curse. You don't deserve to walk among the daylight."

"Suit yourself, but when Dravian gets his hands on you again, you'll have no choice but to break it. You'll see." As Alerice finished speaking, she stopped walking and gasped, staring at something in front of us. Before I could ask why she had stopped, my voice caught in my throat as my eyes peered upon the same thing that had her pinned in silence.

"What the fuck is that?" I whispered.

"You wanted to know what broke all those trees back there. Well, that is what did that." My body stiffened at the sight of the creature, its titanic black body towering above the treetops, pelts of fur trailing along its thick skin, but as I stared longer, I could tell that its body was almost like a shadow. Whatever this creature was, I could see the anger flashing within its eyes, the way it seared into me.

"What is it?" I asked again.

Alerice chuckled and in a quiet voice said, "We call them bloodstalkers. I have never seen one in person. They hunt for blood, just like I do." My grip on Alerice loosened as fear consumed me. This beast towered over me, and it was glaring right at me like it wanted a taste for itself.

Before I could speak, a blaring roar echoed through the lands as this creature slammed its clawed feet into the ground before hurtling itself full speed at us. I screamed and fell backward as Alerice shoved her body away from my grip. Without a warning, she took off running, but right now, my worries were on what was imminent. I had nearly a second before this creature's massive feet crushed me. My body rolled to the side just missing its attack. I scrambled to my feet and began to run as fast as I could. I tried to call out for help with my magic, but the forest didn't listen to me. The only response I got back in return was the anger that seeped into the lands, infecting me with a heaviness.

"Fuck!" I yelled as the bloodstalker threw a fucking tree at me. I ducked just in time before being smashed by the massive trunk. I craned my head back as I ran forward, the beast now catching up. A reverberating growl pierced through the air, vibrating my chest, as it leapt into the air and came crashing down on me. I ducked, but not fully in time to miss being hit. The claws of the massive beast smacked me across the land and into a neighboring tree. Pain cracked within me, my back seizing, as I lay there motionless.

How am I going to get out of this? I thought. Survive this? I could smell the saliva dripping from its sharpened teeth as it approached me with hunger. I tried to move but my body betrayed me, pain shooting through me like lightning. The look in its eyes was nothing short of fury, and I could tell that this anger was directed at me. The tips of its teeth protruded forward when it snarled its mouth back for a bite. It was coming. My end. My death. I never got to kill the vampire who murdered my father, or to kiss Nyx one last time. My heart ached for the unfinished promises that I made myself. I closed my eyes as I prepared to be eaten alive, but when the pain didn't come, I stopped.

"That was quite the show, wasn't it?" a voice said. Dravian's voice. I opened my eyes to see the beast glaring at me with that same hunger, but it was as if it were being forced to hold back. When I glanced to my right and looked upon Dravian standing there, he had his hand held out and palm open. My eyebrows narrowed in confusion. He must have noticed. "It must obey me. I could let it kill you, but we need your blood to be fresh for this to work."

"Should I be thanking you then?" I snarled.

Dravian flashed a wicked grin and said, "Oh, darling. You won't be thanking me when we get started." His eyes traced me up and down, brightening as he noticed the cuts and bruises that decorated my skin. An obvious amusement for my suffering. "Looks like you made it through the Trial. Tell me, *human*, do you feel it yet? Your magic?"

I didn't want to tell him the truth. That he was right. That surviving the night out here under the full moon had activated my magic, but my silence was clear enough for him. He knew it worked and now I was his prisoner once again. Dravian snapped his fingers and two of his guards rushed me, pulling me to my feet. Whimpering from the pain, I dropped, sagging into their bodies.

"Take her back to the dungeon for now while I get the ceremony chamber prepared. It must be perfect for this to work." And just like that, Dravian disappeared into black mist, leaving the monster behind in our presence. The guards dragged me back toward the castle, no one speaking a word this time.

As I was pulled onto enemy territory, leaving the Dark Lands behind, one thought repeated in my mind. *Kill them. Kill them all.*

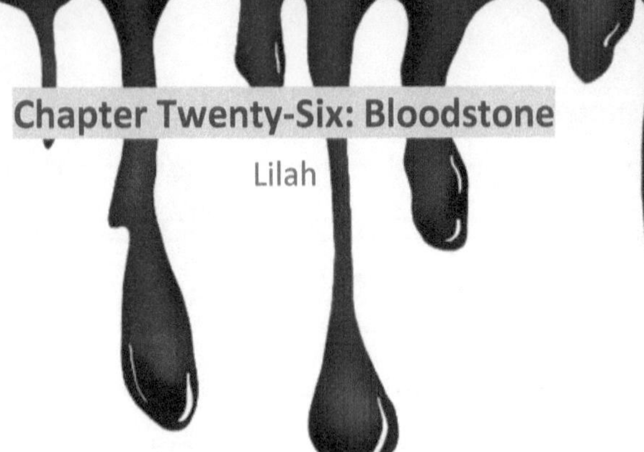

Chapter Twenty-Six: Bloodstone

Lilah

My knees smashed into the gravel beneath me as the guards threw me into another cell. I groaned from the pain that shot through my body. Laughter taunted me as the guard watched my suffering from the other side, shutting the door in my face. "Whenever he is done with you, I would like to have a little taste for myself." The other guard chuckled and then sauntered off, leaving me along with this one.

I clenched my teeth and snarled. "You won't come near me again. I can promise you that."

"Oh, what? Do you think you are going to escape and run off with your little boyfriend?" My head shifted up at the mentioning of Nyx, but immediately I cursed myself under my breath for letting them see that I had a weakness.

He tilted his head to the side, as if analyzing me, and then flashed me a half-smile. "So, it's true then. The Dark Prince has finally found someone to tame him.

And now look, both prisoners. Just where they belong. I'll have fun making you watch as we kill him later." Anger roared through me, and I slammed my fists into the metal cage door.

I pressed him with a seething stare and dropped my voice low so that only he could hear me. "When I get out of this, I will make sure that you suffer. Don't underestimate a mere little *human*. You might regret it." I pushed off the door and slowly stepped away, not once taking my eyes off of the guard. If he was frightened, he didn't show it. Instead, his face was stone cold. Emotionless.

My eyes traced the fine silken black shirt he wore, carefully hugging his muscles, and as he lifted his hand to fix his collar, that was when I saw it. A snake tattoo peaking slightly from under his sleeve. Hatred boiled inside me, rage threatened to explode from my head, because after all these years, I was finally standing before the creature I promised to kill. This was the same tattoo that I saw coated with my father's blood. The same hand that held his throat in his grip as he licked it clean. I had never felt more like a caged animal in this moment, my inner predator begging to be released.

"Keiren," I seethed.

His flat expression shifted as he arched his brow and turned his gaze toward me. "Did I tell you my name?" he asked flatly. My body lost control. I lunged forward and screamed, clawing at him with my bare hands through the metal bars, red now clouding my vision.

"You killed him! It was you! I will fucking kill you for what you did!" I screamed helplessly, sorrow and fury mixing inside my mind like a rolling storm. My entire life I promised to find this vampire who tore my life apart and now that I was standing in front of him, all I could do was lose control.

His lips corked up in a sly smile. He stopped adjusting his collar and turned to face me head on now, letting me scream out my fury. Once I collapsed onto the ground in exhaustion, he stepped forward and spoke. "You were there," he said, more of a statement of realization. My watery eyes met his and as he looked down upon me, lying on the dirty floor, he snickered. "All that time we were searching for you, and you were there, watching. Tell me Lilah, how did you escape us for all these years? Hiding like some rodent among the streets. Was it your magic?"

My breathing hitched, the air now feeling as if it were too thick to inhale. A loud ringing in my ear started as my heartrate thrummed with anger. I dug my fingernails into the palms of my hands to try to keep myself from losing control again, and as I pulled myself back to my feet, I met Keiran's gaze, and said with a seething voice, "Oh, I was there. I watched you rip out my father's throat. You mocked him. Back then, I had no idea what you were. What *I* was, but I swore to myself that I would find you one day and get my revenge, and don't you think that I won't follow through with that promise. You will get what you deserve for what you did to him."

I spat on the ground at his feet and growled at his presence. Keiran only smiled and stepped away slowly as if my threats were nothing more than a child's promise. As he went to walk away, his last words to me—before I was completely alone—were, "Good luck."

Lilah

They left me to rot in this dungeon for what seemed like an eternity, leaving me to suffer from my mind's worry. All I could think about was Nyx and Sadi, Ryker and Eldrich, the only people who had ever been close enough for me to call them a friend.

Were they alive? In pain? It killed me not knowing and it killed me more knowing that I could have helped stop this and yet here I was, trapped like a fucking prisoner. Dravian said he had to get the ritual chamber prepared—whatever that meant—and then my time would come. Down here in this cell, my magical powers felt diluted, weak, as if something were suppressing my abilities. I could no longer feel the energy of the ground or hear the whispers of the souls.

I lifted my hand and tried to levitate a small rock in the corner, but nothing happened. I huffed out an exhale and sighed. My throat tightened, my chest heaved, and tears began to well up again.

I couldn't cry. Not now. I needed to be strong. I needed to be the Huntress I knew I was. My body was covered in gashes and cuts, blood still coating my clothing like war paint. I bet it smelled divine to my captors; my fingers scraped away the dried red flakes of blood as I watched them flutter to the ground like fallen Winter leaves.

As I sat there sulking in the inevitable, a sound from down the hall stole my attention. "Who's there?" I called out; my voice bounced off the walls and faded into the shadows. I was only met with silence at first but then someone emerged under the torchlight. My eyes traced over the silhouette before me, taking in the dark clothing and dark hair, but when I met the gaze of the eyes before me—blue as ice—I gasped.

"Nyx! How are you here? I thought you were dead." I ran forward and immediately began to cry as I reached for him. He stepped forward and let my hands pull him in as he cupped my face through the metal bars.

"Lilah," he breathed. His eyes weren't hopeful or bright, instead, they held sadness in them. Despair. Regret. I interlaced my fingers with his and let my body embrace the warmth of his skin one last time, my tears running down my cheek. "I am so sorry little flower. My father…he figured out our plan. I don't know how, but he did. Are you okay?" As I shifted my body, the torchlight showed him what I truly looked like in this moment.

"You're hurt…" he growled. His eyes flicked down at my feet and that growl rumbled louder. "They took your shoes?"

I stepped back and turned my head to hide the cuts along my face and neck. Nyx immediately began to seethe from his clenched jaw. "I will make him suffer for what he did to you." He reached for my chin and gently pulled it close to him so that I was looking into his eyes again. I didn't want him to see me like this, to see me weak. His finger stroked gentle circles along my skin, and I leaned into his touch.

I shifted and stepped back a little. "Nyx…How? How are we going to get out of this?" I paused for a moment, thinking. Then, something dawned on me. "How are you here right now? The last I saw you,

Dravian had you and Sadi on your knees ready to kill you."

His mouth parted, as if he were going to speak; no words came out, but his eyes, I could see right through them, and they were telling me that something was not right. His shoulders tensed and then he sighed deeply, heavily. "My father is using his magic against me. He ordered me to come take you to his ritual chamber. Being in these walls, in his castle, it makes his magical hold on me stronger somehow. I don't remember being like this, but it is as if I can't say no to him."

Nyx glanced away as if the shame was too much for him to look at me. "We will figure this out. I will find a way to break us out of here. Where's Sadi?" I asked.

Nyx blinked and said, "She is held up in another part of the castle grounds." A small metal key dangled from his hand as he pulled it from his pocket. Flashbacks of that night I found Sadi ran through my mind. It seemed so long ago now, but I could still feel the lingering kiss of Ryker's lips on mine. I wondered if he was searching for me. If he were going to the ends of the world to find me. Did he know about our Queen and her evil secret?

I shook my head. "No, I am not going anywhere. We need to get out of here. We need to come up with a new plan," I begged.

Nyx stepped forward. "I'm sorry Lilah, if I try to resist the magic, it will take over me, turn me into something far worse than the creatures out there. I must do what he says. I don't want to hurt you, but Lilah, you aren't bound by his magic. You can disobey his orders. He is going to take your blood when we get you to his ritual chamber. If you can find a way to evade this somehow, do it. I can't intervene. It's like anytime I try to help, I am constricted, meeting a wall that stops me before I can get close enough. The guard farthest to his right has a sword sheathed on his side. If you can get it somehow, you might be able to fight your way out of here. This curse on my father, on me...it feels like it is pulling me into somewhere dark that my mind doesn't want to go."

Nyx's eyes were begging for mercy, for anything to stop this situation from happening but as his words spilled out, my heart sank deeper in my chest. He was bound by his father's dark magic. Bound by the curse on this land and bringing him back here has made him a prisoner to it just as much as me. I knew that it was up to me to save us from this fate. To save everyone.

"Lilah, we must go." Nyx opened the door, the metal creaking loudly through the hall, and then he reached out his hand for me. Reluctantly, I slipped my fingers into his, a simple touch, a simple pleasure, I never thought I would be able to experience it again. As Nyx pulled me forward through the darkness to my inevitable doom, all I could feel now was the racing pulse of my heart.

Fear burned hot within me. Despair had a firm grip on my chest. And anger consumed every corner of my body. I felt defeated, but the last thing that I would do was give up. There must be a way out of this. There must be. I would be damned to let Dravian win at his own game and when I was standing before him, I would find a way to kill the Vampire King. I would spill the blood of all of his loyal subjects for what they had done to me.

Nyx pulled me farther, deeper into the darkness of the castle until we came up on a dimly lit door, towering higher than some of the trees out in the Dark Lands. "This is it," his voice said hoarsely. "I'm sorry…" he croaked.

I squeezed my fingers tight against his. This wasn't his fault; I had to remind myself of that. He was just as much of a prisoner as me. "I'll find a way to stop this Nyx. To free us both from your father. Don't you—"

The creaking door opened and immediately I noticed the white moonlight spilling onto the ground before my feet, followed by loud chanting ringing around the room. I sucked in my breath as I peered into the ritual chamber, my heart skipping a beat as Nyx pulled me forward.

Chanting—in a language I had never heard before—rang through the chambers like echoing thunder, causing an uneasy feeling to coil in my gut. Darkness consumed every inch of this forsaken room except for the center, which was under an open skylight, allowing the full moon's light to spill in. Nyx slowly pulled me forward as the chamber's darkness swallowed me.

A decaying scent drifted through the air, the smell of spilled blood lingering like a starving predator lurking in the shadows. This was a place of death. Of torment. Dark red streaks were smeared along the cobblestone ground, forever soaked with the spilled blood of their victims. As I plodded forward, my bare feet scraped against the cold cobblestone ground.

Nyx had no choice but to keep moving forward, although I could feel his body slowing down the closer we got to his father. Dravian stood right in the center of the room, holding an object in his hand, smiling down upon me like some twisted proud father. It made me want to hurl.

"At last," his voice echoed.

My gaze shifted around the room again as the line of guards along the wall began to chant louder now, as if my presence had set them in motion. I lifted my chin until I was gazing into the night sky once more, my eyes noticing something dangling from the stone ceilings— chains. Were those for me?

Dravian began to chuckle, which brought my attention right back to him, his face plastered with an evil grin. Nyx clutched onto my hand so tight that I thought it was going to break, but I didn't pull away. I craved his presence, his touch, and this may very well be the last time I felt his hands on mine.

Dravian stepped forward and spoke loudly. "After a century of searching for a Veyl to break this curse, our prayers have been answered." He lifted the object high above his head, letting it soak in the milky moonlight as the crowd cheered. Their grunts and screams rang loudly around my head, causing a dizziness to settle in.

The chanting faded and then Dravian was once again coming closer to me, pinning me with a deathly stare. "My child, your blood will be a gift to my kingdom. Your sacrifice will give us the gift of sunlight again. The Dawnstone needs your blood as an offering to the cursed lands to rid us from its binding." His voice dropped an octave, almost to the point of a growl as he spoke quietly in my ear, "And my child, I will make this hurt."

An unnatural feeling clawed at me beneath my skin, constricting me with a fear I didn't know was possible. Every instinct in my body told me to run but it was as if I too were bound by Dravian's demands. I sucked in my breath the closer he got to me, terrified that he would kill me right here. I needed to get myself out of this.

Where is that guard? My eyes shifted to search for the guard that had the sword. I needed to somehow get close enough to him without being noticed, but…*fuck!* It was too dark to see who was along the walls of the chambers; the only thing that I could notice were their glowing eyes pinning me.

Dravian snaked out his hand and snatched my arm into his grip, my pulse thundering in my ear from the iron grip of my captor. "Let go of me!" I screamed. His grip only tightened until it felt as if my bones would snap. I screamed from the pain, from the rage that boiled inside me. When I glanced over my shoulder,

Nyx instinctively went to reach for me but one of the guards pulled him to the side, securing *him* in chains.

"Nyx!" My watery eyes were back on Dravian, begging, pleading for mercy. "Please let me go. There must be another way." When I glanced through my matted hair, all I could see was the smug look on Dravian's face, his cold, glittering eyes fixed on me as if I was his prized kill. The cloak he wore was tailored, just like his suit, and his hair was black as death—just like Nyx's.

I sucked in my breath as he closed the space between us again. I felt myself shrinking more into myself the closer he got to me. His lip curved, the tips of his fangs taunting me as he spoke. "Why would I do that now? We are just getting started. And don't worry, you won't be able to use your magic against me. If you haven't felt it already, my castle has a spell over it, to weaken your magic. That way it will be easier for me to harness." He sauntered off and continued. "I can't have you starting a war within my chambers now, can I?"

"I don't care what you do to me, I won't help you break the curse," I growled. My eyes desperately sought for Nyx. One of the guards was pulling him off to the side and he looked as if he were in physical pain watching me like this. I could tell his body wanted to run forward and take me away from this place, but he said that Dravian's magic was holding him hostage. Before I had time to process what was going on, Dravian snapped his fingers and ordered, "Chain her. It is time."

Keiran and one of the other guards rushed me and pulled me across the hall. I fought as hard as I could against their weight, but I was no match for the two vampires and their supernatural strength. A bloodcurdling scream ripped from my chest as I tried to break free from their iron grips. "Looks like she is a feisty one," Keiran said.

The other guard raked over my body with his predatory eyes and snickered. "I can't wait to taste her blood." He licked his lips as if tasting me on his tongue. Bile threatened to rise up my throat, but I swallowed it back down.

In the center of the room, there was a stone table and above it were chains hanging lowly from the ceiling beams; above it was an open skylight, revealing the full moon's beauty. Dravian stepped off to the side and directed Keiran and the others to hook my arms to the chains. "Hurry!" he hissed.

I tried to pull back, but it was no use. Before I knew it, my body was dangling from these chains like butchered meat, my feet barely scraping the stone table beneath me. "Please!" I begged.

Dravian pulled out the Dawnstone and set it under my dangling body and began to chant in a language I had never heard before. There were symbols etched into the ground that surrounded us, encasing us in a perfect circle, and as the room echoed loudly with this chant, the symbols began to glow. An ethereal light emitted from under me, lighting up the ritual chambers like hundreds of lit candles.

Nyx was shaking his head, terror flashing within his gaze. I only stared back at him in defeat. The chanting was now raging around me, infecting my head with its energy. My body began to thrum and vibrate, a steady humming rhythm pulsating under my skin. Pain exploded in my toes, in my fingers, in my head, and then before I knew it, it felt as if I were burning in the underworld's inferno. I screamed at the top of my lungs as I watched Dravian flick his wrist until his fingers turned into claws.

He walked over to my dangling body and yanked down on my leg and exposed my skin. "Curse for blood," he said. Then the room echoed his chant in a roar.

"Curse for blood! Curse for blood! Curse for blood!"

Dravian lifted his hand and sliced down until his nails cut a deep gash into my calf. I yelped out in agony as I watched the blood start to pool onto the Dawnstone beneath me. My blood soaked into the porous stone, staining it the color of deep red. A dim glow illuminated the symbols on the stone, almost creating a perfect circle. Tears streamed down my face; my throat constricted as I cried out for mercy. "Please!"

Dravin didn't even slip a glance at me as my pitiful cries faded into the madness. His attention was fully set on the Dawnstone before him. He lifted the stone into the air and smiled, whispering something under his breath. Silence fell over the room, not even the slightest of sounds daring to break through. Keiran was standing off to my right while Dravian was on my left, and as they were distracted from the Dawnstone, I tried to pull the chains free from the stone. I could feel that where the chain met the stone was becoming loose. If only I could wiggle it...

My arms shook from side to side. Right. Left. Right. Left, until I felt a chunk of the stone ceiling crumble down on me. I sucked in my breath. *It's working*. I kept yanking my arms from side to side, pulling as hard as my aching body would let me until I heard a crack.

Everything happened so fast. I dropped like a rock, my body slamming onto the table. I kicked my feet as hard as I could and knocked Dravian right on his ass from the surprise hit. Before Keiran could react, I was already whipping the chains attached to my wrists around his neck. His eyes went wide, and I smiled. "I told you I would—"

I yanked down on the chain until Keiran's neck looked as if it were going to pop from the pressure and before he could rip it away, I yanked harder, twisting it until I heard a snap. Keiran dropped like dead weight, crumpling to the ground and slamming hard. I was seeing red. My mind was consumed with anger. I bellowed out a scream, piercing the air with my shrilling voice and then turned my gaze to Nyx who looked completely and utterly shocked.

"Nyx—"

Before I could step forward, I felt a hand wrap its fingers in my hair and pull my head back. "You fucking bitch. Did you really think you could get away with this?" Dravian's voice slithered over my skin, causing goosebumps to erupt along my body. I recoiled from his touch, but he pulled me closer until his lips were pressed onto my ear. "You will pay for what you did Lilah. Now, I will make this unbearable for you."

Dravian dragged me back to the center of the room and with his other hand picked up the Dawnstone and grunted. "It should have worked!" I could feel him shaking with anger, I could hear it in his voice. He was fucking furious, and I wasn't sure if it was because I just killed his second in command or if it was because the Dawnstone wasn't working.

Something took over me and out of all the craziness of the room; I started to laugh. "It didn't work. After one hundred years of longing for this and it didn't work. You will forever be cursed to burn in the sun." I let my head fall back as laughter boiled out of me.

A low growl rumbled from his chest and his fingers dug into my skull. He pulled me into him and hissed in my ear, "You think this is funny? You won't be laughing at what I do next." Dravian snapped his fingers, and another guard rushed over to me and took the chains that still dangled from my wrists and pulled me back to the center of the room. My leg ached terribly as the gash on my calf throbbed, blood still seeping into my clothing.

I limped until I was led back to the stone table and once again, my chains were secured, forcing me to drink in the moon's light. I drew in a shuddering breath as I watched Dravian circle me with a wicked look in his eyes, his lip curving in an unnatural smirk. "Let's see if you laugh at this," he growled.

His fangs dropped, his eyes went wickedly cold, and his grip on my head was firm and filled with rage. Dravian yanked my head back and forced my neck out. I knew it was coming, the sting of his fangs sinking into my flesh, but suddenly, I heard a rageful scream.

"Dravian!" Nyx's voice boomed throughout the chambers. "Let. Her. Go." Nyx's eyes were consumed with darkness, his body looked as if the vines of the forest had woven themselves into his skin, and they were *glowing*, hues of faint blue emitting from him. Nyx's leg was shackled to the ground, but it was as if it were nothing more than a piece of string as he leaned forward and ripped it clean from the concrete.

Dravian sucked in his breath, gasping as if he had never seen anything like this before. "How?" his voice quivered. I felt his grip on my head loosen and that was when I pushed myself away from him but instead of charging me, he stood completely still in the presence of his Dark Prince.

My mouth dropped, Nyx, strode forward, pinning Dravian with a stare that promised death, his black shirt ripped and now exposing his defined abs. My eyes raked over his body, watching how he looked as if he had some kind of newfound power. I'd be lying if I said it didn't turn me on seeing him like this. The crowd of guards gasped and whispered while Nyx strode over to his father. While never once breaking his furious gaze with his father, Nyx reached out his hand until his fingers found mine. I closed my eyes and gasped from the slight touch of his skin. Something about his touch grounded me, made me feel complete.

"Son, what are you—"

Before Dravian could slip out his words Nyx's hand was around his throat causing his voice to hitch. "But—how?" Dravian croaked out, his eyes darting from Nyx's body to the broken concrete. Vampires were strong but they weren't strong enough to shatter concrete. Nyx cocked his head to the side and smiled.

"Father, looks like your plan didn't work." I watched as Dravian's eyes shifted to the Dawnstone that was still in his hand, my blood still dripping from the porous material. Nyx's nostrils flared as if scenting the tangy smell of my blood and growled. Nyx opened his mouth as if he were about to speak but suddenly, chaos ensued.

Dravian manage to yell out, "Guards!" and then the army of lurking vampires exploded and crashed into us, moving like streaks of darkness. Nyx flung his father to the ground and immediately began fighting off the guards that rushed him. Everyone moved like shadows, disappearing the moment I thought I could see them, but I could hear the guttural moans of rage echoing around the room. I tried to break myself free, but I was still chained to the center of the room. The air was alive with the sickening sound of cracking bones and gargling. It was the same sound my father made as Keiran ripped out his throat.

Immediately, a gut-wrenching pain coiled in me as the memory of my father came rushing to the surface. I curled my fingers into my stomach to keep myself from hurling on the floor. He was trying to protect me that night from meeting this fate, gave his life to keep me safe, and for what? I was exactly where I shouldn't be.

In the darkness of the room, the symbols along the floor emitted a dim glow, but only half of the room was lit up, creating a half circle around the stone table in the center. Then I looked at the Dawnstone that hung in

Dravian's hand and realized that it mimicked the same design, only half lit.

Why didn't it work? Why only half? My mind tried to figure out why the ritual only half worked but before it wandered too far, the snarling stopped, silence snatching my attention to the army in front of me. The sea of vampires parted until it was Nyx kneeling before me with his hands pinned behind his back. The glowing veins along his body had disappeared now. Instinctively, I stepped forward to reach for him, but Dravian's claw-like finger dug into the underneath part of my chin and pulled my head until I met his gaze.

Fury burned in his eyes, along with a wicked gleam of amusement. "Enough of this. You cannot defeat my army, Lilah, and your little Dark Prince can't either. No matter what kind of magic you gave him. It won't last. Once his body absorbs the last of your magic, he will be weak again. Vulnerable." Dravian let go of my chin and tapped his finger along the Dawnstone.

"The ritual didn't fully work. Something was missing, but I think I know what." His voice lingered on that last word, as if savoring the torment, it gave me to hear his wretched voice. A low, guttural chuckle escaped his chest, his eyes lighting up as if realization had dawned on him. "I figured it out. My Dawnstone is only half of the Veyl's artifact. There was a dagger that she used to bind us with this curse too."

Dravian's finger glided over a small slit at the top of the stone and smiled. "Here." He pointed. "The dagger must fit into here. Once I have both of the Veyl heirlooms, then it must work."

His eyes burned into me. He stepped close enough that I could feel the heat of his breath wash over me. "You are going to get that dagger for me, Lilah. And if you don't, I will burn the only people you care about." His threats rang in my ear, causing my breathing to come in uneven shallow breaths. My watery eyes went to Nyx as I gazed upon the broken Dark Prince. Already, Dravian's guards were shackling his wrist and ankles with more chains, and as I got lost in the dread that consumed me, Dravian's hand clamped down on my arm, snapping my attention back to him.

"What makes you think I can get that dagger from the Queen? I have never even met the Queen."

"Because if you don't, your precious Dark Prince and your redheaded friend are going to burn in the sunlight. I will place a curse on their souls, and when the next full moon is highest in the sky, they will be forced by the powers of the Dark Lands to let their bodies burn in the sun. No matter if I have them chained or if they were wandering free. They will burn." My eyes went wide with his threat. *Redheaded friend?* As soon as my brain realized who he was talking about, the doors burst open, followed by Alerice dragging Sadi in by her hair.

"I believe this is yours," she purred.

I seethed her name. "Alerice. But—"

She tilted her head and scoffed. "Did you think just because you already gave yourself up to the King that I wasn't going to offer myself to him? It was me after all that told him about your little plan with the Dark Prince."

"How did you know?"

"I hear everything. The forest tells me things when I give it something in return. All I had to do was give it a gift. I've gotten what I wanted. My King has given me a place within his castle for the information I have brought him. It will feel good watching your little Sadi and Nyx burn."

My throat choked; a sob welled in my chest. I should have killed her. Sadi growled as Alerice pulled her forward and handed her off to three guards that held more chains. They clamped them down on her wrists and ankles, just like Nyx, and brought her to her knees before us. She wouldn't look up at me, as if shame were forcing her gaze to the floor.

"You have until the next full moon to bring me that dagger, or else your little friends will burn right here under the sun's light. Secure them to the center," he roared. Dravian unhooked my wrists and pulled me away from the stone table so that his guards could lock Sadi and Nyx to the center. Their bodies were forced to dangle above with their arms pulled above their heads.

"I'm so sorry," I cried.

"Little flower, don't cry. None of this is your fault."

Sadi didn't speak but her eyes spoke loud and clear as she burned into Dravian with a deathly stare. Then her gaze shifted to me and softened; they were telling me that it was okay. That I didn't have to do this, but I did have to. I couldn't let them burn.

"You better hurry Lilah, before the next full moon rises," his breath slithered in my ear. "Don't try anything stupid. You know what will happen." Dravian shoved me forward and dragged me down the carpet and back to the entrance door. I tried to crane my head back to have just one last look at the man that I have come to love, and at my new friend, but his grip on me was too strong.

He shoved me through the doors and yelled, "Follow her! Make sure she doesn't do anything stupid." He pulled on a chain and the room suddenly was blanketed with darkness as the dome in the center closed up. Now, only a sea of glowing eyes glared back at me causing me to sink into myself.

"Go!" he yelled. I staggered backward until I eventually bumped into something. I turned and ran for the front of the castle, toward the outside. My heart vibrated in my chest, my head thrummed with so many emotions, and I gasped for a steady breath as my hands pushed through the front doors of the Vampire King's castle.

Darkness enveloped the land, only the moon's beams lighting a path before me. The Dark Lands were ahead; my prince and my friend were behind, chained, and ready to be sacrificed. There was only one thing I could do now and that was go back into the very lands that tried to kill me and make it back to Eldoria. I'd have to steal the Queen's dagger all before the next full moon.

I wasn't sure what to expect, my body and mind gripped in fear, but there was nothing else I could do besides accept this quest. If I didn't, my world would once again be shattered into a million pieces. There was still a burning hatred for my Queen Margarethe, a desire to cause her pain that ravaged my soul. She was the one who murdered my mother, who has been murdering and sacrificing her own people for the sake of her power, and so, I might as well slit her throat with her own dagger.

I was coming for her. I was coming for Dravian. I was coming for every evil, vile creature that crossed me and when I was done reigning terror upon our lands, I would have my Dark Prince all to myself. Don't underestimate a woman raging in fury. She might just burn your world down.

Author Note

If you loved A Court of Blood and Sacrifice, make sure to follow me on social media to stay up to date on the release of book two, A Court of Blood and Oath, and on *all* my series and new releases when you follow me:

TikTok: kaymarrie_author

Instagram: kaymarrie_author

Facebook: Kay Marrie Author

Website: https://kaymarrie.com/

Other Books by Kay Marrie

City of the Damned

Era of the Damned

Thank You

I would like to first thank my amazing family and friends for supporting me through my writing career. This book was so fun to write, and I just can't wait for my amazing readers to delve into this series. Thank you to my wonderful editor, Michael, and my new friends that I have made along my journey of this book. Everyone's support has meant the world to me. I can't wait to continue to build my relationship with everyone and grow more friendships along the way.

About the Author

Kay Marrie lives in central Florida with her three young children, husband, and two cats. When she is not juggling playtime with the kids, she spends her time dedicated to working for a charter school. Her true passion is writing and storytelling, and she has found a way to pursue her dreams of being a writer in her busy life. When she is not changing diapers or typing away, you can find her nestled up with a book, enjoying the warm Florida sun from her front porch.

www.ingramcontent.com/pod-product-compliance
Lightning Source LLC
Chambersburg PA
CBHW031202310726
48969CB00001B/183